Also by Nadine Gordimer

The Pickup

Nadine Gordimer

The Pickup

Farrar, Straus and Giroux

New York

Farrar, Straus and Giroux
19 Union Square West, New York 10003

Extract from 'Another Country' from *Collected Poems* by William
Plomer, published by Jonathan Cape. Used by permission of The Random House Group Limited.

'Happiness', edited by Stephen Kessler, copyright © 1999 by Maria Ko-
dama; translation copyright © 1999 by Stephen Kessler, from *Selected
Poems* by Jorge Luis Borges, edited by Alexander Coleman. Used by
permission of Viking Penguin, a division of Penguin Putnam Inc.

Library of Congress Cataloging-in-Publication Data
Gordimer, Nadine.
    The pickup / Nadine Gordimer.
        p.   cm.
    ISBN 0-374-23210-5 (hardcover : alk. paper)
    1. Illegal aliens—Fiction.   2. Arabs—Foreign countries—Fiction.
3. Women—Arab countries—Fiction.   4. Children of the rich—
Fiction.   5. Ethnic relations—Fiction.   6. Married people—
Fiction.   7. Arab countries—Fiction.   I. Title.

PR9369.3.G6 P53 2001
823'.914—dc21

                                              2001023041

Designed by Jonathan D. Lippincott

For Reinhold
Oriane
Hugo

Let us go to another country . . .
The rest is understood
Just say the word.
                                   —William Plomer

The Pickup

Clustered predators round a kill. It's a small car with a young woman inside it. The battery has failed and taxis, cars, minibuses, vans, motorcycles butt and challenge one another, reproach and curse her, a traffic mob mounting its own confusion. Get going. Stupid bloody woman. *Idikazana lomlungu, le!* She throws up hands, palms open, in surrender. They continue to jostle and blare their impatience. She gets out of her car and faces them. One of the unemployed black men who beg by waving vehicles into parking bays sidles his way deftly through fenders, signals with his head—Oka-ay, Oka-ay go inside, go!—and mimes control of the steering wheel. Another like him appears, and they push her and her car into a loading bay. The street hustles on. They stand, looking musingly beyond her while she fumbles for her purse. An expert's quick glance at what she has put in his hand assures the street boss that it is more than adequate. She doesn't know how to thank them enough, etc. He hitches his body to get the money stowed in trousers cut to fit somebody else and smiles with his attention on the lookout for the next vehicle seeking a place to park. A woman wearing a towel as a shawl, enthroned on a fruit-box before her stock of

hair combs, razor blades, pumice stones, woollen caps and
headache powders, yells out to him what must be a teasing
remark in a language the young woman doesn't understand.

There. You've seen. I've seen. The gesture. A woman in a
traffic jam among those that are everyday in the city, any city.
You won't remember it, you won't know who she is.

But I know because from the sight of her I'll find out—as
a story—what was going to happen as the consequence of
that commonplace embarrassment on the streets; where it
was heading her for, and what. Her hands thrown up, open.

The young woman was down in a thorough-
fare, a bazaar of all that the city had not been allowed to be
by the laws and traditions of her parents' generation. Breaking up in bars and cafés the inhibitions of the past has always
been the work of the young, haphazard and selectively tolerant. She was on her way to where she would habitually meet,
without arrangement, friends and friends of friends, whoever
turned up. The L.A. Café. Maybe most people in the street
throngs didn't know the capitals stood for Los Angeles; saw
them as some short version of the name of a proprietor, as the
old-style Greek corner shop would carry the name of Stavros
or Kimon. EL-AY. Whoever owned the café thought the chosen name offered the inspiration of an imagined life-style to
habitués, matching it with their own; probably he confused
Los Angeles with San Francisco. The name of his café was a
statement. A place for the young; but also one where old sur-
vivors of the quarter's past, ageing Hippies and Leftist Jews,
grandfathers and grandmothers of the 1920s immigration
who had not become prosperous bourgeois, could sit over a
single coffee. Crazed peasants wandered from the rural areas
gabbled and begged in the gutters outside. Hair from a bar-

ber's pavement booth blew the human felt of African hair onto the terrace. Prostitutes from Congo and Senegal sat at tables with the confidence of beauty queens.

Hi Julie—as usual, beckoned. Her welcomers saw a graceful neck and face, naturally pale, reddened with emotion of some sort. Black and white, they fussed about her: *Hi Julie, relax, what's up with you*. There were two of her friends from university days, a journalist out of work who house-sat for absent owners, a couple who painted banners for rallies and pop concerts. There was indignation: this city. What shits.

—All they care about is *getting there . . .*—

And where is it they think they're getting to—this from the hanger-on with a shining bald pate and a cape of grey locks falling from behind his ears; still unpublished but recognized from childhood as a poet and philosopher, by his mother.

—Nothing gives a white male more of a kick than humiliating a woman driver.—

—Sexual stimulant for yahoos—

—Someone else shouted something . . . like *Idikaza . . . mlungu . . .* What's that, 'white bitch', isn't it?— Her question to the black friend.

—Well, just about as bad. This city, man!—

—But it was black men who helped me, of course.—

—Oh come on—for a hand-out!—

Her friends knew of a garage in the next street. With a wave from the wrist she left them to take the necessary practical step.

She feels hot gassy breath. Steel snouts and flashing teeth-grilles at her face. Inside her something struggles against them. Her heart summons her like a fist under her ribs, gasps rise within her up to her collar-bones. She is walking along the street, that's all, it's nothing. Walking round a block to a garage. It's nothing, it was nothing, it's over. Shudder. A traffic jam.

There's the garage, as they said. As she walked in she saw its ordinariness, a landing on normality: vehicles as helpless, harmless victims upon hydraulic lifts, tools on benches, water dispenser, plastic cups and take-away food boxes, radio chattering, a man lying on his back half-under the belly of a car. There were two others preoccupied at some noisy machinery and they signalled her over to him. The legs and lower body wriggled down at the sound of her apologetic voice and the man emerged. He was young, in his greasy work-clothes, long hands oil-slicked at the dangle from long arms; he wasn't one of them—the white man speaking Afrikaans to the black man at the machine—but glossy dark-haired with black eyes blueish-shadowed. He listened to her without any reassuring attention or remark. She waited a moment in his silence.

So could you send someone to have a look . . . the car's round the corner.

He stared at his hands. Just a minute while I clean up.

He carried a bulky handleless bag with a new battery and tools and it was awkward to walk beside him through the streets with people dodging around them, but she did not like to walk ahead of the garage man as if he were some sort of servant. In silence, he got the car going and drove back to the workshop with her as his passenger.

There's still some—I don't know—in the ignition. Your car will stall again, I think.

Then I'd better leave it with you. I suppose it needs a general service, anyway.

When was the last time?

She was culpable, smiling, I don't remember.

How long?

I suppose I just drive until something goes wrong.

He nodded slowly, did not speak: of course, that's your way.

I'll give a call to find out when it's ready—you're Mr . . . ?

Ask for Abdu.

She allowed the garage two or three days to do whatever was needed. When she called and asked by name for the mechanic who had taken charge of her car she was told he was out but it was certain the car was still under repair. This didn't matter, there was her father's third car at her disposal, a handsome old Rover he'd bought at a Sotheby's auction and had refurbished, then seldom used. It was a car from The Suburbs, of a kind that wouldn't be ventured down in the quarter of the EL-AY Café. When it was parked there under the admiring care of a well-tipped street man, people stood around to gaze at it, a denizen from another world, affluence as distant as space. She was not over-concerned that it would be stolen—it was too unique to be easy to get away with undetected, and too grandly obsolete to be a profitable source of parts, if broken up. She was only uncomfortable at the idea of its exposure—and hers, as its family occupant—before her friends. She did not live in The Suburbs, where she had grown up, but in a series of backyard cottages adapted from servants' quarters or in modest apartments of the kind they favoured, or had to, being unable to afford anything better. On the Sunday when she came to dose on therapeutic mineral water and coffee with the friends after a night at a club in Soweto where one of them was blowing the trumpet, she found three happy children and a baby in arms sitting on the gleaming bonnet and playing with the silver statuette of Mercury that was its figurehead. Her father just might have been amused by this new game on his vintage plaything, but she did not relate it because it wouldn't do to reveal to his young wife that the car was being driven around in unsuitable places—that one was vigilant in protection of his possessions.

In the week that followed—she had not yet bothered to call the garage again—when she got out of her father's car there was the mechanic, in the street, turned looking at it.

That's a car . . . Excuse me. As if he had accosted someone he did not know.

It's not mine! She claimed her identity: I'd like to have my own old one back! And laughed.

He seemed to recall who this was among clients under whose vehicles' bellies he lay. Oh yes—. Ready by Thursday. They have to get a distributor from the agent.

He was looking at the Rover from another angle. How old? What is the model?

I've really no idea. It's borrowed, I don't own it, that's for sure.

I never saw one before—only in a photo.

They used to be made in England ages ago, before either of us was born. You love cars? Even though you work with their insides all day?

'Love'—I don't say. That is something different. It's just it's beautiful (his long hand rose towards his face and opened, to the car). Many things can be beautiful.

And mine certainly isn't. What else's wrong apart from the whatever-it-is you have to get from the agent? Sounds as if it's going to be a major overhaul.

Why do you keep it. You should buy a new car.

He was turned from her, again looking at the Rover: the evidence gathered that she could afford to.

She lobbed the accusation back to him. Why should I when you can get it going again for me?

He screwed his eyes, very liquid-black in the sun, authoritative. Because it can be a danger for you to drive. Something can fail that can kill you. I can't see (he seemed to reject a word, probably that came to him from another language—he paused uncertainly)—know to stop that, in my work.

And if I were driving a new car, someone else on the road could fail in some way, and that could kill me—so?

That would be your fate, but you would not have—what do I say—looked for it.

Fate.

She was amused: Is there such a thing? Do I believe in it. You do, then.

To be open to encounters—that was what she and her friends believed, anyway, as part of making the worth of their lives. Why don't we have coffee—if you're free?

I'm on lunch. He pulled down the corners of his mouth undecidedly, then smiled for the first time. It was the glimpse of something attractive withheld in the man, escaped now in the image of good teeth set off by clearly delineated lips under a moustache black as his eyes. Most likely of Indian or Cape Malay background; like her, a local of this country in which they were born descendant of immigrants in one era or another—in her case from Suffolk and County Cork, as in his from Gujerat or the East Indies.

EL-AY Café.

The friends probably at their usual table inside. She didn't look, and made for a corner of the terrace.

In casual encounters people—men and women, yes, avoiding any other subject that may be misunderstood, compromising— tell each other what they *do*: which means what work is theirs, not how they engage their being in other ways. A big word had been brought up from what was withheld in this man—'fate'— but it was simple to evade its intimate implications of belief, after all, steer these to the public subject: the occupations by which she, driver of the Rover (even if, as she insisted, it was borrowed), just as he, his place the underbelly of other people's ve-

hicles, gained her bread. Whatever his ancestry, as a local of the
same generation they'd share the understanding of 'bread' as
money rather than a loaf. Nevertheless she found herself speaking rather shyly, respectful of the obvious differences in 'fate' between them: she in her father's (having lied by omission about
this) Rover, he trapped beneath her small jalopy.

*What I do, what you do. That's about the only subject
available.*

I don't know how exactly these things work out. I wanted
to be a lawyer, really, I had these great ambitions when I was
at school—there was a lawyer aunt in the family, I once went
to hear her cross-examine in that wonderful black pleated
gown and white bib. But with various other things on the way
. . . I quit law after only two years. Then it was languages . . .
and somehow I've landed up working as a PRO and fund-
raiser, benefit dinners, celebrity concerts, visiting pop groups.
Everyone says oh great, you must meet such famous people—
but you also meet some awful people and you have to be nice
to them. Sycophantic. I won't stick to it for long. She stopped
short of: I don't know what I want to do, if that means what
I want to be. That was a lead into the confessional, even if the
ethic were to be open with strangers.

It's good money, isn't it?

Commission. Depends what I bring in.

He drank the coffee evenly in swallows and pauses, as if
this were a measured process. Perhaps he wasn't going to
speak again: it was patronizing, after all, this making free encounters out of other people's lives, a show of your conviction
of their equal worth, interest, catching the garage mechanic
in the net, EL-AY Café. When he had taken a last swallow
and put down the cup he'd get up and say thank you and
go—so she had to think of something to say, quickly, to
mend, justify, the pickup.

What about you?

It was the wrong thing—there! She'd done it, it came out god-awful as Showing Interest, and she thought she heard him take a breath in order to deal with it, with her; but he only put out his hand for the sugar-bowl, she hastened to hand it to him, he helped himself to another spoonful for the dregs in his cup. He would keep silent if he wanted to, he could speak if he wished, it wasn't up to her.

Many things, different countries.

Perhaps that's the way.

It is if they don't want you, say it's not your country. You have no country.

Isn't this our country. That's a statement, from her.

For you.

Oh I thought you were—like me—this's home, but it's good to get out of it. I was in America for a year—some other country would have been a better idea, for me.

I go where they'll let me in.

And from . . . She was tentative. It couldn't be avoided now.

He named a country she had barely heard of. One of those partitioned by colonial powers on their departure, or seceded from federations cobbled together to fill vacuums of power-lessness against the regrouping of those old colonial powers under acronyms that still brand-name the world for them-selves. One of those countries where you can't tell religion apart from politics, their forms of persecution from the perse-cution of poverty, as the reason for getting out and going wherever they'll let you in.

Things were bad there. Not really knowing what she was talking about.

Were, are.

But you're all right, here? Are you?

Now he neatly replaced cup in saucer, placed spoon, and did get up to leave.

Thank you. I have to go back to work.

She stood up, too. Thursday?

Better if you call before you come. Thursday.

It's Julie.

But he said, Who, who d'you want to speak to.

I'm the one whose car you're fixing, you said Thursday.

Sorry, there's a lot of noise—yes, it's all ready for you.

At the garage he handed some sort of work-sheet over to the owner at the office, and she paid.

Everything okay now? You're sure.

He gave the slight shrug of one accustomed to dealing with customers' nerves. You can try it out with me if you want.

He got into the passenger seat; she reversed swiftly between obstacles on the workshop floor, to show him she could do it. They drove around the quarter, splashing through overflowing drains, pulling up behind the abrupt stops of minibus taxis, nimbly squeezing between double-parked vans, avoiding pedestrians darting in and out of the streets like a school of fish. She was at ease; now she was part of the stampede, riding with it, chattering.

You still think I should buy a new one.

It makes sense. Next time something else will go wrong; you'll have to pay again to keep the same old thing.

I'd buy a good second-hand car. Maybe. Maybe it's an idea? D'you think perhaps you'd vet it, if I did? I'd have to have it seen by someone who'd know what to check under the bonnet.

If you want. I could do that.

Oh wonderful. Do you perhaps know of someone who would have a good car they'd like to sell? You might get to hear . . .

People sometimes come to the garage . . . I can look
around. If you want. What kind of car?

Not a Rover, you can bet on that!

Yes, but two-door, four-door, automatic—whatever.

There was a space before the EL-AY Café. She obeyed the
man-child who signalled her in with his glue-sniffer's plastic
bottle in hand. Arguing about the model of car, the level of
possession appropriate for her, they left hers and took the
steps to the terrace. This time went inside, this time he was
taken to the friends' table.

Hi Julie; a rearrangement of chairs. —This is Abdu, he's
going to find new wheels for me.—

Hi Abdu. (Sounds to them like an abbreviation of Abdu-
rahman, familiar among names of Malays in Cape Town.)
The friends have no delicacy about asking who you are,
where you come from—that's just the reverse side of bourgeois xenophobia. No, not the Cape. They have his story out
of him in no time at all, they interject, play upon it with ex-
amples they know of, advice they have to offer, interest that
is innocently generous or unwelcome, depends which way the
man might take it—but at once, he's not a 'garage man' he's
a friend, one of them, their horizon is broadening all the time.

So that's where he's from; one of them knows all about
that benighted country. The 'garage man' has a university degree in economics there (the university is one nobody's heard
of) but there isn't a hope in hell (and that place *is* a hell that,
because of god knows what, probably the religious and political factions he did or did not belong to, or lack of money to
pay bribes to the right people) he could get an academic appointment. Or a job of any kind, maybe; no work, no devel-
opment, what can you grow in a desert, corrupt government,
religious oppression, cross-border conflict—composite, if in-
accurate, of all they think they know about the region,
they're telling *him* about his country. But then she hears an

explanation for something he had said to her she hadn't understood. He's telling them: —I can't say that—'my country'—because somebody else made a line and said that is it. In my father's time they gave it to the rich who run it for themselves. So whose country I should say, it's mine.—

With them, his English is adequate enough and they have not been embarrassed to ask from what mother tongue his accent and locutions come. One of them enquires hopefully of this foreignness, since she has adopted the faith that is a way of life, not a bellicose ethnicity. —Are you a Buddhist?—

—No I am not that.—

And again, he has risen, he has to leave them, he's a mechanic, he belongs to the manual world of work. One of them ponders, breaking a match over and over. —An economist having to become a grease-monkey. I wonder how he learned that stuff with cars.—

Another had the answer.

—Needs must. The only way to get into countries that don't want you is as manual labourer or Mafia.—

A week went by. She would never see him again. It happened, among the friends, with the people they picked up: —Where's that girl you brought along, the one who said she'd been a speech-writer for some cabinet minister who was sacked?— —Oh she seems to have left town.— —And the other guy—interesting—he wanted to organize street kids as buskers, playing steel drums outside cinemas, did he ever get that off the ground?— —No idea where he landed up.—

Two weeks. Of course the man from the garage knew where to find her. He approached the friends' table on a Saturday morning to tell her he had found a car for her. The garage workshop was closed on Saturdays and now he was wearing well-ironed black jeans, a rose-coloured shirt with a paisley scarf at the neck. They insisted he must have coffee; it was someone's birthday and the occasion quickly turned the coffee to red wine. He didn't drink alcohol; he looked at her lifting her glass: I've brought the car for you to drive.

And the friends, who were ready to laugh at anything, in their mood, did so clownishly—O-HO-HOHOHO!—assuring him, —Julie has a strong head, not to worry!— But she refused a second glass.

—The cops are out with their breathalysers, it's the weekend.—

The car was not to her liking—too big, difficult to park— and perhaps it was not meant to be. He had a contact who was on the lookout, he would bring another the next weekend. If that was all right.

First she said she didn't know if she'd be free; and then she did it, she told him her telephone number. No paper to note it on. The celebration with the friends was still warm upon her, she laughed. Put it on your wrist. And then was embarrassed at her flippancy because he took a ballpoint out of his pocket, turned his wrist face-up, and was writing the number across the delicate skin and the blue veins revealed of himself, there.

He called, brief and formal over the telephone, addressing her as 'Miss' with her surname, and the arrangement was for an earlier date, after working hours. That car, again, was not quite right for her. They drove a short way out of town to confirm this. It was as if freed of the city it was not only the road open to them; with her face turned to that road ahead she was able to ask what the friends had touched on—*needs must.* How does a graduate in economics become a motor mechanic? Wasn't that quite a long training, apprenticeship and so on? And as he began to speak, she interrupted: Look, I'm Julie, don't call me anything else.

Julie. Well, Julie. His voice was low although they were alone, on the road, no-one to overhear. He was hesitant, after all, did he really know this girl, her gossiping friends, the loud careless forum of the EL-AY Café; but the desire to confide in her overcame him. He was no qualified mechanic. Luckily for him he had tinkered with cars since he was a small boy, his uncle—mother's brother—fixed people's cars and trucks in his backyard . . . he learnt from him instead of playing with other boys . . . The garage employs him illegally—'black', yes that's the word they use. It's cheap for the owner; he doesn't pay accident insurance, pension, medical aid. And now the seldom-granted smile, and this time it rises to the intense, solemn eyes as she turns her glance a moment to him. All the principles of workers' rights I was taught in my studies.

What an awful man, exploiter.

What would I do without him. He risks, I must pay for that. That's how it works, for us.

The next car was the right one—size, fuel consumption, price—and perhaps it had always been available, kept in reserve for the right time to be revealed. She was pleased with the car and also had the satisfaction (although she could not say this to him) he surely would get some sort of kick-back from whoever the owner was—unqualified, working 'black' he couldn't be earning much.

We must celebrate. Good you convinced me it was time to get rid of the old rattle-trap. Really. I'm just lazy about these things. But you don't drink wine . . .

Oh sometimes.

Fine! Then we'll christen my new car.

But not at the café.

He had spoken: with this, a change in their positions was swiftly taken, these were smoothly and firmly reversed, like a shift of gears synchronized under her foot; he was in charge of the acquaintanceship.

At my place then.

In quiet authority, he had no need to enthuse accord.

Even though it passed muster with the whites among the
friends that her 'place' was sufficiently removed from The
Suburbs' ostentation to meet their standards of leaving home
behind, and was accepted by the blacks among them as the
kind of place they themselves moved to from the old segrega-
tion, her outhouse renovated as a cottage was comfortable
enough, its under-furnishings nevertheless giving away a
certain ease inherent in, conditioned by, luxuries taken for
granted as necessities: there was a bathroom that dwarfed
the living-cum-bedroom by comparison, and the cramped
kitchen was equipped with freezer and gadgets. It was un-
tidy; the quarters of someone not used to looking after herself; to seat himself he removed the stained cup and plate and
a spatter of envelopes, sheets of opened letters, withered
apple-peel, old Sunday paper, from a chair. She was making
the usual apologies about the mess, as she did to whoever
dropped in. She opened wine, found a packet of biscuits,
sniffed at cheese taken from the fridge and rejected it in
favour of another piece. He watched this domesticity without
offering help, as her friends would, nobody lets anyone wait
on anyone else. But he ate her cheese and biscuits, he drank
her wine, with her that first time. They talked until late;
about him, his life; hers was here, where they were, in her
city, open in its nature for him to see in the streets, the faces,
the activities—but he, his, was concealed among these. No
record of him on any pay-roll, no address but c/o a garage,
and under a name that was not his. Another name? She was
bewildered: but there he was, a live presence in her room, an
atmosphere of skin, systole and diastole of breath blending
with that which pervaded from her habits of living, the food,
the clothes lying about, the cushions at their backs. Not his?
No—because they had let him in on a permit that had expired more than a year ago, and they would be looking for
him under his name.

And then?

He gestured: Out.

Where would he go? She looked as if she were about to make suggestions; there are always solutions in the resources she comes from.

He leant to pour himself some more wine, as he had reached across for the sugar-bowl. He looked at her and slowly smiled.

But surely . . . ?

Still smiling, moving his head gently from side to side. There was a litany of the countries he had tried that would not let him in. I'm a drug dealer, a white-slave trader coming to take girls, I'll be a burden on the state, that's what they say, I'll steal someone's job, I'll take smaller pay than the local man.

And at this last, they could laugh a moment because that was exactly what he was doing.

It's terrible. Inhuman. Disgraceful.

No. Don't you see them round all the places you like to go, the café. Down there, crack you can buy like a box of matches, the street corner gangs who take your wallet, the women any man can buy—who do they work for? The ones from outside who've been let in. Do you think that's a good thing for your country.

But you . . . you're not one of them.

The law's the same for me. Like for them. Only they are more clever, they have more money—to pay. His long hand opened, the fingers unfolding before her, joint by joint.

There are gestures that decide people's lives: the hand-grasp, the kiss; this was the one, at the border, at immigration, that had no power over her life.

Surely something can be done. For him.

He folded the fingers back into a fist, dropped it to his knee. His attention retreated from the confidence between

them and escaped absently to the pile of CDs near him. They
found they did share something: an enthusiasm for Salif
Keita, Youssou N'Dour and Rhythm & Blues, and listened to
her recordings on her system, of which he highly approved.
You like to drive a second-hand car but you have first-class
equipment for music.

It seemed both sensed at the same moment that it was
time for him to leave. She took it for granted she would drive
him home but he refused, he'd catch a combi ride.

Is that all right? Is it far? Where are you living?

He told her: there was a room behind the garage the
owner let him have.

She looked in—didn't allow herself to ask herself why.

Looked in on the garage, to tell him that the car was going well. And it was about the time of his lunch break. Where
else to go but, naturally, the EL-AY Café, join the friends.
And soon this became almost every day: if she appeared
without him, they asked, where's Abdu? They liked to have
him among them, they knew one another too well, perhaps,
and he was an element like a change in climate coming out of
season, the waft of an unfamiliar temperature. He did not
take much part in their unceasing talk but he listened, sometimes too attentively for their comfort.

—What happened to Brotherhood, I'd like to ask? Fat
cats in the government. Company chairmen. In the bush they
were ready to die for each other—no, no, that's true, grant
it—now they're ready to drive their official Mercedes right
past the Brother homeless here out on the street.—

—Did you see on the box last night—the one who was a
battle commander at Cuito, a hero, he's joined an exclusive
club for cigar connoisseurs . . . it's oysters and champagne instead of pap and goat meat.—

The elderly poet had closed his eyes and was quoting something nobody recognized as not his own work: —'Too long a sacrifice makes a stone of the heart.'—

No-one paid him attention.

—Doesn't make sense . . . why should people abandon what they've believed and fought for, what's got into them between then and now?—

What was he thinking, this intelligence dressed up as a grease-monkey—when he did have something to say it would puncture one of their opinions or trim one of their vociferous convictions. If he did speak, they listened:

—No chance to choose then. Nothing else. That porridge and for each one, the other. Now there is everything else. Here. To choose.—

—Hah! So Brotherhood is only the condition of suffering? Doesn't apply when you have choice, and the choice is the big cheque and the company car, the nice perks of Minister.—

—That is how it is. You have no choose—choice—or you have choice. Only two kinds. Of people.—

And they choose to laugh. —Abdu, what a cynic.—

—So come on David, what kind are you, in his categories—

—Well at the moment my choice is pitta with haloumi.—

—There's no free will in a capitalist economy. It's the bosses' will. That's what the man's really saying.— The political theorist among them is dismissive.

—You say that because you're black, it's old trade unionist stuff, my Bra, and meanwhile you're yearning to cop out and be the boss somewhere.—

The two grasp each other by the shoulder in mock conflict.

They all know one another's attitudes and views only too well. Attention turns to him, among them, again.

—You agree about the capitalist economy?—

—Where I come from—no capitalist economy, no socialist economy. Nothing. I learn about them at the university . . .—

And he's made them laugh, he laughs along with them, that's the way of the table, once you're accepted there.

—So what would you call it—what d'you mean 'nothing'?—

He seems to search for something they'll think they understand, to satisfy them.

—Feudal.— He raises and lowers elbows on the table, looks to her, his sponsor here, to see if the word is the right one; to see if, by this glance, she will be ready to leave. —But they call themselves ministers, presidents, this and that.—

The friends watch the two make their way between other habitués masticating, drinking, crouched in a scrum of conversation, cigarette smoke rising as the ectoplasm of communication not attainable through the cellphones clasped to belt or ear. —Where did Julie pick him up?— A member of The Table who had been away when Julie caused a traffic jam had to be told: that garage in the next street, that's where.

Her companion had paused a moment on the terrace and she turned to see: a girl with sunglasses pushed back crowning her hair, thighs sprawled, stroking the Rasta locks of a young man passed out, drink or drugs, on her lap.

He walked away with a face closed in distaste. Her: Well?—was more tolerance than an enquiry of his mood.

People are disgusting, in that place.

She said, as if speaking for them: I'm sorry.

You're not there; I'm not there: to see. It's not a traffic tangle in the streets, hands going up in culpability, surrender, owing this, open to the public.

It's not the spectacle available late-night on adult TV.

She still joins the friends as usual at The Table to which she belongs—they are, after all, her elective siblings who have distanced themselves from the ways of the past, their families, whether these are black ones still living in the old ghettoes or white ones in The Suburbs. But her working hours are flexible and she's there at times when he's under one of the vehicles round the corner; he doesn't always come along with her to sit over coffee or the plonk that the EL-AY has available. The friends are not the kind to ask what's going on, that's part of their creed: *whatever you do, love, whatever happens, hits you, mate, Bra, that's all right with me.* People come and go among them; so long as they remain faithful among themselves: gathered at The Table.

There was that day when this was something surely he would realize for himself, the day he was with her when one of them told The Table he had just been diagnosed: AIDS.

Ralph. Same wealthy suburban provenance as Julie herself, clear yellow-grey eyes, shiny cheek-bones, adolescent sporting feats that had given him shoulders so muscular his shirts seem padded: they gazed at him and it was as if the old poet saw something they did not, on the unmarked forehead. The old man spoke to The Table in the groans of an oracle. —It's an ancestral curse.—

—For Chris' sake! What is this now—

There's a time and place for the old crazy's pronouncements. Murmurs: shut him up, shut him up. But when The Table poet has something to say he doesn't hear or heed anyone.

—We are descendants of the ape. The disease started with primates. Then hungry humans in the forests killed them and ate their flesh. So the curse comes down to us from the revenge of our primeval ancestors.—

The Buddhist convert stirs in agreement: meat-eaters, breakers of the code of respect for creature-life.

Ralph the victim suddenly bursts into laughter. No-one had dared even to smile encouragement at him; a mood of bravado takes The Table. What has befallen one of their own isn't going to be something they can't deal with alternatively to the revulsion and mawkish sympathy of the Establishment, after all. They will always have the solution—of the spirit, if not the cure.

He, Abdu, does not join them; perhaps he didn't quite understand this is not just a matter of this model of athletic good health being HIV positive, a gamble with the future, but of the disease—that curse the poet's babbling about—already in possession.

On the street, subdued, later she began to explain.

I know, I heard. Your friends—they laugh at everything.

Difficult to tell whether he was envying or accusing. She was silent.

That's their way.

Yes, we don't go in for lamentation.

And after she had said it she saw that might be taken as a dismissal of what she supposed would be the reaction in his hidden life.

She arrives at the garage about noon and he comes out to the waiting car he found for her. She drives to a park away from the quarter of the EL-AY Café and they walk round the lake and buy something from a mobile stall—hot dog for her and chips for him. She asks about his home, does he have photographs—when she makes assumptions, she doesn't even have a photograph to go by, faces to learn from. His figure, a slim taut vertical as he comes out of the dank dimness of the place he works in, the lines of his back, in the sun, as he strolls to the water to give some left-overs to the ducks—he's a cut-out from a background that she surely imagines only wrongly. Palm trees, camels, alleys hung with carpets and brass vessels. Dhows, those sea-bird ships manned by men to whom she can't fit his face. No, he has no photographs.

Nothing much to see. It's a village like hundreds of others there, small shops where people make things, cook food, police station, school. The houses; small. A mosque, small. It's very dry—dust, dusty. Sand.

There are brothers and a brother-in-law, sisters older and younger than he—a big family, of course, he expects her to understand, in that part of the world. There's one brother who's away over the border at the oil fields. The sister-in-law and kids live with the family.

The one—the uncle—with the backyard where you learned about cars?

Oh it was in the village. Next to my father's house.

You must miss them, all so close, and here— She becomes

him, as she walks to his rhythm, she has forgotten how she
has removed definitively, removed herself from the family,
such as it is, in The Suburbs. But she has no idea (if there's
not even a photograph) of what the people he could be missing might be like.

I would bring my mother. Here. I wanted.

All that he said. And—*of course*, again—that was impossible, he himself was not here: had disappeared under the
name in which he was born to them.

Perhaps of her I have a photo—my things, in the room.

She had never seen the room. For her he was detached
from it, as he was from that other place she had never seen,
the village in that other country.

When it rained one Saturday they did not go to the park
but to her elected place—her cottage. She wore a raincoat;
his shirt was soaked, clinging to his skin in the moments they
ran from the car to the door. Running in the rain makes for
laughter. Take it off, take it off, we'll dry it in the kitchen.
You can have one of mine, they're unisex, you'll see. His chest
and back gleamed as if the rain had caressed him with oil, a
chill shuddered under the muscles of his breast, and he found
what it appeared was, for him, the presumption to ask something of her.

Can I have a hot bath?

His manner suddenly made her realize that she had never
given a thought to how he managed in that room, that room
behind the garage—there would be no bathroom?

Go ahead. I'll get you towels. And the shower's great, if
you'd like that.

A shower's what I get all the time—there's an old thing in
the garage and sometimes it works, sometimes no water
comes. I'll take the bath, if you don't mind.

Fill her up to the hilt! You'll find foam stuff and herbal
soap and whatnot. I'll make coffee meanwhile.

She heard him in there, the slap of water against the bath
sides as his body displaced it, a little groan of pleasure as he
wallowed, the gush of a tap turned on again, probably to top
up with more hot water. His occasional presence in this
dwelling-place moved further into the nature of its containment of herself. The pad became a home—at least for the
Saturday afternoon.

He came out barefoot, in his jeans, smiling, the towel
neatly folded in his hands.

Don't bother about that.

She approached to take it from him. It dropped and the
hands, his and hers, held one another, instead. She moved
her palms up his arms in happy recognition of his well-
being; so simple. They embraced. All was as it should be. The
living-room was also a bedroom, so no awkwardness in finding a place to make love. If they really had desired one another so much it had not evidenced itself before—no
hand-holding or kisses, or intimate touching over clothes in
titillation; probably due to him, some tradition or inhibition
in him, foreign to her—she had been accustomed to playing
at love-making since she was twelve years old, had had the
usual quota of lovers common to the friends around their
table, and took her contraceptive pill daily with her vitamins.
Yet he must be equally experienced; they made love beauti-
fully; she so roused and fulfilled that tears came with all that
flooded her and she hoped he did not see them magnifying
her open eyes.

He did not spend the night, that weekend. When he had
gone—took her car, she wanted that, he would bring it back
in the morning—to fetch your shirt and give me mine, she
said, head on one side—when he had gone she wandered
about the room in the echoing of their presence together. She
had made love so many times before. But she squatted at the
bookshelves and found what she vaguely knew she was look-

ing for. In an anthology of poetry were the lines that expressed what she was aware of in herself: *Whoever embraces a woman is Adam. The woman is Eve. Everything happens for the first time. . . . Praise be the love wherein there is no possessor and no possessed, but both surrender. . . . Everything happens for the first time but in a way that is eternal.*

He drove back to the locked and deserted garage, the room redolent of fuel and grease, in the calm and passing content that follows love-making as it does not, he recognizes, what her friends round The Table call a fuck. That's the word that comes to him although there's its equivalent in his own language. He knows that at least he gave complete satisfaction. He resists residue feelings of tenderness towards this girl. That temptation.

It was taken for granted that any event or diversion in the lives of the friends would include the presence of the latest live-in preoccupation of one of their number: girl and her guy, gay and his gay—whatever combination currently had something going between them. This Abdu was at gigs with her which began in night clubs, so called, that were rooms in run-down houses of the quarter turned cheerfully into bars with ikon posters   BOB MARLEY LIVES   HUGH MASEKELA   BRENDA FASSIE IS BACK   stuck to the walls; some served pap and *morogo* spinach along with beer and whisky (high-priced), as the oysters and champagne of what the friends' political guru termed unalienated values. All night the friends decamped from one to the other of these modest houses that had once been built by white small-fry speculators aspiring to become affluent, and paid off monthly by working-class whites with genteel aspirations, all fallen into dilapidation as gentility at this humbly snobbish level became part of lost white privilege. There were arguments about which joint was cool, with much lobbying from those friends who had a special connection with or weakness for one rather than another, because the woman who ran it was an incredible per-

sonality from West Africa, a singer had a voice that could take
the roof off, some guy played the marimba like you never
heard, or tonight there might be two bands jamming together.
Some of the bars, opened one month and gone dark the
next—Paris du Sud, Montmartre Mon Amour, a one-act of
enterprise—were run by French-speaking Congolese, Sene-
galese, Côte d'Ivoireans who perhaps also had disappeared
under their own names, and were living as he did—but with
more style. Maybe with the hand (not in self-exculpatory surrender, her palms thrown up) of those who could pay into the
open-hand gesture he had demonstrated. On these intimate
pub-crawls drugs were on sale and there could be some rowdy
punch-ups that didn't have anything to do with the friends,
they might get a little high on drink or (certainly the poet,
tagging along, and the Buddhist convert who had shaved her
head) on what—marijuana—went under all the names, local
and known to the varied clients, grass, dagga, pot, but they
took care of one another and everyone had a good time. Except him, apparently, Julie's find. Sometimes he would sit in
the shadows, drink nothing; at others he would suddenly
swallow alcohol with determination, as if set on a strange kind
of reverse discipline. If the theorist among them had concerned himself with this, he would have found it a survival
technique. Then Julie's man would dance wildly with her, she
laughing with amazement, welcoming this persona, excited,
intrigued to know where the expertise, the energy came
from—discotheques in the dust of that village—hardly! When
he was a student at the university nobody had ever heard of,
or working wherever in Europe—must have been then; the
performance was marvellous but a touch retro, people danced
like that ten years ago, fashions would take time to filter all
the way to where he came from.

   If this partying looked to come about during the week, he

had a valid reason not to go along: the garage; the garage—
lying under the belly of a vehicle, that was his justification,
his reason-to-be, *here*, at all. He had to be at work at 7 a.m.;
whatever it was the rest of them had as an occupation, a matter of earning bread, it seemed adaptable to their other, pri-
ority needs. Often the friends were pressing; there was the
unspoken code—theirs against the sentimental mores of the
world, friends are there for each other while lovers are transi-
tory: the claims of friends come before lovers. D'you mind if I
go? No enthusiasm in her request; probably the hope that
there would be an objection.

He lies in the bed and waits for her, wakes for her. For
her, the return is the best part of the night.

7 a.m. he's at the garage in the grease-stiff disguise of his
overalls. Or is it that when he climbs out of them, leg by leg,
in the evening he steps from his only identity, *here*, into a disguise, the nobody Abdu—he cannot ask himself, such questions are luxuries he can't afford. As for the garage room he
was told he could use, just keep quiet about it, he has been
warned—as if every disused storeroom, shed and lean-to in
the quarter isn't squatted in by somebody—he kept a few
blankets and cardboard boxes there to suggest he still lived in
it; but the complaisant proprietor knew differently. That
young lady who hung about every day, coming in to talk to
him low-voiced while he paused in his work, tools in hand,
there to fetch him in her car every evening: she had class, you
could see, never mind the kind of clothes all that crowd at the
cafés wear, not all the whites had class around these streets,
but she had. As a white father of daughters himself, it was a
shame to see what she was doing with this fellow from God
knows where, nothing against him, but still.

The proprietor took the opportunity one day when she
came up to the office counter to ask whether the fellow was

out—she hadn't found him in the workshop and she had an urgent message for him.

His employer took the folded piece of paper. Looked at her.

—He's bad news.—

The nerves in her hands began to twitch; a confusion that he should think he had the right to infer he knew who occupied her bed, anger at the assumption that she shared human standards in common with the lout, like-to-like, white-to-white; and dismay: something she might not know about the man she had taken into her life.

—Don't get me wrong. For your own good, you're a nice girl, a somebody, I can see. He's not for you. He's not really even allowed to be in the country. I give him a job, poor devil, I mean, God knows who it can happen to, and it's the other kind, the real blacks who get what's going nowadays.—

Her temper hit her like a lash. She was ready to attack him with the arrogance of the 'somebody' in her he recognized—but there intervened at least something she had learned of an alternative reality to her own: the indulgence might lose her lover his cover; this place where she had discovered him under a car.

—Please give him the message when he comes in.— As if the man behind the counter had not spoken.

He drew a snotty-harsh breath through his nostrils, rubbed a forefinger slowly up from the base of his nose, and turned away.

There follows a space of time that she, and perhaps he, are going to return to in examination—now remembering this aspect of it, then that, for the past has no wholeness, it has been etiolated by revised explanations of it, trampled over by hindsight—all their lives.

What gave it its particular character? He put on the mechanic's overalls and went to the garage every day. She went much later to the tenth-floor suite of offices and occupied her custom-designed chair (gift of one of the clients) at a modular desk with a splendid view of the city given a foreground of computer, communication console, and subtropical pot plants supplied monthly on contract, or she met the current arrival of a pop group at the airport. They left their bed and parted knowing that at the end of each working day they would be back in it again, unknown to and unreachable by anything and anyone who claimed him. Apart during those days, at weekends they often drove into 'the veld', as he became accustomed to hear her calling the countryside, whether it was grassland or mountains. There they walked, lay watching the clouds, the swoop of birds, were amused, as lovers are, by the difference in their exchanged perceptions of what each took for granted. They were never far enough away not to have the surf of some highway they'd turned from, sounding under the sough of air and the passing calls of the birds that ignored them in contrast with the inescapable inclusion calling upon them, at The Table in her haunt, the EL-AY Café. She laid a slack hand on his smooth throat and marvelled, to him: To hear silence. We never do.

To him this was not silence, this lullaby of distant traffic she took for it! Silence is desolation; the desert.

Round the village?

Everywhere. As soon as you walk some steps, some few yards from your house.

Your house?

Of course.

And you used to go and play there, with your friends?

No, no—not out there, never. In the street.

What'd you play—football? What were the games, oh, when you weren't learning about the guts of cars!

Then they can laugh at the impostor mechanic, and she smooths the straight thickness of his moustache shining in the sun, and kisses follow. She brings along books as well as food to these hours when they double the disappearance of his identity, they disappear together, this time, in the veld, but the writers she favours are generally not those known to him from his courses in English at that university (in the desert? in a postcard oasis?—there are no photographs). He is a reader of newspapers; he buys, from the last street vendor as they leave the city, all the weekend papers, and they billow and crackle about them, sails in the wind, as they lie on an old groundsheet she keeps in the car. He reads the newspapers with an intense concentration and a discipline of disbelief as first principle in testing the facts. Sometimes he asks her for the meaning of an unfamiliar term or word. She surreptitiously watches him while he is unaware of her—it's one

of the tranquil pastimes of loving: he reads as if his life depends on what is there. The book she has been reading lies on
her breasts, open face-down at a page where she has come
upon a sentence, a statement, that seems to have been written
for her long before she came into existence and came to this
space in the time of her life. She has read it over again and
again, so that it is written, read, on the air around her,
around him and her, on the sky looking down upon them. 'I
decided to postpone our future as long as possible, leaving
everything in its present state.'

Sometimes there is something quite different, in the veld. An
expedition, no less, of the EL-AY Table. Once a camping
weekend, all the friends and the usual changing roster of
hangers-on. She enjoyed herself immensely, that was obvious,
everybody drank a lot of wine and beer and exchanged stories of past weekends together that sent the battle for attention by excited voices, laughter, mock jeers resounding across
the veld, a pack in full cry. He worked with practical matters,
breaking wood and tending the fire, bringing water from the
river; he had not been one of the company on those previous
adventures, sleeping out on the beach in KwaZulu, being ordered off a bushveld farm by a sjambok-wielding farmer, and
had no anecdotes to add to these. He was listening, or was
not listening at all; absent in his own thoughts. Now and then
in a moment to catch breath, they noticed, and felt him, they
thought, studying them. Then she went over, torn between
the familiar warmth of her place among the friends and the
presence of her other, private intimacy, to draw him into that
warmth by making some sort of show of the love affair, hanging on him, whispering in and nibbling at his ear. He re-
strained her gently, as if she were an over-affectionate pet.
The friends were accustomed to sex-play among them on

these weekend transportations from The Table at the EL-AY, no-one would have thought anything of it; it was his—his unfamiliar response that disquieted. There was talk: That relationship's getting heavy, our girl's really gone on that oriental prince of hers. Where was it she picked him up, again?

To continue in their present state: his situation in itself, alone determined this. He is here, and he is not here. It's within this condition of existence that they exist as lovers. It is a state of suspension from the pressures of necessity to plan the way others have to plan; look ahead. There is no future without an identity to claim it; or to be obligated to it. There are no caging norms. In its very precariousness the state is pure and free. The state the friends of the EL-AY Café table would like to attain by some means they are not sure of, can't define, only argue over?

So she is taken by surprise, off the perfect tightrope balance, when he suddenly speaks out of one of his silences.

You have a mother and father. Why don't you take me to know your parents.

Ah yes, and his are far away! Even further away, farther than sea and land, in her idea of them. She wants to respond with a surge of tenderness and guilt at having to have been reminded of this—the nostalgia she thinks he is expressing. But at the same time her self-protective instinct—which is the image of herself she believes to be her true self and that she

has contrived to project to him, prompts her to head him off
with an explanation commensurate with that image.

Four of them. A father and stepmother, a mother and
stepfather. As I've mentioned. So I'd have to subject you
twice over. Both couples and their sets; very boring people. I
haven't wanted to do that to you.

Julie. We are together—five months now, yes. We are still
all the time only with your friends.

No. I thought we're alone together.

Yes, we are together, living in your place, everything . . .
More than five months. If a woman chooses a man for this, or
a man chooses a woman, it is time for the parents to know.
To see the man. It's usual.

Maybe where he comes from. For the first time, the difference between them, the secret conditioning of their origins,
an intriguing special bond in their intimacy against all others,
is a difference in a different sense—an opposition.

I have to tell you. You'll hate it. I wouldn't know which to
choose first, my father and his new wife, my mother and the
casino owner who's her latest husband.

Just to confirm: You have no sisters and brothers.

No, she is not part of that constellation of siblings which,
she sees, he probably knows himself in even though it is not
visible from under these skies where he and she lie together.

My life is my life, not theirs. And she repeats, not knowing
how to say more: I didn't want to subject you to them.

He sulks; or is it lonely sadness in that profile? She is distanced and distressed. Love engraves a profile definitively as
the mint does on a coin.

She is ashamed of her parents; he thinks she is ashamed
of him. Neither knows either, about the other.

The next time her father invites her to Sunday lunch (without for some months at least a telephone call from his daughter) she says she'll be bringing someone with her. The phrase is intended as a hint, a preparation: the ordinary formulation would be that she will be with a friend. Not that this was customary, anyway; her father rarely was brought into contact with whoever these friends were, though he no doubt could judge, by her attitudes towards him and his wife, what sort of alternatives they might be.

—Will that be all right? With Danielle.—

She knows that the elaborate social life of her father's house is convened by the social talents of his wife.

—Good Lord, of course. You can bring anyone you like, your friends are always welcome, you know that.—

He hasn't caught the nuance; and there is one of his own, here: the slipping in of a reproach that his daughter keeps him out of her life.

In order to start off on the right foot in her father's house it is a good idea to observe some convention for guests—even if she is supposed not to be a guest in her own father's house, her 'someone' is—so on the way she asks him to stop the car

at a corner where a flower-seller has a pitch, and she buys a
bunch of roses. You dump them in the hands of Danielle so
that she may not raise them, so to speak, against you. This is
not something one shares with the young man she is beside.
Another hint she thinks—hopes—might be caught by anyone
seeing her car come through the security gates to the house, is
that he, the Someone, not she, is in the driver's seat.

Don't be too sure you know what's to come, that set struck
and rebuilt for the same scene every Sunday all over The
Suburbs. These guests are not exposed, in every sense, half-
clad to the sun on plastic chairs round a swimming pool, her
father is not bending a belly over grilling meat. This is a different level of suburban entertaining. The guests are on a cool
terrace opening from a living-room that leads through arch-
ways to other reception rooms of undefined function (to ac-
commodate parties?), and the cushioned chaises longues and
flower arrangements are an extension rather than a break
from the formal comforts, mirrored bouquets and paintings
in the rooms. The food, already set out by the time the
daughter of the house arrives, is the cold poached Norwe-
gian salmon with sauces and kaleidoscope-bright salads that
Danielle has taught the cook to produce perfectly. The margaritas (host's speciality) have their rime of salt and the
pewter beer mugs and wine glasses are misted by contrast of
temperature between the warm day and their chilled contents. It is all very pleasant, the offering of this kind of Sunday, make no mistake about it; Julie comes upon it as always:
sinking into a familiar dismay. But *he* is at her side, one of
those invisible shields that turn aside arrows and keep the
bearer intact.

When her father was introduced to her Someone there was
across his face a fleeting moment of incomprehension of the
name, quickly dismissed by good manners and a handshake.
What was the immediate register? Black—or some sort of

black. But what she read into this was quickly confused by what she had not noticed—there already was a black couple among the guests—amazing: the innovation showed how long it must have been since she came to one of the Sunday lunch parties in that house Nigel Ackroyd Summers had built for his Danielle. Her father's pragmatic self-assurance knew easily how to deal with half-grasped names now common to the infiltration of the business and professional community by those who bore them. She might have realized by now that her father, as an investment banker in this era of expanding international financial opportunities and the hand-over-fist of black political power on the way to financial power at home, must have to add such names to the guest lists for a balance of his contacts. He let her complete the introductions: —This is my daughter Julie, and her friend . . .—

It was the name that was not his name that he responded to.

There was the bob this-side-and-that against her cheek that Danielle would have given without noticing, if she had a figure from a shop window placed before her for greeting, and then she turned to whoever it was Julie had brought along: her welcoming upward tilt of the head and smile. Either no reaction other than hostessly; or more likely one of no surprise that the girl would turn up with what was no doubt the latest wearying ploy to distance herself from her father. The Someone Julie produced smiled back, and this convention matched that which each one had at hand, in the reflex, purely aesthetical, sincerity irrelevant, the facility of a particularly beautiful transformation of the visage. (He smiled at Julie, out of his reserve, in the sombre greasy shades of the garage, or was it in the street, that first time.) And Danielle— her smile was a kind of personal announcement of her beauty. She was beautiful; trust the father for that. Her social intelligence was well managed to suggest, to anyone able to

appreciate this, that her real intelligence went drier and
deeper. Her stepdaughter saw her, as so often, drawing away
with the bait of some flattering request a female guest from a
man being bored by chatter on matters the poor thing knew
nothing about; moving with a sway of her graceful backside
(she had been an actress, interpreter of sophisticated come-
dies set in London, Paris or New York, out-dated now by the
changes that had also changed her guest list) as she mingled
the guests like the deft shuffle of a pack of cards, slipping in
a remark here and there (. . . I want you to come and tell that
amazing . . .) particularly among the men, to show that she
read the newspapers, was privy to gossip about entrepreneurs
and politicians; picking up, among the usual three or four
women whom nothing could induce to leave their huddle,
variations on domestic anecdotes, and teasing an unsuspected
elderly feminist who suddenly stood, glass in hand, to heckle
two males who were enjoying men-talk witticisms about
women members on their Board.

Apart from replenishing his rounds of margaritas, her father left this general company to his Danielle. He and what
must be the principal guests he was cultivating (his daughter
believes she knows him well) were gathered round the issues
of the day, the week; for her, their lives were always in control, these people—talk around her, 'buying into futures'
(whatever that might be) was a mastery they took, from the
immediate present, of what was to come: the future, of which
any control for the Someone beside her did not exist. The em-
anation of his presence, bodily warmth and breath, was
merely a haze which hid him from them; their reality did not
know of his existence.

—Gold . . . hardly the issue any more. When you think of
the crisis, nearly floored us not so long ago . . . first London
sales that sent the market crashing . . . —

—a full vault somewhere doesn't earn anything—

—well exactly. Wasting asset. For any country. Sell it, sell, sell for dollars deutschmarks whathaveyou and buy blue-chip stocks. Assets must earn, law of survival, ay!—

—pretty sure AngloGold's going to reduce its forward hedge position within a year . . . more than fifty percent of production's probably there, with a big drop likely in the physical market—

—thirty-three thousand tons of the bright stuff in the vaults—

—Shift over and make room for platinum, wha'd you think—

—No profitable future in mining gold here, anyway—

—all that outcry about robbing the poor of their jobs, killing the industry—the unions, the government must face facts—economics of the past don't work, unemployment's not going to be solved by shoring up an industry that's lost its place in terms of global finance. It's the end of an old industrial era, not just something on a calendar—

—With an increase in operative efficiencies some mines—

—strikes? Huge labour problems?—

—Look, it was a bad day, sector down twenty-three percent—

—relief buying, block traders—

—I don't know . . . pretty broad-based recovery, a dedicated programme of expansion . . . chromium . . . —

—software—more hostile take-over bids—

—oh and more unbundling coming, you'll see—

—You must have at least a whole day for Ellora and Ajanta even though the road, my God, you can't believe your bones won't rattle apart.— A counterpoint of voices was exchanging enthusiasm about a holiday in India; as if she had spied a familiar artifact or perhaps out of a well-intentioned move to draw into conversation someone who did not seem to be heard anywhere in the company, a woman wearing indi-

vidual handcuffs of silver bangles turned, jangling, to speak
to the stranger.

—I long to go again, can't explain, so *belonging* there, I
think I'm some sort of old soul who once had a previous existence . . . I suppose you were born here, but your ancestors
. . . have you ever been home to India?—

—I'm not Indian.—

He doesn't offer an identity. She jerks her head in dismissive apology (if that's what's called for) and makes some remark about the delicious food; —I'm on my way for seconds
of Danielle's fish.— The set of her back is the conclusion:
some sort of Arab, then.

—but when the Dow and Nasdaq differ significantly—

—a twenty-one percent rise in headline earnings, four billion—

—ah but that's well below expectations—

—how'd the Minister put it—'toughing it out against in-
flation'—I mean three and six percent as a test case at the
whim of the global financial system—

—how to hammer into their thick heads . . . their survival,
privatization's the only answer, when a service must make
profit it's made to work cost-efficiently, and that's when the
public gets what it needs—

—I have a hunch, everyone rushing in, it's going to boom
or bust with IT—

—our company's been reaping the benefit of rising exports
in base metals and chemicals, pretty satisfying—

—look, nothing—zero—*nada* will happen unless the Reserve Bank—

The other black man among the guests was sitting forward in his chair, palms on knees. —Ah-heh . . . I don't dispute diversification, no no not at all. But our real problem is
that there is not enough venture capital. Not enough in equi-
ties.—

—no question, global buffeting has queered our pitch for growth in many ways, currency down-down, oil prices up-up—

—turnover more than thirteen billion, futures dominating—

The enthusiastic interruption by the guest returned from India has deflected Julie's companion's attention only momentarily; his reply a polite aside. She watches how he listens to this intimate language of money alertly and intently—as he never listens at the EL-AY Café; always absent, elsewhere, entering whatever discussion only now and then, when confronted. She is overcome by embarrassment—what is he thinking, of these people—she is responsible for whatever that may be. She's responsible for *them*.

Suddenly she has left, through the living-room, through the shadowy indoors and up the staircase.

But it is another house she's running away to hide in; she has never lived in this one. This is not the upstairs retreat of the house where she was a child. Each room she looks into up there—no one of them is the room that was hers, with the adolescent posters of film stars and on the bed the worn plush panda her father bought for her once on an airport. It is not that house she is wandering, pausing, listening to herself. The shame of being ashamed of them; the shame of him seeing what she was, is; as he must be what he is, away beyond the dim underworld of the garage, the outhouse granted him, the anonymous name she introduced him by, his being in the village where the desert begins near your house. Rejection implies hidden—her rejection hid this origin of hers now expansively revealed before him, laid out like the margaritas and the wine and the composed still-life of the fish-platter, salads and desserts. She blunders to one of the bathrooms; but cannot succeed in retching to humiliate herself.

—Enjoying yourself, sweetheart—it's an order to settle

down again, after wherever she disappeared to, from her father who is standing up apparently about to propose a toast.

—We're not going to weep and implore don't leave us, we're not even going to complain about being deserted, but we do want to tell you we'll get flabby on the squash court without your smashing serve, Adrian, not to mention the darts with which you hit—infallibly, you shrewdy—prediction in the rise of interest rates and fiscal matters. Always been there for us before the tax man cometh . . . and Gillie, her open house down at the coast in summer, her open heart . . . Danielle and I have brought friends together just to wish you enormous luck and happiness, may you triumph over Down Under, Adrian, with the huge expansion in relocation of your interests, this splendid recognition of your global-class expertise the communications giants have had the good fortune to take advantage of. You don't need any advice— just don't eat kangaroo meat if it's patriotically served at Aussie corporate dinners, that's strictly for Gillie's two labradors I hear she's taking with you . . .—

With laughter and clinking of glasses the talk is of Australia, in place of Cisco Systems, gold or India. The women show appropriate interest in the house the emigrants will choose, suburban or out-of-town, lovely climate anyway. The man explains that he has a complete set-up ready—excellent Australian staff chosen by himself on preparatory visits. —You'll perhaps not be surprised to hear of the exception, my old driver—Festus, remember? Yes—his wife died recently, he wants to try a new life, he says, so he's being relocated with anything else we feel inclined to pack up.—

The young foreigner (coloured, or whatever he is) moves from Nigel Summers' daughter's protection into the general exchange.

—Was it easy to get entry?—

Nobody must laugh at this: the idea that a man of such

means and standing would not be an asset to any country. The executive director of a world-wide website network, kindly, only smiles, gives a brief assuring movement, the chin and lower lip pursing, at the naïvety.

The foreigner looks back from a no-entry cave of black eyes: —I don't mean you. I mean your driver.—

—Oh I left that to my colleague here, Hamilton—Mr Motsamai. Hamilton's a wizard, he knows exactly what one has to get together, whom to approach, documents and so forth. Bureaucratic stuff. It's been tremendously useful, in our operation here, to have a top lawyer on the Management Board, a bonus quite apart from his invaluable financial nous, of course—

The voice was raised for the benefit of the compliment to reach the ears of Mr Motsamai but he was too centred in other animated company to hear it above his own bass. Glances turned to place the one so favoured and a woman pleased to be in the know offered an aside. —That's the black lawyer who saved the son of the Summers' great friends. Such nice people, awful affair. Got him off with only seven years for that ghastly murder a few years ago—the son shot the homosexual who seduced his girl, and he'd had an affair with him, himself. Could have been life in prison.—

'Relocate' they say. The couple are 'relocating'.

If one were to overhear this—do they know what they're talking about?

When in doubt go to the dictionary.

'Locate: to discover the exact locality of a person or thing; to enter, take possession of.'

To discover the exact location of a 'thing' is a simple matter of factual research. To discover the exact location of a person: where to locate the self?

To take possession of—a land-claim, a gold mine, etc.?
The land-claim, the gold mine—the clever lawyer who's just
been praised can tell how to go about taking possession of the
land, the gold mine, (if it's worth possessing at all according
to present inside information) may be gained by a take-over
or merger. To discover and take over possession of oneself, is
that secretly the meaning of 'relocation' as it is shaped by the
tongue and lips in substitution for 'immigration'?

'Relocate' they're saying. It's the current euphemism for
pulling up anchor and going somewhere else, either perforce
or because of the constrictions of poverty or politics, or by
choice of ambition and belief that there's an even more
privileged life, safe from the pitchforks and AK-47s of the
rebellious poor and the handguns of the criminals. It's not a
matter of unpacking furniture in new premises. Some of the
dictionary definitions of the root word 'locate' give away the
inexpressible yearning that cannot be explained by ambition,
privilege, or even fear of others. Promised land, an Australia,
if you like.

A farewell is also a celebration of immigration as a human solution. No-one here brings to mind it's not the first
time. Giles Yelverton. Hein Straus. Mario Marini. Debby and
Glen Horwitz. Top (nickname) Ivanovic. Sandy and Alison
McLeod. Owen Williams. Danielle (née Le Sueur) and Nigel
Ackroyd Summers and his daughter Julie. Generations have
buried this category of theirs along with the grandfathers but
all these are immigrants by descent. Only the lawyer Motsamai, among them, is the exception. He was here; he is here;
a possession of self. Perhaps. Lawyer with the triumph of
famous cases behind him, turned financier, what he has become must be what he wishes to be; his name remains in unchanged identity with where his life began and continues to
be lived.

The fêted couple are about to be immigrants. Sitting

among the gathering Julie is seeing the couple as those—her
father's kind of people—who may move about the world welcome everywhere, as they please, while someone has to live
disguised as a grease-monkey without a name.

Her father appeared as they walked towards her car. They already had said their obligatory goodbyes. He halted her a
moment with a staying gesture barely touching her shoulder.
She turned to meet a face restored from childhood. —You're
all right?— The voice for her alone. And in the moment that
would instantly seem as if it never happened, there was in her
returning gaze, for him only, the understanding that she was
asking the same: about him, her father, that there was between them this question to be shared, to be asked of him, his
life, too.

That Sunday ended. There never need be another; he should be convinced, now. Her mother lives in California; that introduction, if he thought it necessary, would take place sometime if she accompanied her husband to his casino investments back in this country. That would not add much; all there was to tell him, confess, had been shown before him today. In the car he had found for her, going home to her cottage, they were silent, needing rest. She was grateful he said nothing about the experience; not yet. She placed her palm on his thigh and he took a hand off the wheel and touched hers lightly, returning his hand to the business of driving.

In her place—their place—she stood a moment almost giddily and looked at him, an assertion of her reality, before her. He was glancing about the small all-purpose room with its three chairs, table to eat off, bed to receive them, unmade from the morning, as if looking for somewhere to place himself.

Absolutely stuffed with all that food. What about you? Something to drink? Tea?

He lifted a hand—no, no. He let himself down spread-eagled on his back, on the bed. She followed his eyes round the room to discover what he was planning to say; then she went over and sat on the bed. And twisted her body to lean and kiss him, on the forehead and then, tentatively, on the mouth. She was at once heated, like a gross blush all over her body and face, by a fierce desire, which she was at pains to conceal, folding away her hands that urged to thrust down over the flat dark-haired belly that she knew under his pants.

Interesting people there. They make a success.

Those were the words he was looking for round the room. The wonderful desire drained from her instantly.

They'd stamp on one another's heads to make it.

The document must have been lying on some-body's desk, that weekend. Or maybe in the post office from where whatever mail he received was to be delivered in the name that was supposed to be his, care of the garage that was supposed to be his only address. She was to visualize this closed and deserted Sunday post office, uselessly, afterwards, a daymare in sunlight, a conjuring up of foreboding in the dark bed at night. To dignify the piece of paper as a 'docu-ment' was more than the brusque demand it made in the guise of citations from this law and that, this paragraph of that section, as promulgated on one date or another. It had come to the notice of the Department of Home Affairs that (his real name) was living at the above address under the alias (the name the grease-monkey answered to) in contra-vention of the termination of his permit of such-and-such a date to reside in the Republic. This was a criminal offence (paragraph, section of law) and he was therefore duly in-formed that he must depart within 14 days or face charges and deportation to his country of origin.

These letters that come unstamped, Official Business. She has never received one; her income tax papers, a citizen's routine fiscal matters, go to her family's accountants. He came to the cottage still in his dirty overalls, carrying this—thing. The envelope had been raggedly torn—he knows what to expect from such missives. He had read the news and come just as he was from among the eviscerated cars and the amplified pop music in the garage. —Here it is.

She had almost forgotten; the months that had passed since she bought the car he found for her, his coming home to her every evening, the night club jaunts with the friends from The Table, the weekends away in the veld, lying side by side in his silence, the excitement and following peace of love-making, nights and early mornings—these had lulled her. These (what were those lines that came back to her) post-poned the future . . . leaving everything in its present state.

She sat suddenly on their bed to read the thing over again. He stood in the room as if he were already the stranger ejected from it. And so she wept and flung herself at him and he had no reassurance for her in the arms that came about her. They were unsteady on their feet. She struggled free and drew up the piece of paper. She took him by the hand for them to sit and read it over again, together. But he sat beside her, lifted his shoulders and let them fall, did not follow the lines with her. He knows the form, the content, the phraseol-ogy; it is the form of the world's communication with him. She looks for loopholes, for double meanings that might be deciphered to advantage, that he knows are all stopped up, are all unambiguous. Out. Get out. Out.

Then she became angry. Who told them? How did they find out? After how long? How long? Two years—

Two years and some months.

Who? But who would do it, what for?

Anyone. Someone who wants my job, maybe. Yes. Why not.

Why not! What harm do you do anybody, what did you take away from anybody, that lousy job and a shed to live in!

Julie. Somebody who's here in his own place.

And now his eyes were penetrating as searchlights seeking her out, his lips were drawn back in violent pain in place of that beautiful curved smile. Even this I'm wearing, this dirty . . . even whatyoucallit, a shed, a corner in the street to sleep in, that's his, not mine. That's how it is. Whatever I have is his.

A gust of what was unknown between them blew them apart. In distress she wanted somehow to reach and grapple with him as he was borne away, as she was borne away.

Why do you take it like this! What are you going to do about it! There must be something—protest, apply—this Home Affairs place, can't you go to them right away, tomorrow morning—how can you just—

Leave me, leave me: he knows that is what this girl is really saying; to her—of course—expulsion means she loses her lover, this bed will be empty, at least until—she's free, secure and free, she finds another lover. To calm her—and himself: I go there. Nothing will be done. They'll look up the other paper from nearly one year and a half. They know I was supposed to get out then.

So you knew this would happen. Even after so long.

I knew, yes. I thought perhaps, they lost the paper, maybe they have so many papers of people like me, they could forget me. That was my chance. That's how it is. I could go there to them, but what for. It will be better if I do nothing, I didn't get the letter, I'm not at the garage any more, I'm somewhere . . .

Well they don't know you're here with me. You don't live at that address, that's something.

I think they'll know.

That horrible man at the garage! *He's bad news, he's not for you, he's not even allowed to be in the country.* What about your job? Even if no records are kept . . . you'd have to disappear from that as well . . .

Disappear (she has given him the word he needs), yes. Again. Again! And again another name!

He sees her turning her head this way and that, in the trap. That's how it is.

If he says that one more time! So how it has to be is not what he will do about this letter, this document passing a sentence on his life, but what we are going to do. She has friends, thank his gods and hers, anybody's; her friends who solve among themselves all kinds of difficulties in their opposition to establishment officialdom. They have alternative solutions for the alternative society, and there is every proof that that society is the one to which he and she belong: that letter makes it clear. She abrogates any rights that are hers, until they are granted also to him. This means she will follow no obedience to truthfulness ingested at school, no rules promulgated in the Constitution, no policy of transparency as in the Board Rooms where the investment business code applies.

Julie does not tell him this; only by pressing herself against him, he's palpable, he hasn't disappeared from her, and holding her mouth against his until it is opened and lets her in, to the live warmth and moisture of his being.

He receives her, but cannot give himself. She understands: the shock, the letter finally come, followed him, tracked him down; for her, outrage, high on alarm, for him a numbing. Let's go to the EL-AY. We have to talk about this.

Ah no. No, Julie. Not now, tonight. Let us stay alone. Strangely, he began to take off the grease-darkened overalls as if he were shedding a skin, letting them fall to the floor and stepping slowly out of them. Perhaps he meant to get into bed, bed is the simplest offer of oblivion? But no.

I want to take a bath.

She heard the water gushing a long time. She heard it slapping against the sides of the tub as he moved about within it.

She picked up the paper and sat with it in her hand. That first time; he asked to take a hot bath, she heard him there; when he came out holding the neatly-folded towel he was barefoot in his jeans and she saw his naked torso, the ripple of ribs under shining smooth skin, the dark nipples on the pad of muscle at either side of the design of soft-curled black hair.

That's how it is.

They are to meet at The Table in his lunch break. That's the arrangement; she would not come by at the garage for him to join her—if one did not know what was to be done, at least here was a procedure begun, that trail that led through her from the garage to the cottage must be deflected. Look for him somewhere else.

She was there before him.

It's happened. See her face.

The friends in the EL-AY Café also had been lulled by his presence become accepted in their haven; they received her with gazes of alarm and curiosity, darting suppositions. (It's bust up. He's walked out on her. She's seen through her oriental prince and told him, enough. Her dear papa's heard about the affair and cut off her allowance. What else?)

So she had time to tell them, to discuss what had happened before he joined her. Their reactions duplicated hers when it came to surface manifestations; the others, the depths of fear and emotions, they hesitated to approach so precipitately—even the habit of intimate openness quails before situations not in the range of experience. Indignation went back and forth across the cappuccino. That bastard at the garage!

That man! Must have been him, who else! You can't tell me
any of the fellows he works with would want to go near to report to the fuzz! What a shit!

—Wait a moment.— The political theorist thinks before
allowing himself to indulge in hasty accusations. —The
garage owner would not be the one to report that kind of employee. If he did, he'd be reporting himself as hiring an illegal. That's a criminal charge, you know, my Brothers.— His
quick, hard laugh is not offensive—a correction of the limitations of his white friends' awareness of the shifty workings of
survival.

—The first thing, make an application for the order to be
reviewed. You don't take it lying down.—

—You go with him to a lawyer, not one of those divorce
and property sharks, a civil rights lawyer, what about Legal
Resources, they must know a hell of a lot about this kind of
situation.—

—No, no, you *do* go to a shark, and you pay him well—
come on Julie, you can find the cash—

David, who is house-sitting at present, has his time to offer her. —I rather think it's a matter provided for in the
Constitution. Maybe. Could he make the case of political asy-
lum—maybe not . . . I'll go with you to the law library—my
cousin's an advocate and he can do something useful for
once, he'll get us in. You need to know all the relevant stuff,
the small print, ready to throw at Home Affairs, you need to
trip them up somehow—

Their poet laureate has slipped into his usual place, the
cape of white hair tied back with a black ribbon today, catching up quietly, with swayings of the head, on what has happened to Julie's find. —He must go underground. There is a
world underground in this city, in all cities, the only place
for those of us who can't live, haven't the means, not just
money, the statutory means to conform to what others call

the world. Underground. That darkness is the only freedom
for him.—

Disappear. Julie, of whom this elderly man is particularly
fond, among the friends, the one whom he's said he regards
as his spiritual daughter—she has a clutching sense of his divining, affirming her dread. While she tries to listen to everyone at once with confidence in their alternative wisdom, she
keeps erect in her chair looking out for her lover's appearance
among the habitués coming and going in the EL-AY Café.
She returns waves of the hand to those her eye inadvertently
catches; his black eyes at last meet hers, her unique creature
emerging from the forest of others.

Hi Abdu. Today they all get up from round The Table to
receive him. Men and women, they embrace him, this side
and that, in their natural way. It serves them better than
words, now that the subject is there among them. All are
around him, except the poet. He sits contemplating, saying to
himself what no-one overhears, no doubt some quote from
Yeats, Neruda, Lorca or Heaney, Shakespeare, that expresses
the moment, the happening, better than anything said or
done by The Table.

The victim thanks them politely; his hand taken up in
hers, he sits down to listen. To be questioned and to hear his
own replies. There is not much he can tell other than they
drew from him with their brotherly welcoming when she introduced him to The Table months ago; or that he chooses to
tell them? Sometimes she has to repeat to him something that
has been said, as his head has been turned away—what is he
seeking in this phalanstery of wine- and coffee-bibbers? Ever
since he walked in with that piece of paper yesterday, his de-
meanour, his consciousness, by which one human receives
another, has been that of seeking, an alertness that discards
distraction. She orders coffee for him as she sees him glance
at his watch; he's arrived only after half his lunch break is

over. Was there any sign that anyone at the garage knows?
No-one said anything? No clue?

He drank his coffee in an unaccustomed way, spoke between gulps. —Nothing.—

—And the boss. Nothing emanating from him?— The follower of Buddhism thought there would be sensitivity to a
change in atmosphere, even if there was no action.

She was interrupted—Look, man, can't you catch on,
Teresa, I told you it's ridiculous to think the boss could turn
himself in.—

Julie took careful note, in full attention, of all advice
about what these good friends who knew how to look after
themselves suggested should be done. She constantly referred
this to him. He kept quietly gesturing he had heard. Their
support surrounded him; as if he were one of them. As he got
up to leave in the persona of the grease-monkey going back
to the garage, he said without rejection—I have done all these
things before.— There it was: the first time he was ordered to
quit the country, when his permit expired.

She wanted to run after him but her place—it was to be
left behind in the EL-AY Café. Ralph smiled at her, a victim
for whom, when he told The Table he had AIDS, they could
find no solution but the victim's own bravado of laughter.

When he came back to her from the garage that evening she
was ironing a pair of the designer jeans he always wore even
when he was living wretchedly in a shed. A towel was folded
on the table they ate off, the jeans were spread upon it; she
was pressing one hand over the other that held the iron, to
emphasize a seam.

He had never seen her at a domestic task of this nature.
Although they choose to live in a converted outhouse instead
of a beautiful home with shaded terraces and rooms for every

private and public purpose, people like her have a black woman who comes to clean and wash and iron. Since he had moved in he had dropped his clothes into the basket provided, along with hers—she would put apart the overalls, stiff carapace made of the week's working dirt, with a pinned note that they must be washed separately.

She looked up at him from his garment and her eyes swelled with tears.

So it had to come: the tears, sometime. He came over and put the iron aside from her hand and turned her towards him. It's all right. He had to kiss her, this water of hers running salty into his mouth; all the fluids of her body that he tasted, her sweat, the juices of her sex, were there.

Then they went to sit on the sagging concrete step at the cottage door, looking out into the haggard tangle of fir and jacaranda trees darkly stifled by bougainvillaea, that was her end of the old garden where, far behind them a main house stood. She got up at once to go back into the cottage and fetch a bottle of wine—if bed is the simplest offer for oblivion, then among the friends wine is the best way of gathering nerve to tackle problems. She pulled the cork with an abrupt tug and took a swig, glasses forgotten. Handed to him, he put the bottle down on the earth. She began to go over with him the suggestions made by those, her friends, accustomed to get round authority. Again he listened to what he had heard before. Very practical, now, this Julie. She would go with the man David to a law library and familiarize herself with the relevant statute. She would ask around—people had to be wary when they revealed certain connections—about the kind of lawyer who was prepared to handle unconventional ways of evading laws. There must be many, many people like himself—the two of them—in the shit. (She knows he doesn't like to hear her using these words that everyone uses—really there must be the same sort of necessity in his own language but of course even if he wanted to relieve his feelings in this banal way she wouldn't understand.) They also might as well make an appointment with Legal Resources, they'll know about conventional steps to take, human rights fundis must be well up in such matters.

The air was thickening about them in preparation for rain; he breathed it deeply several times. He was speaking to the black thicket of leaves and branches meshing a gathering darkness—Why do you choose those friends. Instead of your family.

For her, it's as if she has overheard something not intended for her. The Table; but why change the urgent subject! Reluctantly she is distracted. I don't know what you mean. Sometimes the limitations of his use of her language bring misunderstanding although she thinks she lovingly has taught herself to interpret him instinctively.

They are people doing well with their life. All the time. Moving on always. Clever. With what they do, make in the world, not just talking intelligent. They are alive, they take opportunity, they use the (snaps his tongue against his palate in search of the word) the will, yes, I mean to say, the will. To do. To have.

The crowd you saw at my father's house. Those?

Yes, your father and the other men. They know what they speak about. What happens. Making business. That's not bad, that is the world. Progress. You have to know it. I don't know why you like to sit there every day in that other place.

The wind that sweeps a path for rain suddenly came between them. She jumped up to go indoors or not to have to accept what he said, let it blow away from them. He came in behind her.

The bottle has fallen and the wine leaks out, its passage catching the light from the windows, a glisten, before the earth drinks it.

Inside, in the atmospheric pressure of the rising storm she sat with her hands in her lap and her eyes on him in a way that asked of him what it was that he wanted.

You can go to your father. He knows many things. They don't know about anything. If they know, they can't do.

Oh no! No. No. That's impossible. No. He doesn't know about such things. No, no.

He moves swiftly into her recoil: afraid, after all, little girl afraid of father. —I don't mean this of me, mine. But other things that are not easy, straight. He knows. Believe it.

Almost weary—You can't understand.

And then she is taken by remorse because by saying this she has made him understand: it's because he is not one of them. He himself said it only a day ago, of the one, *anyone*, entitled to divest him of the overalls and take his place under the vehicles: *even this I'm wearing, this dirt, even a shed, a corner in the street to sleep in, that's his, not mine . . . whatever I have is his*: any one of them, those with the legal birthright, place in the social hierarchy, share of investments advised. Such a man. Already said: *Whatever I have is his*: you, your father's daughter are *his*, not mine.

How could he admire them, those other friends, her father's Chairmen of the Boards, Trustees of the Funds, Directorspiders at the centre of the websites that net the Markets, and at the same time not realize this? For the father, what a timely end to this latest crazy, impossible behaviour on the part of a daughter! The man deported—*finis*, the whole affair solved without any need of parental argument, father-daughter conflict of values, souring of relations, the usual result of any necessary interference on the part of the father. The law will do it. Save her from herself, thank God. Her father need only be there to help put together the pieces of her bereaved state, if she'll accept his love after her pickup (God knows where she found him) is once and for all out of the picture.

They went to bed before long. The kindest thing for both surely would have been to make love. But that's *his* right, that's *his*—the suitable young man who belongs at the Sunday terrace lunches, the inside talk of the men the lover beside her admires so much.

The end; end of a winter, theirs together. The first rain of another season beat on and about the cottage like a surrounding crowd. After brittle months of dryness all the stuff of which their shelter was made—wood, iron roof, plaster on brick—came alive and creaked and shifted as if it crumpled them in a giant fist; as if the hammering of water and the materials given tongue by pressure and expansion were voices of the curious, the interfering, the scornful, the spurious sympathizers and the judgmental, the curt rejectors dictating the piece of paper, gabbling all about them in mimic travesty of the familiar café babble.

In the morning while she lay in the bath and he shaved carefully round the glossy pair of wings on his upper lip, he turned to her without seeing her nakedness. What about that lawyer? He did something for someone who killed. I heard a woman talking about it. You know him—he was there at your father's, he knows who you are. You could find him. The black man.

Well. It touches her with relief like gratitude that he has accepted she will not—cannot—go to her father. Yes, I suppose he would have been someone . . . but does he still practise law? I think he's given it up for money-making, you saw how he was one of the cronies.

You can find out.

Oh I can do that easily. But there's so little time, no time. We must think of everything, anyone who—

Three days of the edict gone by. He is looking at her, placed directly before her as she gets out of the bath aware of her nakedness, wraps her body in a towel. Think, think. She must: because he is there with her, hers; and not there, no name, no address, no claim on anyone.

You've surely heard of him if you are a middle-class woman, or man who lives with that woman, in this city.

Dr Archibald Charles Summers is the gynaecologist and obstetrician, MBBCh Witwatersrand University, Fellow of the Royal College of Surgeons, St Mary's London, Fellow of the Institute of Obstetrics, Boston Mass., with a practice which is, so to speak, always over-subscribed. Call him fashionable, but that would not be entirely just; he is much more than that, he gives more than any regular specialist fees could ever cover. Women talk about him to one another with a reverent sense of trust exceptional between patient and doctor even in this branch of medicine in which the doctor is priest, intermediary in the emergence of new life, and the woman is its active acolyte. As an obstetrician, he is each woman's Angel Gabriel: his annunciation when he reads the scan of her womb—it's a boy. And his shining bald head, outstanding ears and worshipful smile are the first things she sees when he lifts life as it emerges from her body. Between births and after reproduction is no longer part of his patients' biological programming, he takes care—in the most conscientious sense—

of the intricate system inside them that characterizes their gender and influences—often even decides—the crucial balance of their reactions, temperaments, on which depend the manner in which they can deal with the other man-woman relationships—the recognized ones with lovers and/or husbands.

Dr Archibald's consulting rooms are a home: the studio portraits of his children as babies and graduates, the blow-ups of wild life photography, which is his hobby, posters proposing the beauties of the world from museums he has enjoyed on his travels. The bejewelled hands of his Indian receptionist note any change of address of the habituée patient greeted once again, there is a bustle of several nurses with motherly big backsides, Afrikaner and black, calling back and forth to one another, who receive for urine tests the wafers peed upon by the patient in the privacy of a blue-tiled bathroom where a vase of live flowers always stands on the toilet tank.

His patients—his girls, as he refers to them, whether aged twenty or seventy—talk of him to one another as Archie. I've got my six-month appointment with Archie due next week. I've just come from Archie—everything's okay, he says, he's pleased with me. And if everything is not okay, if rose thou art sick, Blake's invisible worm that flies in the night in the howling storm and eats out the heart of the rose has invaded with a cancer, Archie with the knife in his healing hand will cut it out so that blooming continues, for Archie is the deliverer of life.

The doctor has been married to and in love with his wife for thirty years at least. His seraglio of patients has nothing in common with the passion for her which has never waned; the penetration of his expert right hand sheathed in latex into the vaginas of his patients, young and desirable, ageing and desexed, reduced to the subject of a kind of gut-exploration

in the diagnostic divining of his fingertips, might be thought
certain to end in a revulsion against women's bodies. Or
that—what about that?—the sight of parted thighs, the
smooth heat that must be felt through the latex—all this
should be rousing, a doctor is a male beneath his white coat.
But neither professional hazard affects him, or ever has, even
when he was a young man. He is unfailingly roused by the
sight and scent and feel of his wife's body alone (she who was
so hard to win to himself) and it is the man, not the doctor,
who enters her and journeys with her to their joyous pleasure,
as if there is always accessible to her an island in warm seas
like one of those they have travelled to, together. When he
talks to his seraglio women after examination, and sits a few
moments on the edge of the steel table where they lie, he may
be in contact with the body whose exposure he has reverently
re-covered under wraps, he will place a reassuring palm of
the hand on the woman's shrouded hip while he tells her how
she should conduct herself, they discuss the pills she needs to
take, the exercise essential to maintain herself. They are two
human beings equal in their vulnerability to the trials of life
(of which his girls often confess to him their own specific
ones), considering together how best one may survive. She
knows this is not remotely the antenna of sex touching her,
and he knows she understands this. He does not need a nurse
to be present—a precaution most gynaecologists employ—to
reassure his girls of his respect.

'Archie' is also Uncle Archie, brother of Julie's father.

He used to fetch Julie to come and play with her cousins
when she was a small girl. If she could have chosen a father,
then, it would have been him. It still would be. He was a Gulliver over which children could climb and play. Teasing and
story-telling. Her father took her to events on appointed
days, to children's theatre and galas at his riding club; her
mother did not think it necessary for both parents to be pres-

ent, and stayed at home. Or perhaps she went to one of her
lovers—but a child can't be aware of these accommodations
in her parents' lives. (Nigel: poor man: if she happened to
think of it, once herself adult.) She no longer had any contact
with the cousins, but now and then, infrequent perhaps as
her own presence, she would find this uncle among guests
at her father's Sunday lunches. Julie would make for him
among the people who were strangers although she might
know well who were these components of Danielle's and her
father's set—someone she was spontaneously pleased to see
again, one with whom she felt an understanding that she was
out of place in the company of the house built for Danielle.
The working lives, the temperaments of the brothers were
widely different, but he was still part of her father's roots and
perhaps Danielle was one of Archie's 'girls'? Julie herself, of
course, had never consulted him; with Gulliver, a gynaecolog-
ical examination would have seemed, if not to him, to her,
anyway, some sort of incest. She's aware that she retains
traces of the well-brought-up female's prudery, false modesty,
despite the free exchange of all the facts of life at The Table.
     We must think of everyone, anyone who.
     Who?
     Before they go to the famous lawyer together—if he can
be approached at all on the basis of his association with her
father, who must not have the situation made known to him
at all—there must be someone. Not a father, but in place of
that surely outgrown dependency. Someone removed from
themselves—interrogating themselves for a solution even in
their silences, removed from her kind of conventional wisdom, the guidance she relies on from The Table. She's going
to speak to her uncle.
     What uncle is that?
     I've told you about him, my favourite grown-up, as a kid.
     He knows people?

Well, he's prominent . . .

So. If she won't go to her father, she is showing some sense
of family as those his people naturally seek and find action
from when you are in trouble. She comes to be embraced by
him before she sets out; he holds her a moment as one grants
this to a child being sent off to school.

Although she has been privileged to be given an appointment at all she has to wait among women in the bright air-
conditioned room with its images of elephant herds, lion
cubs and Bonnard boating parties. Among women; but who
among them, manicured hands resting secure on pregnant
belly-mounds under elegantly-flowing clothes, diet-slim
middles emphasized by elaborate belts, young faces perfectly
reproducing the looks of the latest model on a magazine
cover, ageing skin drawn tight beneath the eyes by surgery,
elaborately-braided heads bent together—two black women,
wives of the new upper class, laughing and chatting in their
language; who, of all these can have any idea of what her version of a female complaint is, why she is here. In this, they
are not even of the same sex. One of them smiles at her but
her head is turned away as his is, often, in the EL-AY Café.
Girls together. His girls. She has been amused at the way she
has heard her uncle refer to them. But she is in her isolation.

The white-coated version of the uncle has risen from behind his wide desk and come to meet her with a hug. —At
last you decide to see where I hang out, isn't that it! Shall we
have coffee, tea, there's our little kitchen here, we've got them
all, Earl Grey to Rooibos, you know, or is it juice, mango, ap-
ple—

There is the preamble of her apology for insisting on oust-
ing some patient from an appointment, her thanks for his letting her walk in on him like this. —Apology! My dear Julie,
how often do I get to see you! Oh I know from my own brood,
the lives of generations fork out all over in different direc-

tions, the only crossroads we might meet at is at Nigel's, and
neither your way nor Sharon's and mine run that route, we
know. But that's fine. Nigel's such a Big Boy now, he's done so
well, and they're wonderful together, he and Danielle—you
and I must be glad about that, mmh?—

Sharon. At the mention of her uncle's wife's name she recognizes why, in her confusion of thinking of someone, anyone, it was not only the childhood bond that has brought her
here. Archibald Charles Summers in his day betrayed all expectations of his choice of a girl from well-known Anglican
Church families, members of country clubs and owners of
holiday houses at the Cape where he was so popular as polo
player and dance partner, in the old South Africa; it was
when he was actually formally 'engaged' to what everyone
agreed was a particularly lovely and suitable choice, a show
rider, that he suddenly married a Sharon, a Jewess, daughter
of a Lithuanian immigrant who had a luggage-cum-shoe-
repair shop in the very area where the backroom night clubs,
bar hang-outs, the L.A. Café and the garage with its shed
accommodation for an illegal had taken over now. Echoes
of appalled family reaction to this marriage had drifted to
the child's ears; for her, Sharon was the pretty redheaded
mother of the cousins, dispenser of sweetmeats made of gin-
ger and carrots, colour of her frizzy hair, you didn't get
anywhere else, whose embrace was more and more cushioned
by plumpness over childhood years.

The coffee he had summoned (Be a dear, Farida, tell
Thabi we'd like coffee—with biscuits, eh?) provided the comfortable transition of general interests. What career was she
launched on now, she's always so adventurous, quite right,
there are many changes among people, everywhere in the
country, new ways to be active, explore. And they laughed together when she dismissed her present occupation, the old
con jacked up for what is called 'new social mobility', public

relations. —Oh and he must tell her—he and Sharon had
spent the long weekend at a certain guest farm in the Dra-
kensberg—Sharon and I just became renewed, the walks in
the bush, the hot sun and icy pools you can find where there's
no-one—you jump in, in the buff—if you don't already know
of it you two must take off and go there. He doesn't know
who the current partner may be, but he feels he ought to remember, from the most recent news he might have had in encounters with her.

Not much chance of that right now.

In her brief silence, although he never pries—his girls always find in him the right receptive moment when they can
speak what must be broached—he finds the delicacy of an
open, unsolemn response. —Now—you didn't come to see me
here rather than at home because of my bonny blue eyes—

He makes it easy.

Change. —There's something—we, the man you perhaps
don't know of or if you don't happen to have heard from
Nigel that he was with me, there, one Sunday—we don't
know what to do about.—

—Oh, that's it. My girl . . . All right.— The light from the
window behind him, speckled by climbing plants on the sill,
shines through those protruding ears, mapping fine red capil-
laries. That face is still the face of the father you would
choose. The one who would do anything to help you.

And then she sees: he thinks she has come to him for an
abortion.

Unwanted conception—that seems the end of the world to many of his patients. What his niece relates to him of this man she has taken on is a threat *from* the world. The secure world in which, as someone who always has had her in his care, even if he did not see her for months, did not quite know where she might be, he felt himself somehow hoveringly responsible for her in what he has seen as the abrogation of this by the temperament of his brother in his highly-approved first marriage, and her mother's subsequent desertion to her casino impresario. The intricacies of the law are not for him, that's not his field, but he does know, from its physical and mental and spiritual manifestations (he believes in the spirit or soul, this is part of the innocence with which his gloved hand enters its shelter, the body), the indeflectable power of physical attraction in its victims, his patients; its ruthlessness and recklessness. A juggernaut thundering into the personality. He also believes in love (no doubt influenced by his own enduring experience of it)—love is the spirit—which is not necessarily present in physical attraction, but replaced by its denial, cruelty (he sees rape cases, these violent days that do not spare the rich). He knows how love, if mysteriously engendered by physical attraction, develops the characteristic of assuming, to the exclusion of all else, whatever assails the other being; that other has become the self. So in his presence she knows it; that he knows she loves the man who appeared to her, legs, body, finally head from under a car. And about that, he knows there is nothing to be done; although others might think otherwise, and be thankful that the law will do it for them. What there is to be done—he certainly urges engaging the lawyer, lawyers, in fact, any big guns available; as with his own profession, second and even third opinions are needed for alternatives in the need for radical action. Eleven days left of two weeks!

—Shall I go with you to this lawyer you know of? You'd like me to be with you?—

She feels an unwarranted relief from anxiety, based on nothing, just because of this spontaneity from someone who cannot help her. No, no, she and her lover must go together.

—Any time, any time, I'm here. Sharon and I, at home. You can call, you can come. Ask the lawyer if any sort of letter of recommendation—I don't know what the form might be—would be useful. Some guarantee for your man from this respectable and law-abiding old citizen.—

He went with her past the women gazing up to greet him from their place in the waiting-room, leading her along the corridor to the lifts, waiting, so that she would not be alone with doors gliding closed on her.

It is a fact that the Senior Counsel no longer practises law. She finds out in a roundabout way since she could not ask her father without giving an explanation of why she wants to approach the man. One among the friends—it's David—is her source through abandoned connections he takes up on her behalf. The Table is unanimous: get in touch with the guy

anyway, even if he doesn't practise any more, he'll still have
all the stuff in his head, he's not going to refuse advice to you,
he's seen you, he's seen Abdu, you say, at your father's place.
How can he refuse. No way!

Joining them at The Table, the victim, the accused, the
endangered, their friend Julie's pickup—what is he to have
the sense of, as himself?—he has listened to them closely.

—That's what I tell her.—

You know why I'm reluctant. (In case the word escapes
him): Don't much want to.

They are like any of the combination of lovers who come
and go, having a private spat between them in the protection
of The Table.

So if he speaks to your father? That can be something
good. If it comes from him, an important man your father
likes. So if he speaks!

She gets the general secretary on the line when she calls
a corporate headquarters at the number she's been given,
reaches the private secretary, then the personal assistant, and finally Mr Hamilton Motsamai himself. She has had to introduce
herself to the personal assistant as Nigel Summers' daughter.
The lawyer is (in the corporate jargon she's familiar with among
her father's associates) affable, how is Nigel, I expect to be in a
meeting with him next week, very good—of course I remember
you, your father's house is a special place to relax in . . . yes. He
has a deep soft voice, black voice, that sounds as if it would res-
onate from a tall broad man but she remembers he is small and
agile-looking. If it's urgent, of course. Very good. After all, this
is Ackroyd's daughter—but then oddly, as if in contradiction,
she adds something awkwardly.

—I hope you don't mind my asking—would you please
not mention I've called you, if you do happen to be in touch
with my father.—

So at once there is a secret between her and this stranger

that *he*, her lover, will not know of. Although everything in
her, is his. This is a mere filament of the strands of deviousness she is aware of having to learn in a circumstance she, in
all her confident discard of conventional ones, finds she had
no preparation for. He, her find; it was also this one, to be
discovered in herself.

She is asked by the personal secretary, who makes the appointment, to give the registration number of her car so that
she may be granted parking in the corporate headquarters'
underground bays. The good second-hand Toyota the garage
mechanic obtained for her finds a place in the cavern. She
looks for a moment at his avatar, presenting himself aggres-
sively handsome in the silk scarf at the neck of the shirt that
becomes him best. She smiles but he knows she is trying to
measure with other eyes the impression he needs to make.
They emerge through security turnstiles where they slot the
plastic cards given them when the guard at the entrance ver-
ified the registration number; are guided by another uni-
formed man to sign (her name serves for both), time of
arrival and other particulars of identification in a gold-tooled
leather-bound book; are taken over by a smart young woman
programmed to preface with *And how are you today* her instruction of which elevator goes up to the 17th floor. The
doors open on a reception area before interleading halls and
alcoves, like a five-star hotel; palm trees lean up to a glass
dome, a fountain dribbles from the beaks of bronze cranes
and under lamps there are pale leather sofas and chairs
grouped for conversation. Some sort of luncheon is going on,
spilling from one of the alcoves. There is the curve of a small
bar, silver-bright ice buckets on stands, a buffet concealed by
people helping themselves to an accompaniment of laughter
and voices from which the treble jets as another kind of fountain. He and she stand: the lights have gone up in a theatre.

Mr Motsamai's suite is reached through his secretary's office and his personal assistant's office, both women seal-sleekly blonde. He receives his associate's daughter and the young man (foreign) not in the formality of his office where he does business but in his adjoining reception room, not too large for one-to-one contact, amply comfortable, with TV console and a fan of financial journals on its glass tables. His sparse pointed beard, quaintly worn as seen on engravings of ancient tribal kings, is matched in distinction by the fresh white carnation in his lapel beside a rosette of some Order.

It is evident that Summers' daughter will be the one to speak.

His face changes as he listens to her story. It's as if he has been returned by her to another life: this is the withdrawn and acutely attentive face of Senior Counsel, not the affable deputy chairman or whatever-he-is in the headquarters of this banking conglomerate or whatever-it-is. The girl's story becomes a confession in all the detail she has learned carefully by rote and, it's obvious from her wary delivery, she's aware her companion is silently monitoring.

In that other expression of his powers of intellect, of professional mastery, the lawyer has heard and analysed countless confessions while they were in progress. He alternates concentration on her words with unapologetic examining glances resting on the companion—yes, to verify, in his own interpretation of what he is hearing, the likely actions and motivations of this lover.

When she ends—or rather stops speaking—she has to control rising emotion, she wants to go on, to plead, to state her case, her lover's case; the lawyer is familiar with the symptoms in many bearing witness over the years in court. He sits back in his chair and presses his shoulders against the cushioned rest, invisible robes are adjusted round them— Senior Counsel was an Acting Judge for a period, and could be permanently His Honour Mr Justice Motsamai on the bench of the High Court now if he had not decided for that other, more profitable form of power over human destiny, financial institutions. He is also only too well accustomed, from his past career, to the gaze that waits upon him as an oracle. It is one of the rewards of having doffed those heavily-goffered robes in exchange for a custom-tailor's cut of light-weight suit that he doesn't have to be the object of that sort of expectation any more; he himself sometimes had had to fight emotion in knowing, vulnerable man he was himself, black man whose old parents had been supplicants themselves, that nothing more oracular than management of dry facts would come from him.

He let his moments of silence tell them this, these two.

Then he spoke. —You are not married.—

—No. Oh no.—

There comes from him a kind of organ note, something between an exclamation and a groan—an old African affirmation. It could be a comforting or a warning—she is at home with the particular non-verbal expressions that are natural to Africans as Greeks or Italians or Jews have their characteristic ones, but her familiars are the young who have lost the more grandiose, eloquent, traditional African resources in self-expression, and have passed on easily to The Table, the bars, the streets, only those adapted to general usage, across all local cultures, heard all over coming from those of their generation, all colours and kinds.

—The chances of appeal succeeding for Mr . . . ? would have been perhaps marginally better if you had been married. He would have had the advantage of the provision that the spouse of a national—and of course, Julie—Miss Summers, you are unquestionably that—has the right of permanent residence. A moment: wait . . . To resort to marriage now—at this stage—would only prejudice your case further; it would be seen as a device to gain residence, that's all. Mar-

riage to a national as a positive factor in seeking entry to a
country or appealing for permanent residence, a stay of expulsion order, has to have been of a duration—proof that it is
a genuine relationship. You follow. Too many would-be immigrants are ready to pay some woman for a marriage certifi-
cate—the consummation's only on paper, the divorce follows
after a suitable interval. Home Affairs, who presented you
with your order to leave (he points the beard gently at the
young foreigner) is aware of these tricks. So: useless, at this
crucial stage, for you.—

Some sort of guarantees—support of the application—
good character and financial means—would these be of any
help? There's this business of someone becoming a burden on
the state?

Nigel Ackroyd Summers' daughter, of course. But she had
said, don't tell my father I've approached you . . . Well, most
likely the girl has money already settled on her indepen-
dently—common practice among people of means to ensure
death duties are reduced when that bad day comes.

—Letters of support, presumably from people of solid
reputation . . . yes, could have been useful to you in a less,
how shall we put it, already prejudiced situation. Hopelessly
prejudiced. What else can one say. Here is a young man who
entered by dubious means and once his permit was expired
was ordered to leave how long ago—

The beard singles her out and she does not answer; confirming the length of time is like a criminal's admission of guilt.
The beard tips to the young man in question, in the dock.

—One year and five months some weeks.—

—There you are. Ah-heh . . . You were ordered to leave
one year and more than five months ago, you—disappeared—you stayed on in contravention of the law, you
managed to *evade the law*, you made yourself guilty of trans-
gression of the Immigation Act, you defied Home Affairs. And

fortunately for you, because of their inefficiency I'm only too
aware of from the time I was in legal practice, your case
slipped into some crack in a filing system, got lost in their
computers, they smoked their cigarettes and chatted and
looked at their watches for the time to go home and they forgot about you! Perhaps we can say you were lucky. Forgotten! You had your reprieve, your time . . . I don't know if this
was fortunate, if we look at your position now.—

But they are seated before him *now*, the young woman
and the man who came to her from where he *disappeared*,
under a car on a dirty garage floor, months and weeks have
been theirs, *he's not for you, she's not for him* but they have
been, they are, for each other!

His flow can't be challenged, he can't be interrupted, he is
presenting his Heads of Argument, it's habitual, unstoppable.

—You have placed yourself in the position where you have
a criminal charge waiting against you, let alone an order to
quit the country. That is the sticking point. That is what
weighs against however many testimonies to your character,
your desirability as a future citizen, your possibilities of financial guarantees, security etcetera you might submit. I regret
very much to tell you these incontrovertible facts! You were
told your permit had expired and would not be renewed; you
elected to stay on illegally, you shed your identity and took on
an assumed name. If you had left, gone back to your country
of origin or wherever you might have thought you would get
in, if you had re-applied for immigration from there, outside
these borders—then the testimonials from prominent citizens
here might indeed have served you well . . . guarantees . . .
Money is always useful. Yes—(the deep note sounded, drawn
out again). Ah-heh. These people take bribes. You know that.
We all know that. Ah-heh. It is the epidemic that attacks the
freedom won for our country, sickening us from inside, one of
the running sores of corruption. All right. With money no

doubt—enough money—you could buy someone's hands to
tear up that latest order to quit the country. You could keep
your fake name some more months, find another one, disappear once again for—I don't know—maybe another year, but
some other functionary with a grudge against the first will find
your record come up on a computer, there will be another
criminal charge against you, yours will become an habitual
status, evasion of the law plus bribery.—

—So you can't suggest anything, Mr Motsamai?—

He continues to look deeply at her, his eyebrows rise
slowly.

A flush of resentment: *he's not for you*, that's what he's really saying: the famous lawyer is one of *them*, her father's
people and their glossy Danielles comparing the purchase of
Futures and Hedging Funds, sitting here in his corporate
palazzo, it doesn't help at all that he is black; he's been one of
their victims, he's one of *them* now. He, too, expects her to
choose one of her own kind—the kind he belongs to.

She stands up to leave. But it is as if his old skill in reading distressed supplicants has given him intuition of what she
is judging of him; he has ignored her and is turned to her foreigner.

—I know how it is. Man, my people were turned back at
many emigration and immigration gates. Many years, cen-
turies. Myself, when I was young. When I had the opportunity of going abroad for further study. The Sixties—it took
three years—always yes-no, yes-no—for the papers finally
to be refused. Exit permit, one way—out and don't come
back—that's the stamp I had to take then.—

Thank you. Goodbye. She too, has her intuitions, she
knows what he's up to, claiming his rightful brotherhood of
his people's suffering along with his present successful dis-
tancing from it. But he has yet other skills at his disposal,

mastered in court and in the board rooms, he knows how to respond disarmingly to witnesses' hostility and that of difficult trustees. He will answer, in his own time, the question he ignored. —Well . . . I have taken on many apparently hopeless cases in my day, so I suppose I must suggest you go to a lawyer who is stupid enough to take on such cases and clever enough to see what he can do with yours. I could call a former colleague.—

—Thank you. No. Thank you—

She is stayed by the grasp on the forearm of the hand that supplies her with caresses.

—That will be good. Thank you very much. Can it be now? Can you do it? We can go any time, straight away.—

—Well, I have a meeting, papers to go through—but I'll get my assistant to call my colleague the moment I'm free, and when I've spoken to him she'll call you—she has your number, Miss Summers, you have a cell of course—

Thrusts the car keys at him.

All right. All right. There is his beautiful smile, for her, from the first days.

Pompous fart.

All right. All right. Before he starts the engine he does the necessary thing, hooks an arm round her and kisses her tense cheek.

We can find our own lawyer. Shouldn't have gone to him anyway. I might have known what he'd be thinking about all the time: *what my father would say*! And I don't believe he really knows anything about this sort of problem, he wouldn't have been that kind of lawyer, not spectacular enough for him, not murder.

You are wrong, you know. He knows about taxes. How not

to pay, yes. But that also is difficult. That is the world, like
the other friends of your father, he knows how it works the
same kind of all sorts of ways for other things.

David knows lawyers.

What kind of lawyers can David know. This man is important, his people are big. Listen, Julie.

That was the message of that grasp on her forearm: I am
a man. I am the one who is not for you but who possesses you
every night: listen to me.

The call came on the cellphone the public relations people
she worked for insisted she carry with her at all times. This
call was not the chaffing exchange of media jargon which was
the communication they favoured. The name of Mr Motsamai's colleague, his telephone number, his rooms, the date
and time of the appointment made. Julie and her problem
were at The Table. Background music was particularly intru-
sive that day, but everyone shut their ears to it: the friends
followed her lips as she repeated the information. One of
them gave a ballpoint to the lover so that he could take it
down, but he had no paper and the poet, who often wrote
lines that came to him out of his echo-chamber of the babble
in the EL-AY Café, and who suspected that the foreigner
might not get the facts right anyway, noted the information
for her among the tantric doodles in his chap-book.

Somewhere in an illegal's few possessions was something
she didn't know existed: a suit. Perhaps it had been kept
hanging in its plastic bag in the garage shed. He dressed in it
to go to Motsamai's colleague lawyer. He had said he should
go alone, and clearly was confident to do this. He looked at
ease in this fashionable loose-jacketed version of the outfit
that marks the category of respectable citizen as the black
robe marks the category of the judge, and as he did in grease-
monkey overalls. She sees that an illegal has to be some sort
of chameleon, along with all the other subterfuges to be re-

sorted to. She accompanied him, after all. There might be difficulties with language.

When they were in the lawyer's rooms, he did all the talking, the manner an insistent alternation of rapidity and groping, at once frustrated and forceful. He found the words: the lawyer understood them, their gist was another language between the two men. Some papers were produced to sign. The man had a fold of pink loose skin that settled from under thick tabby eyebrows halfway down over his upper eyelids; there was something hypnotic about this feature. There would be an application for the 14 days' grace to be extended, there were particular persons in certain departments to be approached, all this would be done forthwith. Then the real process of obtaining permanent residence status could begin. All considerations were perfectly understood and noted. The client would be kept informed.

Five days, four days, left of the fourteen. Then there was the reprieve—the hypnotist informed his client of an extension of another fourteen days granted on grounds of the legal representative's further investigation of the case to be presented. They didn't appear at The Table. In grease-monkey guise he still went every morning to the garage in a ritual that had lost its purpose. They didn't go out at night. They lay in their bed or sat on the step warm from the day's sun, and talked into the dark of the night garden. They had lived with nothing but the present and now they talked about the future that would come or never come. It was there, theirs, existed for them.

What's it you'd really like to do?

Computer science. Study some more.

We could run a project together, while you prepare . . .

Cape Town would be a nice place.

While you study, there could be a small project, I've thought of it vaguely sometimes, copyright agency on Internet, website not office, so many people I know in the arts and entertainment don't know how copyright works, they're conned every day. I'm fairly familiar with these things through the PR contacts I've had.

Cape Town . . . beautiful place, they say.

Yes, maybe; we could. We should go somewhere away from everything here. Holidays there, of course, all my life—but I've never lived there. Wonderful holidays, as a kid—the sea.

You like it. To live.

Always wanted to live at the sea, I don't know why I didn't find the energy to take myself off somewhere. And you? The sea.

I don't know it. Not at all.

She squeezes his hand that is palm-to-palm with hers: the sand, dust. The sea is the ultimate oasis of the dry world, its depths various with life, its surface free, with crossings that have no frontier, the tides rising on this coastline, then that.

On the seventh day of the reprieve the lawyer leaves a message on her voice-mail. They are to come to him at three-thirty.

He absents himself from the garage without explanation— that doesn't matter now. She drives him to the cottage to change; she doesn't like to tell him it's not necessary to get into the suit, his elegant jeans will do. They both have that strange constriction of the gullet, as if some drawn breath has lodged there. The expression beneath the flap of flesh, the half-hood, is unchanged. The lawyer shakes their hands; hers, his, and they all sit. When he speaks it is only to the foreigner because it is to him that what he has to say applies—the girl is Nigel Ackroyd Summers' daughter, Motsamai informed—there is no threat to her, she belongs. All possible avenues have been explored. Up to the highest level, he might add. Motsamai had been most helpful. There is no possibility that permanent residence will be granted. He greatly regrets to say: nothing fur-

ther can be done, by himself or anyone else. He must tell the
client this in order to save vain hopes and useless expenditure.
—To be frank—even if you were to consider it as a desperate
measure, not even money could find the right hand. As you
must have read in the papers, there is a big exposure of corruption in that very area, that very Department, right now.—

What is left to ask; but they wait.

First the lawyer repeats what he has told; clients often
don't want to hear, don't take in bad news, they've believed
in him beyond professional fallibility, beyond circumstances
of their own making, beyond repair.

Now suddenly he talks to the girl as if what he has to say
needs to be broken to the client through someone close to
him—too blunt to be borne directly. —He will have to leave
the country within ten days. I was able to extend that from a
week, for him.—

They go back—are back—at the EL-AY Café. Where else is there to go, for her? And for him, there never was anywhere, anyone.

She tells their story to her friends over and over, as this one and that joins The Table at different points in the re-counting. They want all the details, it's their way of showing concern; they repeat them, weighing them over, asking the same questions, a part-song. All around, the coming-and-going, the laughter, scraping of chairs, winding of tape-music, tossing back of hair, flamboyant greetings, murmurs, is unabated: The Table might just as well be having a birth-day party.

—Told you before, my Brother, disappear. That's the only way. Like the Mozambiquans, Congolese, Kenyans, what-not.—

—But he'd better make it somewhere else. Durban, Cape Town, clear out of here.—

—Absolutely *not*! This's the only one big enough, it's the labyrinth to get lost in.—

—Of course, else how do all these others get away with it? Tell me. Tripping over their carvings and schmuck on every pavement—you find them everywhere gabbling happily in their Swahili or French or whatever. So many of them no-one can get a hold. Sheer numbers. They can't be caught.—

—It's night in there, man. They're black like me. This guy here, Abdu, he's not one of them, his face and everything—it tells the story.—

—Schmuck—what's that—

—Not some kind of dope, I can tell you—kitsch, if you're able to recognize it when you see it.—

—I still think you had the wrong lawyer. You're just too well-brought-up, Julie, Northern Suburbs clean-hands stuff, God-on-Sundays only sees a sparrow fall, girl, he doesn't de- liver thou-shalt-not to corporate fixings but he ordains it isn't *nice* to use crooked lawyers. You can't tell me something couldn't be fixed. Christ, the top man down at Home Affairs here has just been relieved of his job, grounds of corrup- tion . . .—

Julie is sounding the wood of The Table with spread fin- gers. —I'm not so innocent, not of what's done where I come from or at Home Affairs. It's just what you've suggested that's the problem. When it comes to fixing. No fancy scruples. We've got it on good authority that everyone down there is scared stiff to open a hand, now. He'd only find himself ar- rested for offering bribes, in addition to everything else—

—Naa-arh . . . the higher you go the less chance you have of being reached. You can't tell me that with the right con- nections . . .—

Thinking of her father, yes; there's always been an under- current of keen awareness of her father's money The Table concealed from Julie, in contrast with the lack of vintage Rovers in the background of this speaker and others among the friends. The exceptions—her fellow escapees from the Northern Suburbs—know that Nigel Ackroyd Summers would not approach a cabinet minister with whom he dines

to ask that this illegal alien from a backward country should
continue to sleep with his daughter. From one of them, a
quick dismissal: —That's just not on, Andy.—

—But you can't tell me . . .—

—If all those hundreds—thousands—get away with it,
there *must* be a solution. You have to ask around. Everywhere.—

Where *is* there?

She waits for answers that do not come; the friends have
always huddled together with solutions for everything that
happens to any one of them. The alternative solutions of alternative lives?

Even if it were only, in the life of the one sitting among
them every day under life-sentence of AIDS, to transform the
news from unbearable to the solace of laughter, that time.

—Disappear, my Brother. Like I say.—

Their old hanger-on, the poet, has been present, silent
through repetitions of the story. He folds a sheet torn from his
chap-book on which he's just written something and pushes it
into her hand.

Back at the cottage she comes upon a crackling in the
shirt pocket over her left breast. She feels about the pocket
everywhere, ask everywhere takes out a bit of paper, distrait,
he is drinking water, one glass, two glasses, deep swallows
over the sink, he gasps with the last and slowly shakes his
head. She unfolds the paper and reads what is there.

'This isn't all but it's the first part and it's by someone
called William Plomer you wouldn't know of.

> Let us go to another country
> Not yours or mine
> And start again.
> To another country? Which?
> One without fires, where fever

Lurks under leaves, and water
Is sold to those who thirst?
And carry dope or papers
In our shoes to save us starving?
Hope would be our passport,
The rest is understood
Just say the word.
(Sorry, don't remember how it ends.)'

She has read it aloud to him, but it is meant for her.

Dumb.

Might as well be. When they are talking about matters you know better than they do or ever will. You are dumb if you can't speak—speak their language as they do. You have to use your lips and tongue for the other purpose, your penis and even the soles of your feet, caressing hers in the bed, in place of your opinions, convictions.

What use is that, now?

He can't make love. She has never experienced this with any other of her lovers. Without saying anything to her he takes the car—where has he gone? He comes back with the belongings he had left in his grease-monkey outhouse at the garage. The canvas bag with frayed labels addressed in that unfamiliar script sags on the floor of the room where they have eaten and slept, together.

He asks her if she knows where he can get a cheap air ticket. Of course she knows; her work with those pop groups and conference personnel means she has contacts with travel agencies and airlines. And then she's looking at him, into him, in disbelief, as he speaks.

You'll do it for me? Or find where I must do it.

Her breasts are rising and falling under the sweater and the nostrils of her fine nose (he has never thought her beautiful but has always, since the first day when he came out from under a car, thought it so) are stiffened and flared. Something will happen, tears, an outburst—he must come quickly over to avert whatever it may be, he has his arms around her as you might resort to putting a hand over someone's mouth.

What she is struggling with, not only in this moment of practical confrontation but all the time, the days that are crossed off with every coming of the light through the gap in the curtains above the bed where they lie, cannot be discussed with him. Not yet.

Disappear. Like I say.

Either way. He disappears into another city, another identity, keeps clear; or he disappears into deportation.

They go back again at night to the EL-AY Café, away from the silence in the cottage and the slumped canvas bag, because there's usually likely to be there someone to whom she has always felt closest, among the friends.

The struggle stays clenched tightly inside her. It possesses her, alien to them, even to those she thought close; and makes them alien to her. She feels she never knew them, any of them, in the real sense of knowing that she has now with him, the man foreign to her who came to her one day from under the belly of a car, frugal with his beautiful smile granted, dignified in a way learnt in a life hidden from her, like his

name. Her crowd, Mates, Brothers and Sisters. They are the
strangers and he is the known.

So what's happening?

—A bloody shame. They glide in and out of immigration
at the airports with cocaine stuck up their arse, ecstasy in
their vagina—and I don't mean the kind that makes them
come—but he gets turned down and kicked out.—

Neither the indignation nor the sympathy count; these are
simply tonight's subjects for the usual animation and display.
Let's get some more wine, you need a drink, Julie, come on
Abdu, you too. Someone passes a joint, that's probably more
like what an oriental prince needs. The poet is not there.
There is no-one. There will be no-one, for her, in this city,
this country.

The two don't drink or smoke and they leave early. The
empty space they occupied at The Table is a silence; broken:
—It's not the end of the world. Our girl's been in love a few
times, as we're well aware.—

—This pickup of hers's been a disaster from the beginning.—

—Come on, he's not a bad guy, he just needed a meal
ticket. A bed. And he obviously knew how to occupy it.—

—I've never seen her like this. Bad, man.—

A recent addition to The Table passes a hand over his
shaven head, staring as if to follow the path The Table's intimate and the foreigner are making through Saturday night
partying that buffets them.

—Julie should chill out.—

As there is no longer any sense in playing the grease-monkey
he spends these, his last few days, in the cottage. He has no
appetite but is constantly thirsty; lies on that bed that has

also outlived its usefulness, with a big plastic container full of cold water on the floor beside him.

So he was there when she came home from her work with the envelope from the travel agency. She handed it to him where he lay. He delayed a moment, reading the name of the agency, with its logo of some great bird in flight, as if to convince himself of its portent. He made a slit in the top of the envelope with his nail and slid a forefinger along to open it. Inside, there were two airline tickets.

She stood before him with her hands linked behind her back, like a schoolgirl.

And now's the time: there has been no description of this Julie, little indication of what she looks like, unless an individual's actions and words conjure a face and body. There is, anyway, no description that is *the* description. Everyone who sees a face sees a different face—her father, Nigel Ackroyd Summers, his wife Danielle, her mother in California, remembering her, her contemporaries of The Table, the old unpublished poet; her lover. The face he sees is the definitive face for the present situation. The two air tickets he holds in his hands, turns over, unfolds, verifies, materialize a face, her face for him, that didn't exist before, the face of what is impossible, can't be. So what she was, and now is—what the woman Julie looks like comes through his eyes.

They always want to be told what is beautiful about them—women, anywhere—but I suppose I never did this because I couldn't consider how I should phrase it as I can think of it in my own language now. We also have our poets she wouldn't have heard of, Imru' al-Qays, Antara. Have to understand now what I'm seeing, when I look at this girl, this woman—how old, twenty-nine, one year older than I am. But it's not the days and years, it's the living that calculates the age! She's a child, they're all children, and what she wants to

do now is not something for her, the living she's totally innocent of, hasn't any real idea of, innocence is ignorance, with
them.

She came into the garage like any of their women who
have a car husband or father has given them, and the freedom they're not even aware of to go about wherever they
please and talk to a strange man, giving orders while I get
myself out from under a car and stand up, a dirty fool in
those overalls, to follow her through the streets. Does she realize that a girl like her couldn't go out alone, where I'm being sent back to. I don't think I really looked at her. That day.
Well: European—but they don't call themselves that, they are
not in Europe—they belong here. So—white, young, not
smart but dressed in the style they think disguises the difference between rich and poor, the way my overalls outfit was
supposed to disguise that I'm an illegal on the run. But she
looked at me. I don't know what it was she thought she saw,
there was that invitation to take coffee. And there she was in
that rowdy café, with a strange man, a nobody she found if
not in the street then in a place not much better. I suppose I
saw her as a woman, then. She was not a blonde—I was told
by my uncle and cousins about how attractive blondes were,
for them—hair a no-colour brown, and smooth and straight
falling behind the ears. Later, sometimes in bed with her I
noticed that the ear close to me on the pillow was small and
set flat to the head. Pretty. Eyes water-grey and not large,
always looking at me directly. What else; eyebrows much
darker than her hair, not plucked to the thin line, like the
girls who flirt them at you, lifting, lowering frowning, at my
home. Dark paint on the mouth whose muscles always move
slightly, unconsciously, while she follows what someone is
saying to her. As if she's learning a language. Trying to. As if
she knows, all right, she knows nothing. *Nothing!*

It's impossible, this idea of hers. What could she do there.

What'm I expected to do with her. *There*. Responsible to her
father, she thinks he doesn't matter but he's somebody in this
city and I'll be the filthy wicked foreigner who's taken her to
a run-down depraved strip of a country Europeans didn't
even want to hold on to any longer, were glad to get rid of,
even the oil is over the border. Abducted her; that is what it
would be called in my country. What use will she be. To herself, to me. She's not for me, can't she realize that? Too indulged and pampered to understand that's what she is, she
thinks she can have everything, she doesn't know that the
one thing she can't have is to survive what she's decided she
wants to do now. Madness. Madness. I thought she was intelligent. *Stupidity*. That's it. That's final.

For the first time since the first cup of coffee together they
quarrelled. He who was soft-voiced shouted at her. He who
was beautiful became ugly with anger and scorn.

Who asked you to buy two tickets. You said nothing to me.
Don't you think you must discuss? No, you are used to making all decisions, you do what you like, no father, no mother,
nobody must ever tell you. And me—what am I, don't speak
to me, don't ask me—you cannot live in my country, it's not
for you, you can't understand what it is to live there, you can
wish you were dead, if you have to live there. Can't you understand? I can't be for you—responsible—

She became stiff and clipped with anger.

Nobody has to be responsible for me. I am responsible for
myself.

For yourself. Always yourself. You think that is very
brave. I must tell you something. You only know how to be
responsible for yourself here—this place, your café friends,
your country where you have everything. I can't be responsible. I don't want it.

He saw, could not stop himself seeing—everything change
in her. All that she had been to him, the physical oneness, the
tenderness, the expression of her whole being that had concentrated in the hours with lawyers, the humiliations suffered
before the indifference of official communications, the recognition of him as the man he knew himself to be beneath the
nobody with a false name—this possessed her face and body
in revelation. And his words *I don't want it* struck the stag-
gering blow.

You don't want me.

Not for her to speak those words; he heard them as she
had heard them. Nothing for her to say; she knows *nothing*.
That is true but he sees, feels, has revealed to him something
he does not know: this foreign girl has for him—there are
beautiful words for it coming to him in his mother tongue—
devotion. How could anyone, man or woman, not want that?
Devotion. Is it not natural to be loved? To accept a blessing.
She knows *something*. Even if it comes out of ignorance, innocence of reality.

The capacity returned to him, for this foreigner makes
him whole. That night he made love to her with the recipro-
cal tenderness—call it whatever old name you like—that he
had guarded against—with a few lapses—couldn't afford its
commitment, in his situation, must be able to take whatever
the next foothold might offer. That night they made love, the
kind of love-making that is another country, a country of its
own, not yours or mine.

With the acceptance of love there comes the authority to impose conditions. They have never said the worn old words to one another, for her they are bourgeois clichés left behind; or perhaps it is because each would need a different vocabulary in their two languages. But there is a consequence common to both: if you love me you will want to do as I say, or at least make concessions to please me. It was right that she must inform her father of her decision. The idea filled her with dismay. He insisted. She lived through the whole scene in advance, and the actuality bore this out: she went alone and sat on the terrace where the Sunday lunches were held and the intention she announced gained preposterousness by nature of the setting in which it was heard. *You have always lived your own life and in my love for you I have respected this although at times it has caused me concern— and hurt, yes hurt. You lack consideration for what you do, indirectly, to your family, I suppose I've spoilt you, this happens with one parent or other when there's a divorce. My fault. Be that as it may. Many times I have had to stand by, ready to support you, catch you when you crash, and breathed again only when you've recovered your senses. I've never thought the people you mix with worthy of you—don't smile, that's not to do with money or class—but I've always thought as you grew older you'd find that out for yourself. Make something of your life and all the advantages you've had—including your freedom. You're nearly thirty. And now you come here without any warning and simply tell us you are leaving in a week's time for one of the worst, poorest and most backward of Third World countries, following a man who's been living here illegally, getting yourself deported—yes—from your own country, thrown out along with him, someone no-one knows anything at all about, someone from God knows what kind of background. Who is he where he comes from? What does he do there? What kind of family does he belong to? What we do know, everyone knows, is that the place is dangerous, a country of gangster political rivals, abominable lack of health standards—and as for women: you, you to whom independence, freedom, mean so much, eh, there women are treated like slaves. It's the culture, religion. You are out of your mind. What more can I say. You choose to go to hell in your own way.*

And now he suddenly looks old, her father, helpless in place of anger, it's a tactic he's used before, but she's thankful her lover isn't with her to see this.

The encounter was almost but not quite as bad as she had prepared herself to meet with the unchallengeable confirmation of the two air tickets—no authority remains in the father's love to cancel those—because it seems there is another crisis in the family, one she had not heard of until now.

—My daughter and my brother . . . What more could hit us. Both in danger. You've always been attached to your uncle, he's the one you went to over this whole business of yours, I believe, didn't you. Do you know what's happening to him, do you? But you're turning your back on all that consists of your life.—

When she quickly demands: —Archie—Archie ill?—her father gestures to his wife. —Danielle had better tell you, it's better explained by a woman, you know more about the background to these things.—

After Danielle has said what she was deputed to say, and the daughter had left with an awkward embrace barely accepted by her father, Danielle went over to him and from behind his chair substituted her own embrace about his shoulders. —What did you expect. The kind of people she's always been mixed up with. That Sunday when she brought him, I sensed trouble. This one's not like the others.—

Dr Archibald Charles Summers has been in medical practice for the best part of half a century.

After 41 years your professional ethics are immutable, like love; you've always lived by them.

For 41 years the boundless opportunities of the gynaecologist were there, his harem of beauties passed literally through his hands. That afternoon as every afternoon in consulting hours the anteroom where they waited on his summons was full. His girls. On this day one or two among them were new acquisitions, no doubt brought there by the faith of others in the understanding and healing powers of their 'Archie'. The newcomers were identifiable because they were busy under instruction from the serene and elegant Farida at Reception, filling in forms with personal details. Farida remembers well—trust her efficiency—the two women, one the kind coming along with a first pregnancy, and the other, age on her form set down as 35, a youthful-looking woman— well-endowed in every sense (Farida's image of her, later), expensive clothes and rings, breasts soft as marshmallows falling together in the scoop neck of her dress as she leaned to write. Her appointment was early on the list and she did not have to wait long. Farida knows all kinds: this was one of those who feign not to be aware that there is anyone else, any woman other than herself, in the space around that self. She had not brought a book with her, as the intellectuals do, nor did she delve into her handbag or pick up and toss aside one magazine after another, as others do. One of the tense and haughty ones, plenty on their minds.

When shown into the doctor's room she greeted him as with relief at getting away to find herself with an equal. She sat back confidently in the chair across from his desk furnished with friendly tokens of patients' gratitude, malachite paperweight, embossed diary, clutch of gilt and silver pens, miniature calculator, two statuettes, copies of some god and goddess—he was at once interrupted by an urgent phone call, and she picked up one of the sacred objects and turned it, smiling. As he ended the call with a gesture of apology, she replaced the god. —Like the good Doctor Freud you enjoy having ancient art around you.—

—They are nice, aren't they. The Greek period in Egypt, I'm told.—

—Well, I'm sure they're a necessary change from the present with the troubles of people like me.—

He recognized then, at once, that she was not a woman who must be approached with small talk. —Now let's hear what the trouble is.— He was also smiling slightly as he glanced through the form bearing her statistics and medical history.

—I'm in the middle of a divorce—and you know how that is, the lawyer says if I want the settlement I'm entitled to I shouldn't be found to be having anyone else—if my husband's lawyers knew there was another man . . .—

—I understand. Yes, that generally would be the case.—

—And now. I have a problem.—

—There is another man. Yes. That's also generally the

case. You are—let's see—thirty-five. It is a restless age for
women. If only men would understand that, there wouldn't
be so many divorces.—

They both laugh.

—So you'll know what's coming next, Doctor. I think I'm
pregnant. God knows how it happened, I'm careful. The
usual symptom, no period for two months. I thought the first
miss was, what does everyone blame everything on, now—
stress. I've got a new job—credit manager in a multinational
company and now there's this. I've done that urine test
thing—negative, but I don't trust it.—

—Any children of your marriage?—

—No. An abortion, five years ago. I'm not the motherly
type, that was one of the things—many things—wrong in
that marriage.—

—So if we do find you are pregnant, you don't want the
child. Of your lover. I must ask you, you know. Your answer
affects what we might be discussing for you, after.—

—No child. No. He won't know, either. Anyway, seems it's
over with him. I don't want any complications. I didn't think
you would be one of those doctors who are disapproving
about abortion.—

And so this woman is one of the unhappy ones. She thinks
she's a bad woman, they all do, the girls, when they want an
abortion for her kind of reason, they sound cocky but they
feel they are unnatural, their mother and grandmother would
tell them so, and they still hear the echo. —I'm not, my dear.
An unwanted life hasn't much chance of having a life worth
living. But I have to have some assurance of the options, for
you. Now come, let's see.—

It must have been this way.

She undressed in the cubicle with the shapeless gowns
hung ready to be discreet over obligatory nakedness presented to the doctor, a ritual process very different from, al-

though the consequence of, being undressed by a lover. The nurse, calling her 'darling' and humming to herself, led her to the examining room, Archie's inner chamber, windowlessly private; the nurse withdrew; she lay on the crisp white sheet over a kind of steel bed and looked at the wash-basin with its taps that could be managed by the elbows, and the powdered latex gloves, pots of unguents and a gleaming long instrument on a small shelf.

The doctor entered by another door and closed it quietly behind him, gave her a reassuring nod and went about his priestly preparations with the calm that meant so much to his girls, all of them treated alike with the same respect for their feelings at the surrender of their bodies without intimacy. He opened the gown, placed a linen towel at the belly down over the pubis so that she would not have the embarrassment of gazing at his gloved hand first opening her up, then pressing what must be the long fingers of his warm hand she could not see all the way to touch some resistance inside her; that must be the womb, the centre of all life whose holiness has so long been his mission. The hand caused a small momentary sensation, a vague ache, like sadness; the hand, the touch—all was withdrawn.

He removed the glove, turned to her with the face of good news. —You are not pregnant.—

He saw her draw a great breath and tilt back her head. His girls. If men knew what crises their women face.

—But all isn't quite as it should be with you, my dear, inside. Let me explain. He was covering her completely with the sides of the gown drawn together as he removed the towel. Then he perched on the edge of the steel bed in his customary way, one leg braced to the floor, the other bent at the knee, to comfort his anxious girls by his presence, there for them, no matter how grave what he had to tell them might be. And he laid the palm of his hand reassuringly on

the stuff of the gown covering her hip as he told her—It's
nothing to worry about at present, but your uterus is retro-
verted, that means it's tipped back, out of place—you don't
complain of back-ache, do you?—

He saw—he remembered that—she had her lower lip
caught tight under her teeth, as a child suppresses a sense of
triumph.

—No. No, no.—

—Then we'll let it be. If you start to have aches and pains,
we'll do something about it.— She's an intelligent woman,
she'll enjoy sharing one of his old army quips, all his girls
have heard it. —Don't ask to see the brigadier unless he
sends for you.—

She grasped his hand where it had alighted on her and
pressed it. He gently but firmly withdrew, he was accustomed
to these impulsive moments of gratitude, women indeed suf-
fer much stress.

Back at his desk with the patient before him in her elegant
clothes, the outfit of a woman who thinks of herself, presents
herself, and not without reason, as good-looking, he wrote
the usual prescription for amenorrhea and dismissed her with
a word of caution, half-admonitory, half-joking—But don't
rely on that womb of yours—take your daily pill, eh.—

—I don't need to come back?—

—You're a healthy woman. Just take care of yourself.
That's what I tell all my girls and hope they'll listen.—

—All.— A wry pull of the mouth. —Oh.— She picked up
the little god, put it down. —You don't think I should see you
again. Anyway.—

His girls. As their mentor, sometimes their needs are beyond what he can give. When their time is up—time for the
next one—he kindly indicates this by rising and coming
round from his desk to shake their hands: on this day, with
this woman, as usual.

That weekend he and his wife Sharon indulged themselves in their love of both music and country walks at a nearby resort where a chamber trio gave an all-Mozart Sunday concert. When he came from his morning hospital round to his consulting rooms on Monday a summons was served on him to appear in court on a charge of sexual harassment. His new patient was the plaintiff.

There was no place within their present for anyone or anything but the significance of the two airline tickets, her application for a visa, order of traveller's cheques in dollars, notice to the owners of the cottage that it was to be vacated, abandoned within a week, the tenant would not be returning, no, whatever was left in it anybody was welcome to take. An elegant suitcase with its wheels and document pouches and combination lock (birthday gift chosen by Danielle for her father to give her a year or two ago) was already standing beside the canvas bag from the garage outhouse. She did not know what to think, what to say, when she burst in back from the parting visit to her father her lover had insisted on. That she would return in some sort of state of nerves—inevitable, he accepted that in advance. But now there was total confusion—what was all this about—the uncle, what uncle—not her father and herself.

Archie. The one I went to see, when we were still trying . . . How is it possible! What are they doing to him, what are they doing to all of us, what's happening, what's happening—

What could he be hoped to say. Each society has mores of its own and ways to deal with those who betray them—but he did not know the English words for this. He's an old man, isn't he. You must understand these things happen.

But he didn't understand what she meant by *happening*! He didn't understand! The earth-quaking within that no-one told you could ever come to you: banishment, deportation, an accusation of behaviour that could never, never ever, be held against such a man, the man who should have been her father. And now she was appalled by what he, lover, beloved, was thinking: complacent, not even shocked. You don't actually *believe* he would do such a thing! You can't believe that!

But do I know him. I have never seen this man. I only know about old men. Poor man.

Archie was always there for her. He said, only days ago, any time, come to me, Sharon and me, any time. And now: to be there for him . . . she made for the telephone but it was he, her lover, who knew better. That's no good. To call. You better see him yourself. That is the right way, if you want . . .

Oh yes, she *wants*. This horrible thing can't be allowed to touch Archie.

Sexual harassment—the boss putting his hand up the skirt of his secretary, the politician fumbling at his assistant's breasts—that's for the pages of the tabloids. He listened patiently—or perhaps his mind was elsewhere, she was too distrait to notice—while she continued to tell him again and again who this uncle was, what he was, not only to her but to others, how many years of care and skill and healing, begun even before she was born. Later in the afternoon she went back to the car and he heard her drive away. He knew where to.

Archie's house: hardly changed. Only the trees grown, towering. The same garden where she had tumbled about on the grass over Gulliver. Dogs came shambling and jumping in greeting, she pressed the intercom and out of what she sensed was emptiness the accents of a black woman came through static to tell her the doctor and his wife were gone away, they said they will come back at the end of next week; she must not give to anyone the name of the place where they were.

Next week.

He and she would be *gone away*; the two plane tickets were carried about with her, her passport was at the embassy of his country for the entry of a visa.

She was back at the cottage sooner than he would have thought, and quiet. All I can do is write to him. What else. Who can this creature be who would get such a thing into her crazy head. But the letter was not written. When next day she received *her* official document, the visa stamped in her passport, something else happened. They had rejoiced, embraced, almost losing their footing together, and then suddenly, grave, he said it.

Now before we go we must be married.

Marriage is for suitable matings in the Northern Suburbs, for Nigel Ackroyd Summers and his wives. Whatever the foreigner might think of The Table at the EL-AY Café, other forms of trust have been discovered to her there.

What for. We don't need that.

He looked at her for what seemed a long time.

What for. She said it again. We don't need that. A bit of paper . . . like the one they wouldn't give you . . . to let you stay.

But she felt he would withhold from her his rare smile, for good. Nevermore. The black mirror of his eyes refused to reflect her.

If you must leave with me then we must marry. I cannot take a woman to my family, with us—like this.

Just say the word.

She laughs, with tears.

He took her in his arms and kissed her solemnly as if exacting a vow. Two days before the aircraft took off they went to the Magistrate's Court and before a marriage officer, the first time he had dared show his face in any place of law enforcement. David from The Table was the required and only witness. They kept away from any celebration, that night, at the café where she had taken him, on impulse, out of the

garage, for coffee. He was right about The Table—something
left behind, abandoned like the cottage—The Table was no
more of use to her, to him and his qualities, than the gather-
ings at Sunday lunch on Nigel Ackroyd Summers' terrace.

Let us go to another country . . .
The rest is understood
Just say the word.

I brahim ibn Musa.

He stands at the foot of the stair where the aircraft has brought its human load down from the skies. Lumbered and slung about with hand-luggage and carrier bags, he turns to wait for her to descend from behind him.

He is home. He is someone she sees for the first time. The heat is a gag pressed across her nose and mouth. There are no palm trees.

Ibrahim ibn Musa. They have traipsed across the stony crunch of the airfield in the shouldering of others, entered an echoing babble in which movement and sound are united confusion, and now are before the immigration booths. A man behind the glass partition lowers his stamp. Ibrahim ibn Musa.

Her visa takes a moment's scrutiny. The wife; Ibrahim ibn Musa. That's all; done.

An airport in a country like this is a surging, shifting human mass with all individualism subsumed in two human states, both of suspension, both temporary, both vacuums before reality: Leaving, Arriving. Total self-absorption becomes its opposite, a vast amorphous condition. The old women

squatting, wide-kneed, skirts occupied by the to-and-fro of
children, the black-veiled women gazing, jostling, the mouths
masticating food, the big bellies of men pregnant with
age under white tunics, the tangling patterns of human
speech, laughter, exasperation, argument, the clumps of baggage, residue of lives, sum of lives (which?), in a common
existence-that-does-not-exist. Julie is no different, she has no
sense of who she is in this immersion, everyone nameless:
only him, officially: Ibrahim ibn Musa.

He was very efficient, speaking his own language, making
enquiries, engaging in exchanges of colloquial ease with those
he approached. He retrieved the elegant suitcase and the canvas bag, and pushed and shouted to grab the door of a taxi
before others could get to it. The drive from the airport to the
outskirts of the capital on a pot-holed tarred road was a contest with other vehicles pressing up to overtake one another
like horses on the home stretch of a race. She was suddenly
exhilarated and laughed, feeling for the hand of this new being. I'm here! I'm here! What she meant: can you believe it?
I'm with you.

She dodged about to see through this window and that the
silhouette of the city emerging blindingly beyond—to her
eyes—the decaying few industrial buildings, vehicle repair
shops and tarpaulined nooks under Coca-Cola signs where
men sat drinking coffee. White, white, sunlight was white on
the cubist shapes of buildings pierced by the index fingers of
minarets.

We don't stay any time in town. We go to the bus station
now.

I want to walk about, look at everything.

All right. Not today. There are not many buses where we
must go.

The bus station on the periphery of the city was a smaller
version of the airport concourse. Only here there were cages

of chickens among the bundles of life-time possessions. He discouraged her from going to the lavatory. This's a dirty place.

You forget that I come from Africa? I've camped out all over, stayed in villages, you know my friends—we didn't exactly look for tiled bathrooms—

His brow twitched with impatience. You don't know this.

She was overcome with love for him: he is in shock, coming back home. She must make light of his irritation with her. Ibrahim . . . (trying out the name, listening to it, feeling it on her tongue). So what d'you want me to do? Wet my pants on the bus? But she laughed alone.

Wait. He caught by the arm one of the men in a voluble group and asked something that was enthusiastically answered by all at once. There's a place we can get coffee just down the road; you can go, while we are there, it will be better.

But the bus? Ibrahim. We'll miss the bus?

There is half-an-hour.

They had to load one another again, like the donkeys seen on the airport road, and he grasped her firmly by the hand, dodging her through buses, cars, trucks and bicycles, wily as the roving stray dogs. Pulled along, she did not need to look where she was going, her gaze darted everywhere about her, snatching a collage of bright and dark images, a vendor with bracelets of bread up his arms, a hag-face begging, the beautiful hands of a baby holding tight on its mother's shrouding veil, the bared grin of a man momentarily staring at her, the shop signs with their flourishes touting heaven knows what. But he—it was as if he shut himself away from what he was navigating; he distanced himself as he often had done from that other—how remote—café, The Table where *she* had taken *him*. This 'café' was a tiny shop perceived as darkness by eyes looking in from the white glare; objects strung across the ceiling and a juke-box winding out loud nasal music.

He—Ibrahim—spoke to the white shape of a tunic (the face
of the man could not be made out at once) and had from him
permission to use his personal outhouse. Her husband (another new identity) had to accompany her, a strange man
could not take a woman there, and she was amused to be led,
as across the road, like a child, to a shed with a door hanging
from one hinge. He stood outside with his back to her private
need; a delicacy that would have made The Table laugh, if it
could have seen.

When she came out he drew up his shoulders in distaste
for a moment and pinched in his nostrils as he breathed.
This's a dirty place. Said it again, a judgment of some kind,
not a passing observation on the concrete-rimmed hole in the
ground over which she had balanced herself.

Well I feel better . . . anyway it's cleaner than a seat where
everyone's been on the throne. Of course it's easier for you
guys, we women lack the appropriate attachment, I suppose
there's always the risk that I could have fallen in.

Come. We must take coffee.

He does not like this sort of claim by intimacy, this manner of talk doesn't come well from a woman one makes love
to. A woman who was not even considered to be for him.

She was not aware that she had offended his sensibilities
but she once again took and squeezed his hand while they sat
at a little tin table outside the shop and drank two small glass
cups of coffee. I'm here, I'm here. *We're here.*

He sees that this—the first cup of coffee at the EL-AY
Café, the love-making in her bed, the wild decision to come
to this place, this country, from which she could not be dis-
suaded, even—yes—the marriage he then had no choice but
to insist on—all this was another of the adventures she prided
herself on being far enough from her father's beautiful house
always to be ready for. But how ready, now, for what is at the
end of the bus ride.

They had a bride for him. Of course. Since he was sixteen or seventeen years old there had been a girl marked out. Even before, perhaps; there was a little one all skinny elbows and knees who swung her plait among the children he played with and later she was recognizable, mournful-eyed to attract attention, in the group of girls past puberty. But that one would be out of the way, by now, he had been away too long—there had been refuges other than under the belly of a car, in other parts of the world where he was unwelcome. Girls are married off young in this place that the innocent, this foreign wife thrown against him by the swaying of the bus, called his home: home, you're home! Her adventure wiped out, for her, the anguished weeks of effort to avoid being relegated to this return. But the lurch and retreat of her soft body against his brought a tenderness in irrelevant distraction, he liked plumpness in a woman, the flesh that takes in the sharp edges and splinters of a man's fate. This Julie who was not for him had just the right amount of flesh for solace. There it was, a gentle weight every now and then, comforting against his side. He did not know what he was thinking; he did not want to think about whatever it was, lurching his mind this way and that, along with the efforts of the overloaded bus to stay on the road.

He had prepared them; or warned them. He was coming back and it was not as the successful son who had made a better life, the Western life of television version, bringing them a share of it in his pockets and in his person, but as a reject, with nothing but a wife—a foreign woman.

At least she had some money because she was one of those not for him. But how much that would compensate them, reach them, his family, was doubtful because she had the luxury, of those who have always had everything, to pride herself in not taking money from her rich father even if he were to offer it. The credit card and dollar traveller's cheques in her sling bag representing a limited sum were the preparations made for this adventure just as she was accustomed to do for other trips abroad. Funds that only if she goes back before long will make it possible for her to buy for herself in foreign currency the things she had where she comes from and will find she can't do without—her essentials are not the essentials of this place.

She'll have enough to pay for her food and mine, while she's here. That's what I, their son, bring back to provide for their old age, for my sisters and their children's future, and for my young brother who is hoping to follow a path—away—opened by his elder.

And again he does not know what he is thinking, no, feeling, currents of love and resentment crossing the inevitability of the family waiting to greet him.

She was exclaiming, asking questions—what is this, oh look at that—about the desert landscape they were being transported through, all new to her. But for him nothing is changed. It is all as it was; everything he had believed he could get away from.

As he knew they were coming close to the village where

there was the image of the family waiting, he looked at her, up and down, in a way that made her turn, smiling enquiry.

Have you got something else to put on. In one of the bags.

Put on? What?

He touched at his breast-bone in the open neck of his shirt. Here. To cover up.

But it's so hot. Don't I look all right? She hitched at the shoulders of the indeterminate sort of garment she wore as a comfortable travelling outfit with her jeans, the movement of muscle lifting for a moment into view the soft cupping of her breasts.

A scarf or something.

I don't see how I can get at things—in our stuff—among all these people, I'll be tramping over them. Wait. Wait—I've got a safety pin somewhere—

She drew together, at the base of her elegant long neck which would some day become flesh-ringed, the openings of the garment and pinned them, with some difficulty, on the inner side of the material so that the pin would not be obvious. All right? All right?

With his eyes down, already preoccupied with some other thought, he signalled, a hand raised from the wrist, that whatever makeshift she had managed would have to serve. She was not at home, now, in the EL-AY Café; she had been determined to come here, to this place. It had its rules, as her father's beautiful house and the guests who came there had theirs. She had made her choice; here it was. She was the one with the choices. The freedom of the world was hers.

There they were. In his mind. His mother for whom he had wanted to save the garage money, bring away from the yoke of family burdens in this dirty place, dirt of the politics of the rich, dirt of poverty. His father always with half-curled hang-

ing hands of a man who lives only through the expectations
he places on those he's engendered (they must live the life he
could not), the brothers left behind, the sisters where there
would be one, as usual, swollen with child, the husband
knowing his place is not in the foreground, the sister-in-law,
wife of the brother away at the oil fields, whose reputation of
being difficult he's heard about; the children, babies when he
left who must be gangling by now, the Uncle who no longer
has a backyard workshop but a vehicle sales and repair business, the neighbours, witness to everything in each other's
lives, coming to see what this son has brought from the
world, his baggage and his strange wife.

Ibrahim ibn Musa. His face drew up in a grimace of pain
and anger at the nature of their existence, but his eyes, black
as theirs, swam tears across this vision of his people.

Julie Summers. In the human press of the airport, in the eyes of the man made out with difficulty in his cave of a shop, in the faces turned in curiosity to study her, close by in the bus, it came to her that she was somehow as strange to herself as she was to them: she was what they saw. That girl, that woman had lived all her life in the eyes of black people, where she comes from, but never had had from them this kind of consciousness of self: so that was what home was. She was aware of this with an intrigued detachment. And it meant that when she went forward to his family in this state, with him, the son who belonged to them, she could do so offering herself in an emotional knowledge: if she was strangely new to them, she was also strangely new to herself.

There they were. At the bus terminus, men of the family; they could not have known the exact time of arrival but they were there. The photographs that might have been—he wasn't sure—among the things he had kept at the garage and that she had never been shown—here they were brought to life. The formal group of men made them recognizable, distinguished from the anonymity of the distracting crowd;

apart, they belonged to him, Abdu-Ibrahim, the wave of their joyousness broke over the couple. The elderly men among them, thick-creased faces, but no uncertainty about which was the father, there was a moment of stillness in that face—the moment of unbelief at a longed-for materialization offering itself in the flesh—that made the man unmistakable despite no physical resemblance between father and son. The embraces were long. The rush and chatter of people in the terminus an accompanying chorus; she was caught up in the emotion of these men, did not know if she was part of them or of the chorus. It was as if she had lost sight of Ibrahim. He was presenting her to his father. The man made a speech of welcome, drawn back from the two of them, she felt his attention, he was addressing her, and she opened herself to it while the son, her husband, gave nervous pressures of some sort of impatience or disapproval on her arm as he translated. *Speak English, speak English.* —The interruption was not heeded.— He can speak a little. At least to greet you.

She jerked her arm against the restraining hand, in dismissal; the hoarse flow and guttural hum of the language reached her on a wave-length of meaning other than verbal. The second elderly man, arms stoutly crossed in confidence over his chest, smiling down upon the ceremonial from some vantage of his own, was introduced to her—the Uncle. The names of the others could not all at once match the individual brothers she knew of, and there were cousins to be confused with them, as well. Some wore casual Western clothes, others were in the traditional long white tunics that, for her, gave them undefined stature, the whole party made the path of their event out of the terminus and to four cars in which, arguing theatrically about who should go where, they found room for themselves. She sat at the passenger door, sharing the front seat with her husband who was close up beside the Uncle in his, the best car. The others accompanied them in a horn-blowing procession to their destination: the place, the street, the house where Ibrahim ibn Musa came from to the garage round the block from the EL-AY Café.

In a street, people were outside a house, smiling and stirring when the procession drew up blaring, the Uncle's car in the lead, the other, road-worn ones coming to a stop with shudders and jerks of their battered chassis. More neighbouring male relatives to be introduced, and among them the children of the house. The children stared at the woman Ibrahim brought, giggled, ran away when she laughed and held her arms wide to receive them. The house—its face, facade—she could be aware of only peripherally behind the excited assembly, the carrying of the elegant suitcase, canvas bag and bundles snatched by various hands taking charge. A flat concrete roof with some clutter of living visible up there; women were peering down from behind its wall, eyes eager and smiling.

She passed an empty pedestal flower-urn painted blue, a burglar grille ajar at the door.

Struck from the sunlight outside, centred in blinding dimness was the still darker shape of a solid figure seated on a sofa; the presence of this house.

She was produced before his mother by her husband. The welcome was formal; as her eyes grew accustomed to the change from the sun's intensity, the hushed room emerged, other women there. The presence—this woman with a beautiful face (she knew it was his mother he would look like) asserted beneath a palimpsest of dark fatigue and grooves of unimaginable experience, addressed her majestically, at length and in their language, but her gaze was on her son and tears ran, ignored by her, down the calm of her cheeks. He translated abruptly, probably omitting elaboration, and then his mother engulfed him, the flight of sisters set upon him, upon the woman he had brought as his wife. And at once her impression of his parents' house, his home, into which she

had now truly been received was broken up by activities that
spilled through doorways where people pushed past one another, balancing dishes of food wreathed in steam and sharp-
sweet scents. The women were a swirl of their enveloping
garments, polyester chiffon and braid, bobbing and dodging;
the men were conducting, giving orders. People sat round
small tables on the carpet and cushions and ate—the way
Ibrahim had given up, in the company of The Table—agilely
with their fingers. Not all the dishes could be found room for
on the flowered cloths among glass plates and brightly-
coloured glasses. There were bowls of fruit and sweetmeats
on the television set; small children ate with concentration
between the adults' feet and older ones raced in and out the
front door helping themselves on the run. Ibrahim the bride-
groom was at his father's side, Julie the bride was facing him
across others, with his mother. She touched now and then at
the pin that held her skimpy garment closed at her throat; the
breathing of the powerful presence at her side stirred robes
rising and falling, ample. The food was delicious; when she
had had her fill of couscous and vegetable stew the women
brought in mutton chops, salad, and handed round the hon-
eyed sweetmeats; she at least knew enough to observe the eti-
quette that here it was impolite to refuse anything offered;
the strength of the coffee helped, long part of therapy after
other kinds of indulgence, left behind. Sweet synthetic drinks
took the place of wine; to signal her closeness she had lifted
her glass to him, down there among the men, calling for his
rare and beautiful smile—but it did not come, his glance met
her a moment but he was apparently answering questions
from his father and brothers. It was the Uncle who made him
smile, booming laughter through a full mouth as he told what
must have been a joke or made a salacious remark—this was,
after all, a kind of wedding feast as well as a son's home-

coming. One of the sisters shyly spoke English when urged by the women, in their own language, to come up to Ibrahim's bride. There was a phrase-book exchange so that the foreign newcomer to the family might not feel left out—the men were confidently animated among themselves, round the returned son, the women preoccupied with the replenishment of food, chattering softly as they moved swiftly about.

—How was the journey.—

—The journey was fine, but you know it is very far—where Ibrahim and I came from.—

—We know. He sent us a letter. Some day it came. I hope you will like it here. It is a village only.—

—I hope you will show me your village.—

—Ibrahim will show.—

The two young women looked at one another in deep incomprehensibility, each unable to imagine the life of the other; smiling. It was perhaps right then that she made the decision: I have to learn the language.

One of the doors led from the party directly into the room that obviously had been vacated for Ibrahim and his chosen wife. The elegant suitcase and the canvas bag stood as they had, way back in her cottage. He closed the door on the company clearing up the feast in the communal room.

There was the huge old, high bed with its carved head- and footboards. An array of coloured covers under a crocheted white spread. She was admiring: how splendid. Ibrahim, what a bed.

He saw it; it is his mother's and father's bed, the only splendour of their marriage, the absurd pretension of the start of driven poverty, the retreat into which each has collapsed exhausted every night for all their years. It is the bed in which each will die.

It's the bed in which he was conceived.

Julie began to unpack gifts they had brought.

No. Not now. Tomorrow we'll give them. It's enough for today.

He tugged back the lace curtains at the window. Tomorrow. He would insist that his parents move back into this room, he and she must find somewhere else to sleep.

A little later she went over to him. What I need now is a long, hot bath. Where's the bathroom?

There was no bathroom. Had she thought of that, when she decided to come with him. This place is buried in desert. Water's like gold is in her country, it's got to be brought up from deep, far down, pumped to this village—what there is of it. Had she any idea of what a burden she would be. So there it is. Madness. Madness to think she could stick it out, here. He was angry—with this house, this village, these his people—to have to tell her other unacceptable things, tell her once and for all what her ignorant obstinacy of coming with him to this place means, when she failed, with all her privilege, at getting him accepted in hers. Tomorrow. The other days ahead.

And it was as he knew it was going to be.

She wants to see 'everything'. They haven't been in his parents' house more than two days when she says, if he doesn't feel like coming along, if there are people he needs to consult, things he needs to do, she's quite happy to explore the village, hop on a bus and see the capital, on her own.

Of course. Of course. Independent. This is the way she's accustomed to living, pleasing herself. Again. But that's impossible, here. He has to be with her, some member of the family, if there could be one who could be understood, has to accompany her everywhere beyond a few neighbourhood streets, that's how it is in the place he thought he had left behind him. It's not usual for women to sit down to eat with the men, today was a special exception for the occasion—does she understand. It's enough, for these people, that she goes about with an uncovered head—that they can tolerate with a white face, maybe. He has sharply resisted his mother's taking him aside to insist that his wife put a scarf over her head when leaving the house or in the company of men who were not family; resisted with pain, because this is his mother, whom he wanted to bring away to a better life. And *she*, the one he has brought back with him, all that he has brought back with him, is the cause of this pain.

It's not an alarm clock you fumble a hand out to stifle. The rising wail lingers and fades, comes again as if a dream has been given a voice, or—there's the grey, lifted eyelid prelude of dawn in the room—some animal out in the desert sounds its cry. There are jackals, they say.

It's the call to prayer.

The first adjustment to any change must be to the time-frame imposed within it; this begins with the small child's first day at school: the containment of life in a society commences. The other demarcations of the day set by that particular society follow, commuter time, clock-in time, canteen break time, workout time or cocktail time, and so on to the last divide of the living of a day, depending on your circumstances. Five times each day the voice of the muezzin set the time-frame she had entered, as once, in her tourist travels, she would set her watch to and live a local hour different from the one in the country left behind.

After much discussion in the language she couldn't understand but whose mixed tenors of hurt feeling and obduracy she felt intensely—somehow herself the cause of it—in the presence of the father's and son's contestation and the monu-

mental silence of his mother ignoring her, they had taken the
elegant suitcase and canvas bag and moved to the lean-to
room and an iron-frame bed. There were shifting sounds beyond the house wall and the clang of the front door grille.
The father accompanied by only one of the brothers went
to dawn prayers at the mosque. Abdu-Ibrahim beside
her turned and folded the pillow over his ear against the
muezzin's summons. At noon, afternoon and evening he
seemed not to hear it, either, without having to block his ears.
She asked what were the other functions of the muezzin?

There isn't any muezzin, there's a recording and a loud-
speaker, you see it on top of the mosque, that is what we have
in the miracle of technology in our place.

But he went, without comment, to Friday prayers with his
father and a day after arrival had begun to wear the skull-
cap tossed aside with his clothes she could see from their bed
when the muezzin opened the day for her. The cap was intri-
cately embroidered with silver thread, she guessed by his
mother; he warned her to keep respectfully clear and quiet
when his mother spread her small velvet rug and swayed her
forehead to it over her obeisant bulk in a private trance of
prayer in the sheltered angle of a passage where members of
the household came and went.

So she wanted to see the place. What is there to see in a
place like ours.

Not Cape Town where they were going to start a business
by the sea and famous mountain.

Tourists don't come here, what for. The tomb of Sidi
Yusuf, the holy man from long ago, supposed to be why this
place grew. Not much of a shrine, only people from round
about in the desert come to it.

She put her arms round his back and rested her lips
against the glossy black hair above his nape. I'm not a
tourist.

He took her with his sister, Maryam, to a large vacant lot
with a trampled fence and a gate hanging without function.
Market day. Rickety stalls distorted by heat were stacked and
spread, spilling to the stony sand geometric arrangements of
vegetables, fruit, dried teguments and strips of something
unidentifiable—fish or meat—grain, flat bread, concoctions
of things—creatures?—imprisoned in jars, towers of volup-
tuous watermelons swagged with green and gold stripes, and
garlands of strung bicycle wheels, vehicle hubcaps and battered tools, old radios, gutted refrigerators assembled—an
objets trouvés art work, she told him delightedly. She asked
Maryam about a man squatting at work on an ancient
portable typewriter while a woman spoke volubly at him. —
Many don't know how to write. They pay for a letter.— Another sat with bright powders of different colours in little
dishes spread on a rug—spices rather than potions, she supposed. Cobblers: the piles of old shoes whose mis-shape taken
on from living feet suggest the dead. A man with the appearance the blind have of talking aloud to themselves was inton-
ing what must be religious texts. Ibrahim had to hang about
while she gazed along the stock of a stall selling posters, the
Kaaba in Mecca, the Prophet's Mosque in Medina, the Dome
of The Rock, the splendidly intricate calligraphy of inscribed
verses from the Koran.

I want to know.

He gave a little snort of a laugh, and a gentle push for her
to move on. Third-hand clothes were piled for a fourth-hand
wearing, sunglasses and cellphones were offered by touts;
there were stacked plastic plates, cups, bowls, and enamelled
jugs, cooking pots, kettles decorated with flower patterns of
organic ostentation that seemed tactless in a desert village.

Why does the world dump these hideous things here,
don't the people make much better things for themselves?

These don't break so soon.

But she takes responsibility upon herself. Why do we send only such shit.

The sister with her few words of English was trying to follow, her eyes on him, his words.

Because here there's no money to pay for anything else.

Here is where she has insisted on coming, here she is, with the gaudy tin basins that offend her, the children wearing oddments of the fourth-hand cast-offs, fancy running shoes clumped at the end of bone-thin legs—and who knows how they got hold of those—pestering to sell two or three cigarettes or a handful of sweets.

Later in the day the Uncle came to fetch his nephew and bride for a visit to his house—he no longer lived next door, in the street where Ibrahim was born; other relatives, distant cousins, were the occupants now. The car was hung with amulets, illuminated Arabic texts, and pungent with some washroom scented spray, his laughing guttural voice could have been disc-jockey chatter accompanying the winding incantations of Easternized American pop on the car radio. Ibrahim lowered a window and as they passed she was able to identify the market-place again, emptied, taken over by stray goats, crows, and a scatter of boys playing football. She was oddly conscious of him, Ibrahim, her husband, yes—watching her as if to perceive before she did what she might be seeing. This street was the only tarred one in the village, men were sitting under the drooping slant of rough awnings drinking coffee, some apparently playing a game—difficult to make out what it was, from a moving vehicle. Everywhere, selling and buying. Black-draped women trailed capering children who could have been anywhere—the exuberance of childhood is a universal response to being alive; his, in this village, might not after all have felt so different from hers, climbing over Gulliver in a beautiful garden, falling asleep with plush toys bought by Nigel Ackroyd Summers in duty-free airport shops of the world. It is only with growing up, becoming the man he is and the woman she is, that circumstances come between you. Outside the haphazard stretch of sheds and buildings either half-completed or half-fallen-down, difficult to say which, she sees for the first time in her life two old men actually sharing a water-pipe, the hookah of illustrations to childhood's Scheherazade stories. So much life!

But he closes the smeary window as the Uncle bounces the car off tarmac onto the sand track that must lead to his new address.

The Uncle's house has everything to the limit of the material ambitions that are possible to fulfil in this place—if his nephew, entering, needs to be reminded of this, which is always with him, implacable warning that prods and pierces him, flays him to rouse the will to carry on washing dishes in a London restaurant, swabbing the floors of drunken vomit in a Berlin beer hall, lying under trucks and cars round the block from the EL-AY Café and emerging to take the opportunity—what choices are there—to become the lover of one of those who have everything (the Uncle could never dream of) and who could be a way to fulfil a need—a destiny!—to realize one's self in ambitions hopeless in this place.

The aunt, bound about with gold jewellery on wrists and ox-blood-fingernailed hands, withdrew Julie to the women's quarters of the house, where the daughters remained during the visit. She and the aunt returned to the men—Ibrahim explained afterwards it was not allowed for a male to see his female cousins, although, what seemed in contradiction of orthodox modesty, while one of the young women was dressed in flowing tradition like the mother, the other daughter wore jeans and the latest in high platform-soled boots.

Julie notices that *he* is—can it be!—somehow touched by dread, foreboding, in the rooms that the Uncle is proudly

showing them round. She cannot ask—among all her questions later—what it was that came to him in that harmlessly
vulgar house as they were seated on carved and gilded chairs
and plied with sherbet, dates and sweetmeats. The backyard
repairs have become a large workshop hidden behind the
elaborate tiled wall of the courtyard with its hibiscus and
canopied swing-couches. There, the Uncle explains and asks
Ibrahim to translate for her, he has district government contracts to maintain and repair all official vehicles and ministers' cars, he is the official agent for American and German
cars, American, German and Italian spare parts and, of
course, his is the only service anyone who has a good-model
vehicle comes to from villages even several hours' journey
across the desert.

That is what he has made of himself.

—Remember you used to come to help out when you were
a kid, the wrecks we fixed up? In the old yard?—tell her!—

—She knows. She knows I learned from you how to pre-
tend to be a mechanic.—

This in their language; she could only laugh when they
did, not aware it was at the vision of him, that first time, the
grease-monkey under a car.

Returned to their lean-to he lay on his back on the bed in
his unconscious grace as he had at her cottage, eyes deep as
wells she would feel herself as if straining precariously to look
into. That Uncle's made a go of it, hasn't he.

Yes.

She often has the sense that he is not looking at her when
his regard is on her; it is she who is looking for herself re-
flected in those eyes.

Yes. The success you can have in this place.

But are they talking from the same premise? Is she wryly
admiring the success, on a humble scale, of a Nigel Ackroyd
Summers she has removed herself from, far as she could, by

way of the EL-AY Café and a man without papers or a name; is he drily remarking there is no comparison with the success available to those with access to financial institutions quoted on the stock exchange?

Neither knows.

They make love, that unspoken knowledge they can share; that country to which they can resort.

Where the street ended, there was the desert. Led by the children down the row of houses like the family one, lean-tos and haggard walls, bright motifs of paint, dusty plants, leaning bicycles, cars sputtering from broken exhausts, men lounging, women at windows, washing hooked on a fence, more children who race and skitter, garrulous radio discourse, the man selling bean rissoles calling out—this everyday life suddenly ends.

It was bewildering to her: come to a stop. At the end of a street there must be another street. A district leads to another district. And a road, a highway that links one place of habitation to others. There was the mound of detritus unravelled, tin cans rolled away, spikes of glass signalling back to the sun; and then, in the terms by which humans judge the significance of their presence—nothing. Sand. No shapes. No movement. When she came back to the house: It's not the wind months, he told her. You don't want to be here for that, believe me.

She laughed. We are here.

They are right, those people in the village he is aware see

her as something they never have, a tourist. Tourists don't en-
dure the bad seasons, that's not for them.

Julie is accustomed to being active. He and she can't sit
about in the house all day, waiting for—what to do next. She
wants some little expedition into the desert but is aware of his
distaste—the heat is too bad and you need a four-wheel-
drive. The Uncle has generously lent them—Ibrahim insists—
no it's my gift to your marriage the Uncle pronounces
carefully in English—a car in fair condition and they drive
around the village, the school from which some teacher managed to get him sent on to education beyond memorizing the
Koran, what used to be the sports field, donkeys there now; a
lop-sided sign whose script she had him translate for her indicates a boarded-up communal hall, stalls propped one
against the other—a fall of shavings from a carpentry shop,
men, always men, drinking coffee—the groan of a generator
and thick steam coming from the pipes of a dilapidated hospital, the mosque where she can only picture him on Fridays,
she is a woman, and even she who may go anywhere in the
world, do as she likes, cannot enter. What else is there: this is
his place.

She wanted to buy sandals like the ones his sister-in-law
Khadija wore so they went to look for the shoemaker who might
have them. How get lost in a village he must have known, roam-
ing every turn and twist, as a boy! Landing at empty lots, abandoned workshops, they didn't find the shoemaker but in this part
of the village she saw as a ruin but was the normal state of lassitude in the extremes of poverty, there was no demarcation between what was the thoroughfare and the shacks where goats
were tethered and women squatted in their black garb like crows
brought down wounded—suddenly he had to swerve to avoid a
dead sheep lying bloated in a shroud of flies. Now she was appalled. Ah poor thing! Why doesn't someone bury it!

His foot on the accelerator made the violent pressure of an about-turn, churning up stones and sand.

He lies like a corpse and a fly lands on his forehead.

Dead sheep. Rotting.

He is ashamed and at the same time angrily resentful that she is seeing it (over again, he sees her), it will be an image of his country, his people, *what he comes from*, what he really is—like the name he has come back to be rightfully known by. Not for her; no, that was it.

Often he was away all day. He left early, for the capital. Things to do there; family matters, she was resigned to suppose: he was back home. The family was a graph of responsibilities to be traced, a tree not of ancestry but the complexity of present circumstances. There was the question of the sister-in-law living in the house, wife of the elder brother who was away over the frontier at the oil fields and whose earnings transferred to support his wife and children had for months failed to arrive from the agency in the capital. There was some problem over the father's right to a portion of profit from a small rice crop owned by a collateral; no lawyer in the village to regulate these disputes? No. Responsibilities were expected of the return of a son experienced in the ways of a world outside. There was no suggestion that she should accompany him, these were not occasions to explore the city, what was the sense of her hanging about in queues before officialdom.

She rationed to herself the books provided in the elegant suitcase. Might be some time before she and he decided what they would do, their project (the vocabulary of her public relations period slipped in, like an accent discernible in a second-language speaker)—what a new life, here, was going to be.

A child gentle as a moth came in to the lean-to and stood watching her read.

The second time, the child sat down on the floor, so quiet that even her breath was no intrusion. Then the child brought with her the young woman who spoke a little English.

He had made the list.

Maryam—my little sister's what do you call it, a domestic—she works in a house like my Uncle's. And my sister Amina, who's living here with her children, I don't know what her husband is doing now—what work, if there is any. Ahmad, the tall brother, kills animals for a butcher, you can smell it when he comes in. That water you see being boiled—it's what my mother always prepares for him to wash himself. The other one, that's Daood, he is the coffee-maker in a café. My brother Zayd, Khadija's husband—they say there's no news, don't know what's happening with him. My small brother Muhammad is still at school, he sells cheese to the houses for a shopkeeper, walking everywhere. There, that is my family. Their professions.

It must have been the young sister's day off—Friday, yes, Julie had seen her prostrate, praying beside her mother that morning. The book was put aside and they began to talk, bridging hesitancy with gestures—Julie, with mime—and laughter at each other's attempts at being understood. Her Ibrahim had taught her nothing of the language, dismissing even the conventional polite exchanges. They'll get it although you say good evening and thank you very much. But this young sister seemed to enjoy having the foreigner repeat these banalities become achievements, correcting the awkwardness of a throat producing unfamiliar sounds and lips shaped to expel them. In turn, the young woman slowly arranged the sequence of her English words, and waited attentively to hear of her mistakes. For the meal after midday prayers the child put her hand, a delicate frond of fingers, in Julie's and led her along with Maryam to where in a room with no defined purpose the women of the house cooked food for everyone on two spirit burners—that feast on the return of the son from seeking his fortune must have come from the Uncle's house. Julie wanted to help with washing dishes in the tin basins (the flowered ones she'd seen in the market); the ethics of the EL-AY Café did not allow oneself to be waited on except in a restaurant. But the women crowded about to prevent her from so much as putting her hands in water. The mother stood apart; it must have been her direction—from her son?—that this bride he had brought as that fortune from the other world could not be expected to take on what was the lot of women.

Maryam is such a bright girl.

Yes? He really does not know her; she was a child when first he went wherever it was he could pass immigration.

She says she wants to study. Doesn't seem to know quite what—be a doctor, secretary in a company—glamourized careers she sees on television, for sure. But she *is* so hungry to learn. Why can't she have the chance? Why should she be a nursemaid or whatever it is. She has a brain. You somehow got to the university.

Doesn't she tell you she'll be married next year. It has been arranged with the son of my father's friend, the commissioner of police. The son is a policeman. You haven't seen—they tell me he's posted somewhere else. She will go there.

Julie echoes his customary conclusion: So that's it.

She will be a wife. My mother—you can't talk to her so how can you know. My mother is a very clever woman. She has a brain, as you say.

Oh I see that. It's there in her face.

But you don't know how she fought with everyone for education, that girl, forced her father to let her go to school to
learn to write and read the Koran. In those days she was the
only girl among the boys there. She could read newspapers
and books no other girl could. She could say whole parts of
the Koran—by heart, is it? Many verses. She still can. But it
was arranged, she was married. And here she has been in this
house giving us birth, feeding us, boiling water to clean us.

Julie could not understand the hostility in him at such
times and could not know that he hardly understood it:
whether it was against the bonds of a life he had set himself
passionately adrift from, the sorrow that his mother's life
was, to him, and that he failed to change—and now; look at
his mother—what would she have been, this image of dignity,
all that she had endured and controlled, put down in the
streets between the garage backyard and the company of the
café table! Or was this animus against *her*—the tourist who
like all tourists didn't ever know what it was she really was
looking at. The sense—the *strength*—his, in the possession of
her, had been in the chance that she, her connections, what
she *was*, would have obtained for him in her country what he
could not attain. His animus the protection he must take to
guard against that thing, luxury, people who could afford it
called love—he found himself yielding to feel, for her. *That*
would be his weakness—the day when she packed the elegant
suitcase and went away, this adventure worn thin, as it will.
Him the loser, yet again. He's not for her. Papers refused.

He did not tell her that from the first day what he was doing when he left early on a morning for the capital was seeking out every contact, every strategy of wily ingenuity that
could be got out of such contacts, to apply for visas for emigration to those endowed countries of the world he had not
yet entered and been deported from. Australia, Canada, the

USA, anywhere, out of the reproach of this dirty place that was his.

No point in raising hopes that might not succeed in time: before the adventure was over and the elegant suitcase packed for the EL-AY Café, and the beautiful terrace of her father's house, although she didn't care to call that home.

He is back helping out in his Uncle's vehicle repair workshop.

Ibrahim ibn Musa.

The processes of applying for permission to enter someone else's country from this one are numerous and set no definite period for their conclusion. The verdict—yes or no, and under what conditions—takes even longer. The local consular representative of the country concerned, after the applicant has managed to get past counter clerks and sit before him, has to send all relevant documents back and forth to the Ministry in that country; they slip to the bottom of a pile, get lost in the interstices of a filing cabinet, are wiped out by computer failure, and the process has to start over again. There is no use asking for reasons; and then there are new questions from the Ministry, requiring still further documentation, to and fro. And underlying all this that is taking place openly on stamped forms and computer screens there are other measures, anything and everything that can be tried to wriggle under power-lines of bureaucracy, and that have succeeded, it is legendary, the odyssey of emigration, for some, while

failing—he follows their experience every day, with compatri-
ots at a coffee stall—for others.

She has been only the Siren to his Ulysses. Whereas in her
country it had been up to her to importune the influential
and engage lawyers etc. in the contest with the bureaucracy
of authority—an unsuccessful diversion, even if attractive—
in this place, this situation back here, he is the one who must
have the know-how, or somehow acquire it. What had served
him before, when he managed to get some kind of dubious
entry to a country, might not—did not—work now; the
equivalent national humanitarian symbols of the Lady With
The Upheld Torch, like her, no longer welcome but use the
Light to frisk each applicant blindingly for possible connections with international terrorism—people fighting their own
foreign ideological battles on other nations' soil, or carrying
in their body fluids the world's latest fatal disease. This country which claimed him by his birth, his features and colour,
his language, and the Faith that he had to fill in on forms although he did not know if his mother's son was still a Be-
liever—this country was well known to have a high rating as
a place of origin from which immigrants were undesirable.

She, his foreign wife, was the right kind of foreigner. One
who belonged to an internationally acceptable category of
origin. When he was simply handed a single form for her application for a visa for any of the countries he favoured, he
had now to tell her what his absences in the capital were
about.

I started right away to get us out of here.

But where to. She was reading down the form as she
spoke. What sort of country.

Does she still believe in choice. But he gave her his slow
rare smile that he knew she was, always, moved to coax from
him. Any one we can have.

All right for her. For him, her husband, if other ways were

to be followed where official ones were going to be a no-no, these cost money. She had no scruples about this so long as bribes could be managed, here, without danger to him; the only reason why this course hadn't been resorted to back in her country was the warning of the lawyer that he would find himself in more trouble. There were the tourist dollars she had brought with her; her only hesitation was how would he and she continue to contribute food and other necessities— things his mother certainly needed—if the money ran out? The Uncle wasn't paying him, at present—apparently the old car and free fuel were regarded as compensation for having him back under vehicles. This time the fleet of the provincial administration and now as a mechanic *genuine-trained* in a big city far from us! —This was the Uncle's bonhomie that, once she had Ibrahim translate for her, she began to recognize in its frequent repetition.

We'll be gone before then.

He was fixed in determination as on something palpable, as he stripped himself of jeans and T-shirt. The designer jeans were oil- and dirt-stained now, there were no trade unions with rules for the protection of workers, the kind of business the Uncle owned so profitably did not supply overalls. His determination was an awesome possession she had never seen, never needed to be called forth either in the life of her father's suburb or the sheltered alternatives of her friends. Never known in herself—well, perhaps when she stood in the cottage before him with two flight tickets instead of one.

She picked up the jeans and shirt, and the simple gesture, could have been that of his mother or sisters, sent him over to her. His naked feet covered hers, his naked legs clasped her, and he smothered her head against his breast as if to stay something beginning in her.

No-one can say how long it could take. When you grease a palm (or whatever that business is called here) you have to risk whether the recipient-behind-the-recipient can do what he assures—no problem! no problem!—or won't be seen again, and neither will the dollars.

Life in the meantime.

Life. An unremarked insidious way in which both anticipation and impatience are suspended along with the official refusals and the repeated re-applications to be made. An entry into the state lived by the family, the street that ends in desert, the men sitting at coffee stalls. Everyone is waiting for something that may come sometime—a return from the oil fields, the settlement of an ancient debt, a coup whose generals will not stuff their own pockets—or never.

Julie was teaching English not only to Maryam and the quiet young neighbourhood girls and awkward boys who sidled into the lean-to whispering and making place for one another cross-legged on the floor. Maryam must have mentioned this little gathering to the lady of the house where she was employed; the woman invited the foreign wife to come to tea and be good enough to talk English with other ladies wanting to learn to speak the language. What on earth qualified her to teach! On the other hand, what else did she have? What use were her supposed skills, here; who needed promotion hype? She was like one who has to settle for the underbelly of a car. The books in the elegant suitcase were bedside bibles constantly turned to, by now, read and re-read; she agreed—but in exchange for lessons in *their* language. Why sit among his people as a deaf-mute? Always the foreigner where she ate from the communal dish, a closeness that The Table at the distant EL-AY Café aimed to emulate far from any biological family. Never able better to reach her lover (husband!—she found it difficult to think of herself as a wife) through some sort of contact with the mother to whom was reserved, she knew long before meeting her in the imposing flesh, a place within him out of reach by anyone else. The Table friends were always cash-strapped, even if she had felt like re-entering the cul-de-sac she once occupied with them, not fair to expect an outlay on purchase and despatch; she wrote to her mother, why shouldn't she be asked to order through one of those wonderful Internet book warehouses in California a translation of the Koran, hardback. And send it by courier; the village post office was a counter shared with chewing gum and cigarettes in a shop.

Her mother, of all people, yes. Speaking from within the family where she now found herself, he had made it clear she was remiss in not keeping a daughter's contact with a mother. So there had been an exchange of letters. *My crazy girl, I can imagine your papa's horror . . . you're like me, I'm afraid, you just can't restrict yourself to tidy emotions! But don't forget, darling, if it doesn't work you can always get out.* She had been amused to read the letter to him but skipped the last sentence. A few days later he asked whether she had answered the letter yet.

No of course not. It's not going to be a weekly duty, like when I was at boarding school.

Her mother can get some references. From her friends, her husband. He's an American, isn't he. It's necessary for our visas.

Canada, Australia—America too? Every possibility was being worked at through his contacts. The only country where she might have any of use was England; but he already had against him a record of illegal entry there.

The letters of recommendation she requested—at his dictation, he knew so well the form to take—so far had not come from California. But the book by door-to-door service prepaid at high cost did arrive—somehow—with the driver of the bus from the capital; whoever was supposed to take charge of the package there happened to know the man's route. She hesitated to ask Ibrahim what the verses were that he had told her his mother knew by heart; Maryam would tell her. There was some difficulty in making her request understood, perhaps not because of language problems but of the girl thinking she must be misunderstanding: what would Ibrahim's wife want to know these things for?

The Chapter of The Merciful, the Chapter of Mary, the Chapter of The Prophets.

He was out with men with whom he grew up, some friends said to be able to lead him to the hands open behind officials' backs. There were no hours restricting his quest, no chances of pursuit too unlikely. She was alone with the gooseneck lamp he had bought, saying that at least she could read by the light of some amenity she was used to, while they were in this place. *Suras*, the footnotes said they were called. She read aloud to herself as if to hear in the natural emphases of delivery which had been the passages come upon—for life— in these choices out of so much advice and exhortation, inspiration, consolation people find in religious texts. She read at random; the verses did not come in the order in which Maryam had happened to name them.

And remember Job: when he cried to his Lord, Truly evil

hath touched me: but thou art the most merciful of those who show mercy.

So we heard him, and lightened the burden of his woe; and we gave him back his family.

Turned away from the encircling light of the lamp.

She was beside the majestic figure statue-draped in black at the feast, the first meal. Her lover, the son, cast out by Nigel Ackroyd Summers' world, given back to his family by that silent figure whose authority came from the thrall of his love. How had the girl-child known the verse she was learning to read was: for her. Known by heart.

And make mention in the Book of Mary, when she went apart from her family, eastward

And took a veil to shroud herself from them: and we sent our spirit to her, and he took before her the form of a perfect man.

She said: 'I fly for refuge from thee to the God of Mercy! If thou fearest him, begone from me.'

He said: 'I am only a messenger of the Lord, that I may bestow upon thee a holy son.'

She said: 'How shall I have a son, when man hath never touched me and I am not unchaste.'

He said: 'So shall it be, The Lord hath said: "Easy is this with me; and we will make him a sign to mankind, and a mercy from us. For it is a thing decreed." '

And she conceived him, and retired with him to a far-off place.

Boarding-school scripture stuff.

And when one who was dubbed a Jesus-freak among the café habitués got herself pregnant and said she didn't know how that happened, it had been the banter of the day . . . now which of you randy guys played Angel Gabriel . . .

What the story might mean to the one who still could recite it by heart; well you'd have to have a son of your own to understand.

The light fell again on the pages; turning, skimming; a pause:

The God of Mercy hath taught the Koran
Hath created man,
Hath taught him articulate speech.
The Sun and the Moon have each their times,
And the plants and the trees bend in adoration,
And the Heaven, He hath reared it on high . . .
. . . He hath let loose the two seas which meet each other:
Yet between them is a barrier which they overpass not.

Everyone knows, in texts like these, what is meant: for her. She left this book open on the last two lines.

She lay on the iron bed and waited for him, gone about the imperatives of his world, as he had awaited her, gone about hers, nights in the cottage.

For a while Australia looked promising.

What'll we do there?

Plenty. A country with opportunities, all kinds. Developing. It will be good, for you, you know, very much like your home place.

She shook her head, laughing. I've left that home place.

Julie went along with him to someone who had connections with someone else who knew the Canberra representative in the capital, to give particulars of her own background that might count favourably; wife a citizen of a fellow Commonwealth country, legal and fiscal provenance impeccable, standard of education high.

What about those people, the man at your father's place, that time, who was going to Australia. He was the one who was even taking his black driver with him, you remember the talk.

I've no idea where they are.

There was the summon of his black eyes.

Your father knows.

She raked her hair up the back of her head through

splayed fingers; he stood before her as he had when he emerged from under a car in a garage: here I am.

I can't ask my father.

His silences distressed her more than any argument between them would have, they were retreats into thoughts that barred her; he who had been refused so often had unconsciously taken on for himself the response of refusal.

She went to him where he was suddenly rummaging in the canvas bag—he had never completely unpacked, not allowed her to do it for him, it was there ready for departure from this place, his home, standing week after week, month after month, in the lean-to room. She bent over him, her arms going around his waist and her cheek against his bare back. To her, the essence of him, the odour of his skin, overcame his silence and received her. She wanted to say, I will do anything for you, but how could this be formulated when she had shown there was something she could not?

It wouldn't do anything for us except humiliate us. He'd say no, he wouldn't even think of embarrassing his colleague, his corporate mate, accepted in a country in *high standing* . . . expecting him to recommend some immigrant he's seen once at a lunch party and who was the husband of a daughter whose father had told her she must go to hell in her own chosen way—those were my father's lovely farewell words to me!

I wrote the name of the place they were going to. Somewhere in here, it is. Perth, it was Perth. I think so . . . a bit of paper . . .

The bit of paper was not found. Without the reference from Perth the processes of application continued, the periods of waiting while documents went back and forth.

Entry to Australia was not granted.

Julie was confusedly angry. Apparently with the Australians; with herself for not having been able to 'do anything' for him that—in fact, in contradiction—would have been unlikely to have made any difference.

He kept contingency plans for the next country, concur-
rently with every application that failed. They have enough
trying to keep out others from the East, they don't need
people like me. That's all. That's it.

In the meantime.

Waiting generates a pace of its own; routine, that is supposed to belong to permanence, forms out of the fact that in the meantime there is nothing else to be done. Ibrahim takes the old car the Uncle has lent—given—them and goes to the Uncle's vehicle workshop in the morning, Julie has classes in English at Maryam's employer's house and at a school— word-of-mouth makes more claims on an apparent skill or gift she didn't know she had. In the family house Maryam has gathered her sister Amina, who has just given birth, and Khadija, wife of the son missing at the oil fields; they and others come unobtrusively to join the exchange, picking up Julie's language, Julie picking up theirs, under a torn awning at the back of the house that stretches to an oleander whose pink flowers are thick with dust, like a woman who uses too much powder. There is no palm tree. The shade is thin and the shifting of light across the faces, Julie's and theirs, is a play upon what each does not know, in unfamiliarity, and is

beginning to have revealed, in glances of intuition about the
other. Maryam has become almost fluent, or Julie has become
quicker at understanding what the girl is getting at in the locutions and inevitable substitutions of one English word for
another. Maryam insists that Khadija is the one who can im-
part their language to Julie far better than she can, Khadija
comes from the capital, she finished school 'all the way'. It is
not just the young girl's inarticulacy in the foreign language
that is the reason for this advocacy; everyone in the family
knows, even Ibrahim's wife has seen, that Khadija is in a
state of frustration which swings from being found weeping
in a corner (the one reserved for the mother's prayer mat, at
that) to angry imprecations against her husband, a son of the
house. Ibrahim calls her, privately to his wife, that crazy
woman. She shouts at my brother for being dead, perhaps he
is dead, God knows. Maryam's delicate way of wanting to
help her sister-in-law is to attempt to distract her by recognizing her superiority and flattering her into the obligation to
use it to help someone else: their new sister-in-law, Ibrahim's
wife. —I tell Khadija, she is lonely without our language.—
  Julie repeated this to him.
  Isn't that original? Maryam's such an unusual girl, it even
comes out in her broken English. She's right about Khadija,
though. Khadija never looks at me, you know she's somehow
haughty, but she's listening and then she corrects me, I'm really learning pronunciation from her. Talk to me. You'll see.
We must use your language together . . .
  He was back from the Uncle's workshop and had fetched
the water his mother heated for him. The tin tub was kept
ready in the lean-to; he would not allow Julie to fetch water:
the other women in the house smiled to see him carry the
bucket, women's work; his mother kept her face set against
the spectacle, turned away from him. He might indeed be

away; one of his exiles where he could not be placed in her
mind, only in a biological awareness of him that circulated in
her blood, pumped through the heart.

What are the names—I don't know, the, the . . . you know
. . . the love words . . . I'd like to hear them. You've never
said them to me . . . ?

We must talk English. I need to speak English. I must
speak English with you if I am going to get a decent job anywhere. I can be able to study some more there. Only with
English. He tipped the water to the tub.

Scrubbing at himself as he crouches he feels the grease-
stains of engine innards, the dirt-coating of tools blackened
under his nails, as if all over his body, the condition of his life
she has never known, how could this one, who had taken a
fancy to him in this state he must escape from, ever know.
And he is aware that he is in dialogue with himself in the language she now has taken a fancy to learn, no use to her, to
them, where they would go. But what use—cruelty—to tell
her that in the life she's decided for herself, following him,
nice accomplishments are a luxury. Ramadan was approaching. Who would have thought I'd still have her in this place,
we'd still be here then. The fine suitcase not gone from where
she's pushed it away under the bed, her adventure not over,
we make love on that poor iron bed and I please her, my God
how I please her. And no visas for me.

He told her it was of course not necessary that she should
fast. With his father and the rest of the family, he would: because of his mother.

With the family and the whole village, wasn't that so?

Why should she be the exception? The only one. Lonely
without the language. He ought to be able to understand;
here, here in his home, she was what he had been at The
Table in the EL-AY Café with her friends, at the terrace

lunch party to bid farewell to the couple and their driver welcomed by Australia. Of course I'll fast.

You'll make yourself ill. To be without water is terrible. Don't think only, no food; food is nothing, nothing, not like water. Believe me.

Rubbish, my love! I can do with losing some padding, I eat too much at these family meals, I'm getting a fat backside, look.

Another adventure.

He believes she may never learn; or perhaps never have to learn the rules of survival, always has all choices open to her.

Against the rusty complaints of the iron bedstead under love-making only half-unclothed she murmured, taking up an unconcluded subject, I'm all the way with you. A banal phrase from The Table, but all she had.

The pace of waiting transformed completely. Reaction to the span of the Ramadan day was exactly like the reaction of body and mind to the time-change on arrival in a country whose hours are far behind or ahead of the one departed from. The same vague swaying sensation of seeing surroundings through a distorting lens, not really unpleasant, a lazy resistance against drooping eyelid muscles, the consciousness saying, let me sleep, shut out the light, do not answer the vacuum sucking at the stomach: *satisfy me, it's the hour.* And the strange surprise: the nights now were cold; the picture-postcard place was one of perpetual heat; there had been no Northern Hemisphere season of winter in that desert. She missed the pre-dawn meal for which there was really no designation, it is the meal, ultimate sustenance; she could not goad herself sufficiently awake to ingest. Thought and reaction slowed while the house was a murmuring hive of women

at prayer and the men were at the mosque. However they occupied the other periods of the day, the men of the family
kept to themselves elsewhere in male company. Julie did not
expect to see Ibrahim until they returned after sunset. Sometimes the women visited one another, gathered at this neighbouring house or that. The mother saw her son's wife leave in
the company of Maryam, Amina, Khadija and the children
for a cousin's house; tranquilly watching from her sofa. After
a while, she went to her place of prayer. An hour or more
passed before she returned to the sofa in the deserted family
room, and recognizing, as always, the gait and weight of his
footsteps, heard her son unexpectedly return. She rose, going
to him as he quietly entered. They met for a moment silently;
in their faces each the likeness of the other. Then the tone of
her voice, meant only for him, held the cadence of the
prayers that had filled her afternoon, as a passage of music
continues to sound in the ears: —Are you not well, my son.—

He inclined his head towards his mother in the special
gesture—submission? love?—reserved for her. With his father
he had always a ready exchange, often a combat of controlled
disagreement between them. With the mother there often
seemed hardly need for words. A pause. —I don't know . . .
no, just tired.— He looked towards the lean-to door and
away again.

Between them was knowledge of the taboo, to be observed
absolutely, that a husband and wife must not retire together
to their bedroom during the daylight hours of Ramadan,
when any intimacy between men and women is forbidden.

—Your wife is with Maryam and the others at Zuhra's.—

The gesture of the inclined head towards his mother,
again.

Working with cars and heavy trucks and all the time
back, back to those foreign offices in the capital planning to
go away. When would he ever take care of himself.

—You need rest.—

No need for either to remark that when the women came
back he would hear and leave the lean-to before his wife
might enter. Mother and son sat a few minutes together before she returned to her place of prayer.

He went to the lean-to—and there she was, Julie. He
stayed himself in the doorway, then pulled the ill-fitting door
carefully closed behind him.

You left the other men?

He could have said, You left the other women. He gave his
wife his smile, that of himself which was for *this one*: for her.
I'm tired.

So was I. They're sweet, but the chatter—it gets to be like
being caught in an aviary.

He kicked off his shoes and, a moment's hesitation, doffed
the embroidered cap held with a clip on the thick hair of his
crown, he lay down on the bed, an obedient child sent to nap.
You need rest. She lay beside him, their bodies not touching.
Perhaps she knew of the taboo, Maryam might have told her;
maybe not. It seemed a long time; neither slept nor spoke.

She felt desire rising in her and unfolding, thickening
those other lips of hers, overwhelming the lassitude of hunger
and the drought of thirst. And she was ashamed; she knew
that sexual acts, like other forms of indulgence, were forbidden during these dedicated days, though this abstinence
proved to add deferred excitement to love-making in the
nights. Her hand went out to assure herself that it would only
seek his in the aspect of love that is companionship, but it en-
countered bewilderingly his penis raised under his clothes. She
withdrew the hand swiftly. She didn't know where to place it
in relation to herself after the contact. Again some kind of
measure of time passed at this pace that was unlike any other.
They turned to one another in the same moment, and he divested her of her disguise of clothes and she divested him of

his. But she was the one who put the palm of a hand on his breast to stay him, thinking of the complaining springs of the iron bedstead, and lay down on the floor to receive him.

There was water in the jar they kept beside the tin tub. They washed each other off themselves; maybe her infidel's guilty illusion of cleansing absolution. But he silently dressed, pinned the embroidered cap on his crown, and left. His mother was not in her place on the sofa. She must have been still at prayer, but she would have known, even from the disturbance in the air of the house—made by his body, alone of anyone else's, the passage of her son's presence—that he had recovered his forces and gone to rejoin the men.

Women and children came back, high tide of the house's life over-running its secret streams. Maryam was asking— Has Julie gone out again?—

—She was with you.—

—Oh she didn't stay long, she left to go home.—

Maryam called softly at the lean-to door with her usual one-knuckle tap.

—Yes? I'm coming.—

The sound of the foreign voice choked the mother with a strangle of shock.

There, there in the bedroom. Before her son came away from the men, before she told him his wife was with the other women, she herself, the mother, was alone in the house, for him—the woman had come back, unheard in the concentration of prayer, the alcove of devotion, and she was in that bedroom all the time.

There. Fear and anger hastened breathing to gasps. Amina and Maryam were alarmed by the heaving of the mother's great breast; what was it, a heart attack? Her outspread hand erased them rather than waved them away; the day-long deprivation of water, the sun was setting, she would drink deeply, that is all that is needed.

At the meal to break the day's fast her son was animated
as any of the family in the pleasure of satisfying a hunger and
thirst unique to the time-frame of Ramadan, the reward of
abstention from all indulgence.

The mother did drink deeply. Not only of water, but of the
shame and sin of what he had done: her son; she could not
look at this beloved face, as if she would see it horribly
changed, only for her—others were still seeing him handsome
and full of grace—into corruption and ugliness. And that
face, since she had bequeathed her own features to him,
would also be her own.

If she denounced him to his father and brothers, brother-
in-law, denounced the woman his wife to the daughters, and
the daughter-in-law who would receive it as a triumph
against the honour of the family?

What happened behind the closed door of the room where
the wife was already lying—any woman who had lived long
enough to know men and women could be in no doubt. And
how at ease her son was now, the relaxation of a certain kind
recognized by an old woman who had slept beside a man for
many years.

How would her son be dealt with by the men of the family. The couple—what would happen to them. But she knew,
she knew what would happen. Ibrahim would not take disgrace from anyone here, such edicts were bearings cast loose,
their authority over sons lost in the alien authority of exile,
emigration—that she knew.

Her brother. If his Uncle Yaqub were told. And of course
he would be informed, the senior and most important member of the family. And he was the only one she privately could
have hoped might offer help for her son to stay instead
of seeking another emigration. When Yaqub was informed;
what would happen.

She knew what would happen.

Her son would leave somehow, for somewhere, lost to her in the world once again.

No-one had been in the house. Only she. She had not heard—no—the woman, his wife, enter and go to the lean-to, she had been at prayer. It was only he, her son, whose presence or absence she was always aware of, coming or going. Her daughter Maryam did not know that her brother had come and gone during the afternoon, occupied a bedroom with his wife.

What would happen to her, the mother, if she spoke to no-one of what she knew—no-one.

Aoodhu billah. If she took the sin upon herself, as if she assumed the distorted visage of the beloved face only she knew was evident. *Astaghfar allah.* If he is disgraced, nothing will stop him. He will leave. She will lose him again. Any punishment, *in sha allah*, rather than that.

When one of the men lightly remarks upon her son's disappearance from the company of the men in the course of the afternoon, she responds before he could. —He needs rest.—

She, Julie, was apprehensive about the family meal after sunset, what had she done to him; would he not—both of them not—be shamed to take part, he among the men, she among the women. But he returned from the mosque with his father, Ahmad, Daood, Amina's husband Suliman and young Muhammad, and greeted her as if he had not seen her since morning.

The fuzzy intoxication of being awake when you were used to being asleep and to be sleeping when you were meant to be awake wore off just as the internal clock re-sets itself after a few days in a country across a date-line. She rose in the cold for the pre-dawn meal and the calls of hunger and thirst were a clamour only by sunset. The transformation of time-scale was complete when she remembered: back there, at The Table, friends had weeks ago seen an old year out, getting drunk, stoned; Nigel Ackroyd Summers and his Danielle had started with champagne and oysters their old life over again on a new calendar. A New Year was yet to come, as time is measured here.

I was taught time was divided by the birth of a child in a stable and the calculation B.C., A.D. that followed ever after the great event. *That* was time. And all the blacks had been brain-washed by missionaries and battered by settlers into co-option. So they believed it, too. Had to. Well I suppose my parents had some friends—I must have known a few other kids?—who were perhaps Jewish, but whatever rituals they had didn't count for much with us and they came to Nigel's Christmas and New Year bash anyway, if they were on the right social level. Muslims—we didn't know any . . . but the Indian shopkeepers closed for what we said was the birthday of God's son and the day we'd decided was a new year beginning—oh I know the cycles of the moon and the changes of season were mixed up in it, but this was the Christian cycle. The world's just *their* world, to them, the Christian world.

He was sitting in the lean-to's only chair marking with a ballpoint passages in a copy of *Newsweek* he had picked up somewhere when he was last in the capital for an interview with some consular visa section. The pen kept making only grooves and he scratched it fiercely into the paper to get ink flowing. Paused; to regard her.

World is their world. They own it. It's run by computers, telecommunications—see about it here—the West, they own ninety-one percent of these. Where you come from—the whole Africa has only two percent, and it's your country has the most of that. This one?—not enough even to make one figure! Desert. If you want to be in the world, to get what you call the Christian world to let you in is the only way.

Canada. The end of Ramadan meant for him that without offence to his mother he could take up again his way to go about applications for Canada. Two letters of recommendation (To Whom It May Concern) based, probably calculatedly and correctly on an unknown's marriage to a wife with all the right provenance and papers—the wealthy American citizen mother as well as the wealthy father, cited, this time—had turned up from California. Surprise, surprise; Julie handed them over. She would not have thought Beverly—her mother—would or could have found anyone to put his name to them. The casino stepfather apparently had connections among his gambling cronies, though who knew what their signatures were worth. Anyway, Ibrahim put the letters in the file he kept of documents—applications pending, applications refused—marked in the flow of Arabic script she admired.

In another country it would be called up on a computer, not all these to keep.

He thrust the file back into the canvas bag of his possessions. Canada—there were brothers, in the village sense of community, already established; Toronto, Calgary under glittering glass-splinter snow, these frozen places might crook a finger of acceptance to the desert, where sand was grit between the teeth.

She had been allowed, presenting herself tentatively and ready to be turned away with the sisters' usual exquisite politeness and a stare from Khadija sullenly stern in her abandonment as a wife, to take part in the cooking preparations for the feast of *Eid al-fitr*. For her, the end of Ramadan meant that the sisters and the children came to sit expectantly in the communal space of the house at the accustomed times for the exchange of English and Arabic.

An afternoon after Ramadan his mother was sitting among the women. She did not speak. But she was there. The die from which Ibrahim's face was cast. A statement to be read, if only one knew how to decipher it in what endured, a bronze of being beneath flesh drawn from its fine-boned muscular moorings down round the dark elegantly-pursed mouth, creased beneath the brows, invaded by the growth of wiry hairs on the chin. All Julie could make out, in this presence, was she had gained acceptance by the respect of observing the edict that she neither eat nor drink between sunrise and sunset for thirty days, even if she did not spend those days in prayer.

Even had seduced the son again, now in his family home restored to him, in the forbidden days. Did the face of the mother conceal she knew that, as well. He's absolved: 'He needs rest.'

This foreign woman gives it to him.

Sometimes his mood—when he came into the room where she was among the women or in the lean-to amusing Khadija's and Amina's children with games unearthed from memories of Gulliver's garden—showed that Canada was going well. Other days he would glare round at his sisters and desolate sister-in-law as if at a flock to be shooed away, or say to the children in the language he shared with them—goodbye, out, go!—play somewhere else!

There would have been frustration; no news at the consulate, the failure of a promised contact to materialize. He and she did not talk much about these inevitabilities of waiting; there was an unspoken pact of feeling that this would be somehow a way of attracting bad luck, as if some force were hanging over them, eavesdropping, grinning, tantalizing, holding out closed fists—which one? which one?—enjoying a knowledge that the one reached out for contained: visa refused. Why raise her hopes. Why answer questions about what he was ready to resort to, to get them out of this place. Just do it. Whatever it might be. Any day he might find the elegant suitcase packed. In her hand one ticket this time. Week after week passing; the sight of his sister-in-law, the woman Khadija, so haughtily accusatory of the family who had produced her husband, incensed him. Her mannerism of suddenly covering her well-made-up face with her hands, her nervous tic of despair. What the hell was bloody Zayd doing at the fucking oil fields! (The expletives heard at the garage where his wife had picked him up came back to him in their language.) Yes, that's it. Fucking, he's found another woman there, and my mother has to feed the grand wife from the capital he was so proud of, my father has to pay and send his children to school.

Who would have thought they would still be here when the wind months came. The *rih* is blowing.

He comes back from wherever it is the friends-of-friends take him with what they calculate is probably the right sum of her dollars to place in an opened hand, and there she is wrapped up with a robe round her head like any village woman in the street. She smiles an acknowledgment at Maryam: Wasn't it good of your little sister to kit me out for the wind? She drew the covering over her mouth and nose to show him how well she had been protected from the cutting fury of flaying sand on the way to the ladies' conversational tea at the house of Maryam's employer, for which she had now agreed to modest payment.

He was shouting at his sister, some of the words could be understood as a result of those tea-parties: who do you think you are what are you doing who walks out in the *rih* are you mad take that thing off her, and the gentle girl was swaying this way and that as if she were being slapped.

He disappeared into the lean-to. Julie put her arms round the girl and rocked with her. Maryam struggled free and pulled the robe away from Julie, who was incantatory, apologizing for him, Sorry, sorry, sorry. But the girl comforted her in Arabic and then, correcting herself, in English, licking away a tear that had run down her cheek to her lip and chok-

ingly laughing at herself: —He has many worry—he is too
busy with hard things. I know that. It is not me. Ibrahim—
he—is angry for him not for me.— The two with their arms
again about each other sat on the sofa quietly as if Ibrahim's
wife were a sister.

Of course he's right about the wind; even with the entire
outfit women and even men wore, just their eyes showing,
venturing out in that wind was terrifying, exciting—something never experienced before, beyond imagining back
where the most intense experience of this force of nature was
the wind called Black South-Easter that slammed doors and
kept you off the beaches on Cape Town holidays. This was
the reality of the cosmic blasts issuing from mouths of angry
gods symbolized in prophetic engravings. It's not often, now,
waiting for Canada or wherever it's going to be—with him,
that's all that matters—she thinks of the childhood where she
did have the room with the plush panda she had wandered to
find in the wrong house, that Sunday; of the revamped servant's quarters with gleaming bathroom, organic soap and
bath oils, miniature kitchen with suitably modest freezer and
microwave, weekly washwoman, wide ever-ready bed for
whoever the latest lover might be: trappings of the coterie of
the alternative to Nigel Ackroyd Summers' Sunday lunches,
The Table at the EL-AY Café—what was supposed to be the
simple life. We were playing at reality; it was a doll's house,
the cottage; a game, the EL-AY Café.

The wind to which everything and everyone in the village
was submitted blew itself out after exactly the months she
was told it would. Its time was over; Canada still in the balance, there were decisions to come from the final authority in
Ottawa. Julie knew that he had other initiatives out for the
possibility of other countries; but what countries would be
left to try. It ceased to be a question: an unspoken statement,
conclusive. (That's it.) He was away more and more from the

family house, driving the old car to the capital—an Uncle is
not a stranger, a sister's son cannot be denied time off like
any employee—spending the evenings in the village or perhaps another village, with the friends who knew contacts to
follow up. The father and other men of the family were also
usually out in the evenings; Amina's husband Suliman,
Daood the coffee-maker, Ahmad who worked at the butchery,
and even schoolboy Muhammad, his cheese delivery round
concluded, homework overseen by the mother, disappeared to
kick a football with other boys under the dim bat-circled
street-lights. It was a quiet time in this house that reverberated with many lives; the small children in bed, the women
waiting for the men. The sisters Maryam and Amina would
be talking dreamily as they endlessly knotted a carpet—or
was it the next carpet—on a handmade loom, not much more
than two young trees stripped of bark and branches, crossed
by rough beams. She sat with the women watching subtitled
American soap operas, left carefully, not to disturb, as if
along the row in a cinema, to read under the lamp he had
provided for her in the lean-to. Sometimes Maryam came
hesitantly after her, and settled with legs crossed under her
garment on the floor beside the bed where she lounged.
Maryam had made extraordinary progress; they could talk
now, exchange ideas beyond phrase-book pleasantries; even
confidences. Did Maryam want to marry? The police commissioner's son: did she love him?

The girl showed her clamped teeth, softly giggled, dropped
her head back. —I don't know any other one. Only my father,
my brothers. He looks a nice man. He speaks well. And he is
not fat—you know—I would not want a fat one.— They
laughed together; the girl shuddered, as if in some imagined
embrace. —I think I can love him, we'll see.— She had anecdotes about and reflections on the other women. They all
talked of Khadija, so annoying and yet so shaming in her

hostile despair. Yes, a pain in the neck . . . but that was a colloquialism hard to explain to Maryam . . . —Poor Khadija.
She was—what do you say—awful, oh awful before, when
my brother Zayd was here with her, when they got married
and he brought her from her parents, she did not like our
house, she was the one who said he must go to the oil fields
for money to buy a house for her. Now she is—more awful—
because she is so unhappy. She looks at you like this, she
hates because she is jealous. You have your husband, your
husband will take you to a good country, you have money.
Poor Khadija. In this house no person likes her. And my
brother . . . ? Does he still want her. We don't know. If he
doesn't come back?—

    —But the children are lovely. Your father and mother like
having the children with them.—

    The girl was silent for a while, considering the threshold
between gossip and causing offence. She opened her pretty
face to Ibrahim's wife, the half-known, half-mysterious, about
to tell something. —The others, they wonder why you do not
get a baby. Then perhaps you will first marry here, our way.
They look at you. We talk about it. And now—I must say to
you . . . My mother has asked. She asks me.—

    It was understood: Maryam has been told by the mother
to inform me that she expects me to produce a child.

    It must be passed off lightly. —There are plenty of grand-
children, Khadija's, Amina's just had another, now you will
have babies too.—

    —My mother thinks of a child from Ibrahim.—

She glides out of contact with his back, out of the bed, awake
very early. Perhaps it's a new habit left over from the hours of
Ramadan. She puts on jeans and a shirt over bare breasts,

picks up sandals, slips out of the house with them in her
hand. He's always saying, as if drily repeating an adage, you
can only live in the early morning in this place, his home, but
he never wakes to do so—during the ritual rising before dawn
one of the brothers had to come and thump on the lean-to
door. She squats beside the empty blue urn to wriggle her
toes into the sandals. It is true that the air is a pure element
to walk out into, as different from the element of midday as it
is to immerse oneself, move from dry land to water. The *rih*
has sandpapered the shapes of habitations, the sky; there is
the stillness of perfect clarity. She takes a walk, just down the
street, accompanied for a few minutes by one of those cowed
dogs who know they are despised in this village. Although she
has not threatened it, it turns from her and runs away. She
has come to the sudden end of the street: there is the desert.
Its immensity has put a stop to the houses, the people: go no
farther with your belching cars, your bleary lights in the
majesty of darkness, your street vendors and broadcast babble; go no further in your aspirations.

There was a clump of masonry a few yards out into the
sand, the remains of something that had been built and fallen
down, there, interred. She began to make for it and there was
yet another element entered; the chill of the desert, night-
cooled sand sifting through the straps of the sandals to lave
her feet. She sat on the broken remnant of wall and looked—
if it can be said the eyes are looking at no fixed object, no
horizon to be made out. The sands are immobile. She tried to
think it was like gazing out of the window of a plane into
space, but then there is always a wisp of cloud that comes
across and creates scale. After a while there was an object—
objects—which quickly drew into focus, black marks, spots
before the eyes?—and as they grew became a woman en-
veloped in black herding a small straggle of goats. She came

only near enough into vision for a staff she was wielding to be
made out, taking her goats in another direction. In search of
pasture. Here? This space undisturbed by growth, even while
you lift and place your feet it obliterates where they fall and
covers their interruption as they pass on. The spots before the
eyes were gone. She suddenly thought of a glass of water,
wanted it. And the need was strange. When you thirst, in the
sands, water takes on a new meaning: it's an element that has
no place. She sat a while, hadn't put on her watch, and then
walked back to where the street began, with the feeling of being seen off, although there was nobody. The street was coming to life. The electronic call to prayer wound out from the
direction of the mosque and from one of the houses there was
the sprightly beguiling voice of a radio commercial. The vendor of fritters was coming towards her and she found, as she
hoped, some coins in her jeans and bought a few, pleasingly
warm in their wisp of paper, to her hand, as the cool of the
sand had been to her feet.

What is this.

He gestured at the sight of her, up and dressed. He lay
flushed with sleep under his dark-honey-coloured skin, black
shining eyes shadowed in blue hollows, melancholy or erotic.
Here I am.

Here to come back to from a desert just on the doorstep.

Out to buy fritters. Look, still hot. She waved the fragrant
disks at him.

Ibrahim was shaving. The hot water came from a kettle he
had bought that worked off an extension cord from the house
handy Ahmad had rigged up, which also served for the fan
he'd bought, and the lamp for her to read by—each appli-
ance could be used only when the others were disconnected,
and there were hours when the village electricity failed: cold

water, darkness. The paraffin burners were the resort of the household; nobody went hungry, the slaughterer brother had his bath water heated for him by his mother in the customary way, and Ibrahim's wife, inducted to women's work now, waited patiently for her turn to fetch his; oil lamps turned the house into a shadowy cave of shelter.

He opened his mouth wide, high and taut, and shaved at the corners under the two glossy tresses of moustache. Open on his beautiful teeth, this was like a variation of his rare and awaited smile. He raised eyebrows in enquiry: she was watching him?

They wonder why we don't have a baby.

He goes on shaving the delicate area. The aura of his presence that she has known so well from the first day, contracts in withdrawal; she's come to know that, too.

Who wonders that.

Your mother wants a child from you.

She has not said it, but he sees, he knows, she is suddenly taken with the idea. Another adventure.

What do we want with a child. We are not Zayd and Suliman and the lot. We will be gone. What a way to make a start, you sick, giving birth, a little baby to look after.

Is she reproaching him through his mother.

Are you crazy? And the moment spoken, he feels its cruelty stab back at him. He throws the razor onto the towel, holds his breath and plunges his face to the bowl of steaming water. When he lifts his head, she has taken up the razor and offers the towel. As he dries his face it is as if the whole exchange has also evaporated. Everything as before, as every morning in the existence of waiting; suspended. He goes off to help out at the vehicle workshop that, within the support of the family system, provides a little money (he's now being paid) and the use of a car. She has come to be accepted as one of the women who share household tasks, and she makes use of her education to teach English to schoolchildren and anyone else in the village—word has gone round, there are more and more who would like to improve their chances in what (he has said) is the world. Sometimes, recalling public-relations-speak over a cellphone which used to be attached to her like the tag on the leg of a homing pigeon, she thinks it's the first time that expensive education has been put to use.

The Bedouin woman can be seen only in the early hours. (Maryam, when asked as a matter of casual curiosity from a foreigner, says she must be Bedouin, they have their tents and their goats somewhere out there.)

She goes to sit on the stump of masonry in the hours when he is at the Uncle's workshop, the father of the family away on the benches outside coffee shops where he conducts whatever it is occupies him, the brothers at work and the children in school. The women—except Maryam, cleaning her employer's house—are cooking, watching television or praying— she understands: prayer is the only form of rest his mother allows herself.

No-one would notice her absence. Although it is not proper to go about to the market or shops unless accompanied by one of the sisters or, at least, a couple of children, just to the end of the street apparently does not count. Neighbours, who drop in and out of the family house to visit, are accustomed to her presence among them and greet her if they see her pass; a corner of curtain may be lifted, dropped again: she cannot be going anywhere or to do anything of interest; this direction of the street ends in the desert.

She wears an old khaki hat from camping days with the
EL-AY Café crowd which fortunately she dropped into the
elegant suitcase when looking around for what just might be
useful, before she left the cottage and all non-essentials. The
heat tends to collect beneath the dark green cotton brim, adequate protection where she came from, but not here; when
she reached her place on the relic of a habitation she would
take out of her shirt pocket a sleazy scarf bought in the market and drape it over the hat to her shoulders—people here
knew that the sun was an enemy not to be exposed to as
a sensuous benefice on Cape Town beaches. The Bedouin
hidden in the wisdom of her black wraps was safe from
melanoma, alone with her goats in the desert.

The desert. No seasons of bloom and decay. Just the endless turn of night and day. Out of time: and she is gazing—
not over it, taken into it, for it has no measure of space,
features that mark distance from here to there. In a film of
haze there is no horizon, the pallor of sand, pink-traced,
lilac-luminous with its own colour of faint light, has no demarcation from land to air. Sky-haze is indistinguishable
from sand-haze. All drifts together, and there is no onlooker;
the desert is eternity.

What could/would thrust this back into time? Water.

An ice age—if that were to come. Water is a lost memory:
memory the passing proof of time's existence.

Ice to cover the sands and melt them back into time with
its own melting, over millennia. Drinking an ice age; after the
ages when all life-juices had dried away to purity—only that
which is inactive can attain purity. Nullity is purity; detachment from the greedy stirring of growth. Eternity is purity;
what lasts is not alive.

When the ice age melts, this will be forced to *become*
again: become the vast grassland it was how many thousand
years ago?

Buried under sand the insistence of a broken line of words surfaces to disturb her quiet mind . . . 'and she conceived . . . and retired with him to a far-off place.'

She woke, and with her arm limply open-palmed flung across his breast, eyes still closed, smiling, mumbled something.

I dreamed green.

He doesn't ask what she does with herself all day—the English lessons, all right . . . He did not know of her hours with the desert; she didn't tell him, because he avoided, ignored, shunned the desert. (*Are you crazy?*)

Yes green. If we don't get out of here soon she won't stand it much longer, this dusty hell of my place. She'll go back there. The big trees round her cottage. The grass a black man came to cut. Her kind; that Café. The beautiful terrace for lunch on Sunday. Permanent Residence: so many applications, so many ways, any kind of way, tried, for that status anywhere. Anywhere but here. If she had been one of the ways snatched at when he gave his smile in response to her attraction to him that day in the garage (or was it only on the street), if she had failed him, failed the influence he had counted on through her secure status of birth, whiteness, family position, money, if it didn't achieve any right for his Permanent Residence in her country—she had come (didn't she say it) all the way with him; the way of refusal, failure, buried back here in the cursed village in the sand, *his home*, that claimed him. Love. He had to believe it, existing in her. He felt something unwanted, something it was not necessary, no obligation on a penniless illegal to feel for one of those who own the world, can buy a ticket, get on a plane, present a passport and be welcomed back into that world any time, she will go, with tears and embraces, one last wonderful coupling on the iron bed, any week now; he felt responsibility—

that's it—responsibility for her. Though he had none; he had
not wanted her to come here, she would not let go of him and
he could hardly have told her that her purpose in his life was
ended. So he even married her; had to, couldn't take her to
his mother as if she were some whore he'd picked up in his
loneliness; if he brought his mother, who deserved everything,
an obviously high-class wife (even if a foreigner outside the
Faith), this was at least some mark of her son's worth recognized where he wandered.

One of those elaborate gifts brought home that are not
what is needed, put away in a lean-to. He cursed himself with
some old remembered malediction.

She dreams green. But the thought of the lean-to, without
her, the strangeness and intimacy of her, hollowed him out
with the deep breath it made him take, all through his body,
limbs and hands.

She had been smiling to herself, only half out of sleep, at the
idea of having somehow mistakenly dreamed in green, a
crossed line from the old subconscious store of landscapes,
when she had in fact fallen asleep by transporting herself into
the pale radiance of the desert entered that afternoon, beyond
the colour and time of growth.

On a morning, he also woke from a dream. He couldn't recall
what it was; behind closed eyes, he too put out a hand. There
was the flat empty space. Suddenly, that was the dream, it
had happened: gone.

Out to buy fritters.

Canada had enough Arabs, Pakistanis and Indians—the kind other than the red ones who were the original Permanent Residents. Sweden, small country a generous refuge to the politically persecuted, was more cautious about those whose plea did not have the same kind of justification. He began to feel that his manhood was in question. She was his wife, after all, he had to satisfy her needs not only in bed. Green. He now was demanding a country for her as well as for himself. And he could not admit defeat by discussing this with her. When he was not in the clangour of whirring, grinding, and the stink of fuel helping out at the vehicle repair shop, he was about among a certain group of young men to whom he had gravitated once the ones-in-the-know, who assured that with palm-grease they could get you in wherever you wanted, proved to be living on hopes that couldn't be realized—even for themselves! Else why would they still choose to be here, selling watermelons in the market, mending shoes, slaughtering sheep and making coffee, like two of his brothers.

These other young men have some education—like himself—one has a university degree but is a second-grade clerk in a local government office: he has tried to get out but as he has been refused a passport at this end of the process because there is a record of his having been a political troublemaker, as a student, dissident against the regime, he hasn't the first requirement of the many for visa application. For reasons of the same record there's no hope of him being promoted in the civil service; others in the group that drifts every night to the oil lamps of one of the bars disguised as coffee shops have similar histories. Three—like himself—have been declared illegal and deported, back to this place, from the countries they managed to enter and work at whatever they could turn a hand to. They talk until late in order not to go home to the family warrens they escaped once, and to which they have been returned like dead letters—illegals have no fixed address, no identity. They talk about what it is unwise to talk about, even in this poor hole where the Uncle and the husband of Maryam's employer, neither the ruling party's local mayor nor the Imam, would ever be around to overhear, although you could never be sure that a security policeman in plain-clothes galabiah might not be among the shadows. These young men want change, not the rewards of Heaven. Change in the forms it already had taken for others in the old century, change for what it was becoming in this new one. To catch up! With elections that are not rigged or declared void when the government's opposition wins; hard bargains with the West made from a position of counter-power, not foot-kissing, arse-licking servitude (they bring the right vocabulary back with them from the West, whatever else they were denied); change with a voice over the Internet not from the minaret, a voice making demands to be heard by the financial gods of the world.

    . . . bring the modern world to Islam but we're not going to allow ourselves to be taken over by it, no, forced to—

. . . revolutionary but not like other revolutions, they must understand this is a moral religious revolution—

—but it can only be achieved by the seizure of state power, like any other revolution! What are you—

—Yes yes! No question! Don't think there's any other way to get rid of this government that grows fat on us and tells us this poverty is freedom, *bismillah*—

. . . we can't go on accepting what our grandfathers do, what life is that, Ibrahim—the traditional interpreters of Islam . . . for them Islam hasn't anything to do with the future, everything is complete, forever, you only have to . . .

. . . total Islamization—against world powers?—what a mad dream; no, no—

—we must cross-fertilize Islam with the world if the ideals of Islam are to survive, the old model doesn't fit, any kind of isolation can't stand a chance with what's happening in the world, ask Ibrahim, technological revolution already here while we're just talking, talking . . . !

And as young men do when they drink together they also spoke of women, but not in the way the men in the garage near the EL-AY Café did.

—Look, we don't want to deny our past for the American sex we enjoy seeing on TV (there was a whistle and laughter) . . . but *hijab*, I mean you happen to make love with a married woman, she wants it, ay—and she must be stoned to death, who can accept that it's the law, even if it isn't carried out—who can accept that in this age!—

The university graduate emptied his glass and offered: — I just read it somewhere. 'A Muslim doesn't fall in love with a woman, but only with Allah.'— He kept a gloomy face, perhaps himself a lover in difficulties, while there was more laughter—the others evidently did not regard the cynicism as blasphemous.

—So what's our life? With women? What? You tell me.
What freedom do they have or we have with them?—

—But they're the ones now with their own revolution—

—Oh it's part of ours—

—But they want to decide for themselves. They don't
want anyone to tell them to wear the chador, all right, but if
they do want to wear it, they won't have some Westerner
telling them to throw it away. They want to study or work
anywhere they decide outside the kitchen, the modern world
where men still think we're the only ones to have a place.—

—We must get one of them to speak, you know, next time
we have a meeting—never done that, we are true sons of our
grandfathers—

—Will they dare to come—

—They'll come. They'll come. I know a few . . .

—Ah then you'll really see how the government fathers
get the police to go after us . . .

The graduate of the university where he himself gained
the degree that had qualified him to be employed as, in another country, what her friends called a grease-monkey,
turned to him where he was listening, silent.

—I'll lend you a book. Ever heard of Shahrur Muhammad Shahrur? Written a book, *al-Kitab wa-l-Qur'an: Qira'a
mu'asira*. He says people believed once that the sun revolved
round the earth, but it was then discovered that the opposite
was true, eh? Muslims still believe prejudices of religious
authority that are the complete opposite of the correct per-
spective—conventional religious authority can't exist with
economic market forces today! But take care. Don't leave the
book lying around. You can't find it, here, somebody sent it,
and even then it had to be hidden in the cover of some other
book, some nonsense. A package of anything printed that
comes from overseas, it's opened by the authorities, perhaps
you've forgotten that, my brother.—

He was their brother in frustration. Sometimes he felt
himself fired by them to act, join them to plot and agitate,
risk, for change here—this desert. But within him something
drew back appalled at the submission; the future of this place
the world tried to confine him to was not his place in that
world. Permanent residence; under no matter what government, religious law, secular law, what president in a keffiyeh
or got up in military kit with braid and medals—that was not
for him. The company of brothers in frustration salved his
own, but this secret refusal, *his* refusal, roused in him
strongly as any sexual desire.

Friday is the day for visits and family affairs. The shops are closed for noon prayers at the mosque, so is the vehicle workshop. During the day it was not unusual for the Uncle's silver-blue BMW with tasselled blinds to draw up in the street before the gate. Tea was quickly made, sweetmeats taken from their biscuit tin, Coke from the refrigerator (which like the car for his nephew also had been his gift to the family) because the Uncle's preferences are well-known. He always brings gifts for the children of the house, particularly for those of the son of the house who has not been heard from, disappeared to the oil fields, and he greets everyone with the enthusiasm of a mayor meeting his constituents, and then retires with the mother, his sister. They are left in private, either under the awning or in the parents' room, where a special, comfortable chair for the Uncle is carried in by young Muhammad. It is understood that serious family matters are discussed. The father seldom takes part but this is not regarded by him, or anyone else, as demeaning of what would be his authority. No-one questions the position of Ibrahim's mother.

On this Friday afternoon the brother and sister had

emerged from their privacy and were in the company of the
rest of the family, taking tea and refreshments. Only Ibrahim
and his wife were not there; summoned by the mother,
Maryam was sent to call them, rapping softly with the
knuckle of her third finger on the clapboard door. They had
heard the talk and laughter, orchestrated by the unmistakable lead of the Uncle's voice—impossible not to, through the
thin door—but Ibrahim was on the iron bed reading newspapers; Julie, amusing small Leila, who liked to spend time in
the lean-to decking herself out in the few Ndebele and Zulu
bead necklaces that had somehow been tossed into the elegant suitcase, had sent the child out to join the Friday gathering. Leila, your mummy wants you. The child caught the
gist of English-Arabic pidgin, laughing, and obeyed, first
resting her plump cheek a moment, smooth against the back
of Julie's hand.

After the knock on the door, Julie stretched, peered over
the newspaper, opened her eyes wide and pulled her mouth
down in a closed smile: come. A finger placed somewhere on
a column answered that he would finish what he was reading.
She brushed her hair for the company.

She took his hand as they entered, whether in support of
him, comforting his reluctance to spend any part of his hours
to himself with the voice that reverberated through the workshop, or to support herself in her claim to be one of the family. There were warm greetings; only Khadija seemed not to
see them; whenever the Uncle appeared she sat transfixed,
like that, on him, her children drawn around under her arms,
watching his lips for word that he was going to do something
for her—something to find and bring back her husband and
the father of these children. Others could only look away
from the sister-in-law, not to shame her in the spectacle of
her demanding humiliation. Anyone could see she was expecting an announcement of some kind, believing her situa-

tion, the well-born woman deserted by a son of the family for a woman at the oil fields only after his money, must have been the matter deliberated between his Uncle and mother.

But apparently, unusually, whatever the private talk was about, the father had been present; been required? The three sat ranged together.

Ibrahim's mother's breast, prow of the family, rose and fell deeply; his wife saw it, ominous. At a signal to Maryam, the handing round of tea stopped and talk broke off, the gaiety of children was reduced to whispering.

The mother called her son and his wife over to her where room had been made for them to sit. She drew herself up and leaned forward, took another of her deep slow breaths that customarily ended in a sigh (she would rise from prayer with a breath like that) but now gave weight of importance to what she was about to say. It was an announcement, yes, but not for the one who awaited something.

The mother looked slowly at her son and his wife, singling them out as if her hands were laid upon them, and spoke in the language of which his wife, suddenly inexplicably tense, forgot all she had learnt and could make out only the name of the Uncle—Uncle Yaqub, Uncle Yaqub, repeated, and the familiar invocation, *Al-Hamdu lillah*. When the mother had done, the son, lover, husband stood; at bay. That was what she, who had found him, followed him restored to his family, saw he was. With a lifting of spread-fingered hand to his forehead, and the drop of the hand to his side, a strange kind of obeisance, it seemed he took permission to himself to turn to her and translate in a low even voice from his mother tongue.

He thinks about, he thinks to make me his workshop manager.

The father summoned his own small store of English and

understood what had been left out. —Your Uncle Yaqub, he can take you into his business . . .—

Everybody—poor Khadija is nobody—was animated in congratulatory exclamations, murmurs, a happy confusion of interruption with admiration for the Uncle's generosity and the transformation he has the power to bring close to their lives.

It was hardly necessary for Ibrahim to respond: the family was doing it for him. Wonderful. Uncle Yaqub! In business with Uncle Yaqub! But his mother was gazing at him with proudly raised head. At once the message flashed: she had done it for him.

Julie was surrounded by the excited talk, unable to follow much, hearing approximations she could invent from the joyous cadence, what an opportunity, how lucky, how good, how generous an Uncle. And one of the brothers, Ahmad the slaughterer whose only opportunity was to have blood on his hands, jumped up with another kind of generosity and spoke for the brothers, a voice raised out of normal pitch by emotion. Ibrahim heard in their language: —We are full of joy for you, you deserve this. It's great, my brother, for us to have you back with us as we were when we were kids! It has never been right, without you. Allah be praised. May you and your wife be blessed with happiness and prosperity. And now that this has happened, please—let our parents and your brothers and sisters see you married in our law, let us have a real wedding, we were not invited to the wedding before you came home.—

Laughter from everyone at this last. Maryam quickly translated breathily in her friend's ear, and the two young women laughed and nodded, together.

His mother, perhaps alone of the gathering, was waiting for him to have the chance to speak for himself what every-

one knew he must be feeling, what he wished to say to his
Uncle, who had singled him out among her sons, the blessed
one, the success.

Ibrahim was vaguely lifting and lowering his outspread
hands—to quiet the affectionate voices answering for him, or
to take in those hands—a lovely gesture, some interpreted—
the opportunity offered him. In all the attention that pinned
him down he felt that of his wife and he turned a moment to
her and gave her a version—strange, final, its awful beauty—
a culminating version of that smile she always awaited from
him. He addressed his Uncle in the full formality of their
tongue, as if there were no-one else present: He did not know
what to say. It was an offer he would never have thought of,
never have expected. Never. He knows how much the business his Uncle has created means to him. He thanked him,
with the greatest respect, for his generosity, on behalf of his
mother and father, brothers and sisters, for what he had done
now, this day. He asked, with the greatest respect to have . . .
a little time . . . to realize . . .

He did not turn to her. He sought the eyes of his mother;
now she was the only one present.

And they all understood: overcome! They clapped and
passed him from one to the other, men and women, in their
embraces.

She kept somewhat in the background, although she,
too, was embraced. She had had from him that smile that
couldn't be explained.

Something else was not explained: out of delicacy of feeling, among the family present, although all were aware of
it. The Uncle has decided to take Ibrahim in; workshop
manager? This means heir apparent. Of the vehicle repair
workshop that has valuable contracts for maintenance of
provincial government vehicles, the mayor's fleet, whatever
other notables this poor district has, and a franchise for sales

of parts, a dealership in sales of both second-hand and new models of the best German and American cars. There is no son of the Uncle's own begetting, alive, alas, and the son-in-law and prospective son-in-law of the educated daughters are not interested in learning the business by dirtying their hands—they want to have government positions, sitting on their backsides in air-conditioned offices in the capital. So when Uncle Yaqub retires—long may he be granted life in good health—and dies, Ibrahim will inherit the business, and live in a house with fine carpets and furniture in the style of gilt and velvet French kings used to have, with a maid to clean it all, as the house of the notable employs Maryam to do. That is Ibrahim's blessed future. *Al-Hamdu lillah. Praise be to God.*

Ibrahim has declined the offer to take charge of his Uncle's workshop. The chance of a lifetime.

Are you crazy?

She had said to him, It might still be months before we get visas, at least you'd have something a bit more . . . I don't know, responsible, in the meantime.

Meantime.

Permanent residence. That's what it means.

Like I was back there, under somebody's car.

You wouldn't be doing any of that kind of work yourself, the way you are, helping out, now—

Telling the others to do it, yelling at them like my Uncle has to. Sticking my head under the bonnet to see if they're doing it right, waiting for my Uncle to die. Are you crazy.

At night she felt him turning in bed, rubbing his feet one against the other in affront, in turmoil. And was afraid to comfort him in case she said the wrong thing, or made a ges-

ture that could be interpreted as referring to some rejected
aspect of a conflict within him. He had made the decision,
why was he still tormenting himself? When she made a decision that was the end of it; of leaving The Suburbs, leaving
the doll's house and charades at the EL-AY Café: while they
were waiting she was at peace, at her place in the desert. Yet
she herself was not sure of her reactions to what had suddenly been thrust before him, never thought of, never. Something he had cast himself about the unwelcoming world to
put far away as possible from his life. When he stood there, at
bay: did she think he had already said no, the refusal had
surged and burst, his heart was sending it through the vessels
of his blood. Did she expect anything else?

Brooding in a bed in the dark has a kind of telepathy created by the contact of bodies when words have not been exchanged. Whether she might be asleep or awake—he spoke.
You thought I would take it.

A faceless voice. I don't know what I thought. Yes or no.
Because there's so much I don't know—about you. I've found
that out. Since we've been home here. You must understand,
I've never lived in a family before, just made substitutes out
of other people, ties, I suppose—though I didn't realize that,
either, then. There are . . . things . . . between people here,
that are important, no, necessary to them . . . I don't mean
the way you are to me . . . that doesn't fit in with anybody,
anything else, and that's all right, but . . . You could have
reasons for 'yes' I couldn't know about because they're . . .
unconnected with me, with you and me, d'you see?

So she's talking of my mother. He does not discuss his
mother with her; he will not.

She certainly did not know there would be another family
gathering the week after his decision was made known. She
was aware he must have told his mother of it before he told
her—but that might have been because he believed she, his

wife, surely must have known, from the moment the announcement was made by the Uncle, his decision was a fore-
gone conclusion. Only in the dark had he come to the
possibility of her betrayal—You thought I would take it.

The decision had been conveyed to the Uncle by his
mother. It appeared that such a decision could not properly
be made by a young man on his own. He had ignored the due
process of discussion within the family of whatever reasons
there could possibly be for a rebuff—an insult, considering
the Uncle's position in the family, in the whole community—
of this nature.

The story of the amazing action of a young man from a
poor family like their own, who had taken himself off to foreign countries and made nothing of himself there, come home
with only a foreign wife to show for it, had gone from house
to house and café to market stall, wafted up to homes of the
few wealthy and important people—the wife who employed a
member of the family inquisitively extracted inside information from her maid, the young man's sister, Maryam.

The BMW outside the house again. There was no question
of tea and sweetmeats, or the couple preferring to occupy the
lean-to. He said, we have to be there, and they were seated, a
little apart from the rest of the family, when the Uncle entered and everyone rose. His greetings were less mayoral, but
proper.

It had come to the Uncle's ears that his dear sister's son
and the son of his respected brother-in-law was getting mixed
up in politics. Everyone agrees that a young man must have
friends to meet and talk to, a little pleasure men enjoy away
from the house and the women. His self-confidence allowed
him to make a joke even in this situation, but nobody tit-
tered; the men, knowing their indulgences, of which he
hinted, smoking a bit of kif and taking alcohol in a disguised
bar, the women wise in not enquiring where the men went at

night, and all were subdued, as if sharing some sibling guilt
for the brother's misdemeanours that went beyond these.
Well—kif and whisky and even the occasional woman—the
Uncle had been young himself; he did not need to say what,
for his manhood, he assumed was understood. But Ibrahim—
his sister's son like a son to him—it is known, it has now become known to him, and with sorrow, mixes with a certain
crowd. This comes as a shock to his dear parents, and it is for
them that a senior member of the family speaks now. This
young man the whole family loves is spending his time with a
type of malcontents who blame everything in their lives on
others—on the authorities, on the government. Everything
they do not have the ability to do for themselves, work hard
as the older generation, his generation (a hand flat against his
own breast), was willing to do, sacrifice, for the honour of the
family, raise themselves up—all this is the fault of the government. Government owes them everything. The Lord has
given them what a man needs to live a good life in the Faith,
their families have educated them, they can marry and bring
up children in security, there are no foreigners from Europe
flying flags over our land any longer—what more do they
want? They want to bring down the government, *aoodhu billah*. That's the evil they want. They have in their heads the
ideas that set brother against brother. They want to smash
everything, and they don't know—don't they see what is happening in those countries that have done this?—a country
ends up with nothing, everything lost. The young men already have so much that we, their parents, never had. And
why not? We are glad of it. From outside, from progress. Isn't
it enough to have your car and cellphone and TV. What else
is really worth having out there in the world of false gods?

All he wants to say: it is mixing with this group who are
dangerous, a danger to themselves, to us, to our government—they must be the sad reason for a young man giving

up an opportunity that would bring advancement, comforts, everything anyone could want for a good life, eventually a high place in the community and honour to the family. This opportunity that was offered comes out of sorrow, but was a way of making something joyful result from pain, *ma sha allah*, some good to come to the family out of—he placed his hand on his breast, softly, now—a tragedy. *Inna lillah.*

There was silence in which everyone in the room was alone. The children felt it and gazed about at the grown-ups in awe. Tears were running down the composed face of the mother as some revered statues are said to shed tears on certain auspicious dates, while their features remain cast in stone or bronze.

The Uncle, her brother, had spoken seated beside her; but her son, the nephew, stood up.

—No-one in this village, in this place, has anything to do with why I cannot accept the offer you have honoured me with, Uncle Yaqub. I do not have any interest in the government. It is not going to govern me. I am going to America.—

The Uncle spoke measuredly and clearly—to her ears—in contrast with the quick speech of the young people in the family whom she found difficult to follow, probably because they spoke colloquially while she was studying the language out of primers, and those who had volunteered in the friendly exchange of languages over tea also thought it respectful of theirs to teach her only its conventional formulations.

Afterwards, Ibrahim gave her full account of what the Uncle had said. So she was able to piece together the words and phrases she had understood in the Uncle's own voice and to correct for herself, with that echo, the paraphrase and lack of emphasis in what she was being told in the medium of Ibrahim's English. She needed an explanation to the reference to sorrow, a tragedy, at the end, that had produced such a strong effect on everyone, she had felt it herself?

Didn't she remember that the only son was dead? Ah yes—the heir apparent—she did, how was it?

A terrible thing. He burned in his car, an accident. And no-one says it, but it was when he had taken alcohol. Drunk.

So she understood; the reference was used to wind up with

something to shame the one who was refusing bestowal of a privilege to which he wasn't really entitled anyway. Like the other women of the house, she hadn't known, hadn't expected to be told every time her man was out at night, where he went and what he did; this attitude came naturally to her, from the mores of The Table at the EL-AY Café—everyone free to come and go, particularly in the code of intimacy, no-one should police another; even in the ultimate intimacy called love, monitoring was left behind with the rejected values of The Suburbs. The reference—his own—to America, which she had understood as he pronounced it evenly in his mother tongue, had brought an immediate urge of protectiveness towards him, she had wanted to get up, go to him, shield him from the pathetic humiliation he was exposing himself to before the eyes of the family, when everyone knew, everyone, how since his return, deported from one country, he was always making applications for immigration visas to other countries and coming back from the queues in the capital with a piece of paper; refusal. He was going to Canada, Australia, New Zealand. The neat file in the canvas bag was full of such documents.

To save him embarrassment, she did not refer to the pretext he had given for his refusal; she knew the real reasons. The grease-stiff overalls and the stink of fuel from which he had emerged in the garage round the block near the EL-AY Café. And perhaps he felt it was—what?—distasteful, bad luck, somehow not what should be, to fill the empty space of someone's sorrow, occupy the place of a young man he must have known, a family sibling, as a child. He could not tell them that; he brought up a pretext nobody could believe in.

It was not the end of it, for him, of course. His father had the right and obligation of long homilies addressed to the son, the family kept out, the house subdued to the death-watch-beetle tlok-tlok of the ornamental clock (also a gift from the Uncle). His mother, rising from prayers that he must feel were for him, summoned him aside and their mingled voices were so low it sounded merely as if prayer were continuing. But if the supreme authority of the Uncle could have no influence on their son, no-one, nothing else would.

What passed between mother and son must have been an apocalypse for both, a kind of rebirth tearing her body, a fearful thrusting re-emergence for him. His wife who had never known, never would know, such emotions—Nigel Ackroyd Summers, and the mother someone imagined in California—felt the force of his with humility and offered all she had in recognition: love-making. In her body he was himself, he belonged to nobody, she was the country to which he had emigrated.

In some accommodation reached with the Uncle by family council, the prodigal nephew was continuing to help out at the vehicle repair workshop as if nothing had happened, to have use of the car, and to go off to the capital during working hours on affairs of his own. He also still pursued family matters since it was felt his education made him the one best qualified to, and one day actually was able to bring news of the brother, Khadija's husband, Zayd—at the agency there was a letter, a bank draft. Whatever explanations for the long silence were, the withdrawn Khadija did not say whether or not she accepted them. Khadija used a strong perfume, it was the assertion of her presence in the house, constant pungent reminder that she was deserted by a son of this family; when Ibrahim's wife was impulsively bold enough to approach her and say how glad she was that this sister-in-law's husband was safe and well, the woman gave a proud wry smile—and then, suddenly, she who never touched anyone but her own children, embraced Julie. Perhaps it was because Julie spent

much time with one of the children. Leila had fallen in love
with her, as small girls will with some adult who offers activities different from those of a parent; as Julie had fallen in
love with Gulliver-Archie. Her kind of Uncle.

Almost a year since they arrived at his home. She was fully occupied now. Strange; she had never worked like this before, without reservations of self, always had been merely trying out this and that, always conscious that she could move on, any time, to something else, not expecting satisfaction, looking on at herself, half-amusedly, as an ant scurrying god knows where. In addition to the ladies' conversational circle, the lessons for other adults who sought her out, and the play-learning she discovered she could devise (probably started with Leila) for small children, as well as the classes she taught in the primary school, she had been drawn in to coach English to older boys who hoped to go to high school in the capital some day; she had been able to persuade—flatter—the local school principal to let girls join the classes although it was more than unlikely their families would allow them to leave home.

She performed such unskilled tasks as she could be expected to be able to do, among her sisters-in-law, in the preparation of family meals. The mother directed everything, she was obeyed as the guardian of all culinary knowledge and dietary edicts, the ingredients she chose and the methods of

preparation she decreed were followed. The ingredients of the
food were simple but they were combined and transformed
into something subtly delicious, the so-named pilaffs and
other 'ethnic' dishes fiercely spiced in the alternative cuisine
favoured at The Table turned out to have had nothing to do
with these. Amazing what you could produce on two paraffin
burners. Apparently the mother noted her interest; perhaps a
sign of other recognition from the heights of her black-robed
dignity, began to call Ibrahim's wife over and show her, with
a gesture authorizing her to try for herself the procedures by
which preparation of food, as it should be, were to be performed. The mother smiled—Ibrahim's smile—when she saw
how this privilege of her cuisine and lessons were enjoyed.
Occasionally she pronounced (like a ventriloquist's projection) a few words in English; the exchange with his wife's
halting Arabic might in time even extend to conversation lessons in the kitchen? Amina and Maryam laughed encouragement to her over pots and knives when she spoke to them in
their language. In the evenings they were beginning to discuss
plans for Maryam's wedding, not so distant, and Maryam
liked her to be there with them, translating for her and looking to her for approval, from the outside world, of the style of
the event previewed. In projection of the days of celebration
both set aside that Julie would not be there, any more, then.
Canada, Australia; wherever this brother, who persisted in
pressing for entry, again and again, no matter how many
times rejected, would take her away.

Leila had her by the hand.

    After the child came home from school and had eaten,
neither her mother nor her playmates expected to see her.
The child slipped into the lean-to to find if Julie, too, were
back home; looked for her where she might be reading under

the awning if it were not too hot. When Julie went to the house of Maryam's employer for the conversational teas, Leila (the first time with her mother's permission requested) came along. She sat silently, nibbled cake silently. Ibrahim's wife loves children, the ladies enthused; she had never had anything to do with children, not since the Gulliver games, childhood itself—that had been left behind with The Suburbs. There was another construction—perception of herself formed in—by—this village that was his home. There had been a number in her life; she could sum up—the well-brought-up girl with her panda who would marry a well-brought-up polo player from her father's club; the public relations gal with personality plus, set to make a career; the acolyte of the remnant hippie community, rehash resurrected from the era they had been a generation too young to belong to; experiences, all; none definitive of herself, by herself. So far. Only the day she stood in the doll's house and showed him two airline tickets.

Leila by the hand. So small a folding of little bones and flesh-pads it might be just some talisman in her palm. Leila came like this with her to the desert. Nobody missed the child. Nobody knew where they had gone, went as the day cooled; when they returned to the house everyone assumed, as the child hadn't been seen about, the two had been playing games again in the lean-to; Leila loved the games with coloured pegs and counters Julie had had sent from a shop in London, along with an order of books—she wanted Ibrahim to rig up a shelf for her, could he?

Pack them, you will take them with us.

She and the child walked to the end of the street. Not speaking; Leila sang very softly to herself. Their footsteps had a rhythm and counter-rhythm because Julie's steps were longer and the child took two to her one. Then there was the sand. Muffling; it sank in, between their toes; they left no

trail, it ended in the street, the village dropped behind. They
sat together, hand in hand—the desert was too far and wide
for the child—as the sun, also, left them and such shadows as
they caused in the vastness blurred away. Sometimes the
stray dog appeared; what was it he found in the desert, as the
woman's flock of goats found pasture; but this was not
the place of questions to be asked of oneself or answered.
Sometimes the child leaned her head and might have
dropped asleep; children have an exhausting life, you only remember that when you teach in school. Sometimes hand in
hand they moved a short way into the desert from the stump
of masonry, a smooth dragging gait imposed by depth of
sand, and sat down, cross-legged both of them, in the sand. It
sifted up, sidled round their backsides, her fleshy one and the
child's neat bones. Go farther and even that undulating scarf
of sound, the muezzin's call from the mosque, is taken in, out
of hearing. But she doesn't go farther, with the child.

It is in the very early morning that she goes out into the
desert alone; although—she couldn't explain and does not
want to delve, in the dialogue all beings have within themselves—even with the child she is alone in the sense of not accompanied by what was always with her, part of herself, back
wherever the past was. The books she had ordered and that
had come, once again, in the care of the bus driver from the
capital, made her giggle or abandon half-read—that woman
Hester Stanhope, and the man Lawrence, English charades in
the desert, imperialism in fancy dress with the ultimate con-
descension of bestowing the honour of wanting to be like the
people of the desert. Another game, another repertoire like
that in the theatre company of the EL-AY Café, but with serious consequences, apparently, for the countries where the
man had been. Nothing to do with her; she wrapped herself
in black robes only when it was necessary for protection
against the wind.

On their lean-to bed he slept, mysteriously calm in that familiar other lone region, and if he had awakened while she was gone, did not ask, when she was in the room again, where she had been.

Reading, while it was still cool under the awning. Out to buy fritters. His conscious mood was distracted and concentrated: distracted from her, from their doubled existence, and concentrated on whatever new tactics he was in the process of engaging with authority. What they might be, she did not ask either; she was somehow afraid that what she'd been told again and again by Maryam, by the ladies at the conversational teas, would be read in her face: all said matter-of-factly it sometimes took several years before permission to enter another country might at last be achieved. This was the commonplace experience of relatives and friends.

She walked through night-cooled sands into the desert. No fear of getting lost; she could always return herself from the desert, turn her back and verify the signal finger-beckon of the minaret; the houses flocked together behind her. The goats with the Bedouin woman appeared before her in the desert as if conjured up. She would walk what seemed a long way towards her and her goats but the measure of distance in this element and space was unaccustomed; the figures of woman and animals retreated although they had appeared to be only slowly veering, changing direction. There was one morning when they were discovered close; close enough to be advanced to. The woman turned out to be hardly more than a child—perhaps twelve years old. For a few moments the desert opened, the two saw each other, the woman under her bushveld hat, the girl-child a pair of keen eyes from a small figure swathed against the sun.

She smiled but the other responded only by the eyes' acknowledgment of a presence.

The encounter without word or gesture became a kind of

daily greeting; recognition. After which she would sit on, in
the sands, and forget the Bedouin girl and the goats; or, sometimes summoned in an old habit of focus, would follow their
eclipse like slowed film footage in which the closing of a
flower at night may be followed.

The dog lost its fear of her. It swung its tail if she were sitting on the stump of masonry but did not accompany her if
she went farther than a few yards into the desert; it came to
the stump as part of the dregs of the village, to forage the
rubbish tossed against the traces of someone who had tested
the limits of habitation and been overcome.

At last, she was in the capital. Where, when they first arrived,
she had wanted to 'see everything', as if 'everything' were to
be known there; before they had occupied the grand marital
bed and moved to the lean-to, before love-making on the vo-
cal springs of the iron bedstead, before they had stayed
through Ramadan and the season of wind, before she began
to exchange the sound of one language for another, discover
you could do something other than write advertising copy or
arrange pop singers' itineraries.

I never got round to going with you.

Half a question.

But he was the one who had decided that. When the suggestion had come from her: What will you do there, standing
in offices. And she had stayed behind and—he saw it—occupied herself in the meantime for which he was not responsible. He had done and was doing everything possible to get
them out of this place. And every time something, someone,
brought to his mind the offer of his Uncle, the trap that was
set to snap on him by the family, his mother the beloved—his
body swelled with the blood of accusation and rage, a distress
that gave him an erection, and that with a confusion of

shame and desire, using her, could only be assuaged in wild
love-making which she took for something else, so little did
she know, in her kind of existence, emotions of the kind of
survival you have to fight for, in this place.

Photographs and documents were sufficient as a general
practice for him to submit on behalf of an individual such as
her, a wife with credentials enough to make her an acceptable
immigrant anywhere. Desirable even; one with connections
that mean money. But at a certain stage he didn't explain—so
much bureaucracy, in whose ways he is expert—consulates
must see the applicant's wife in person, verifying the photographs and asking questions already replied to over and over
in documentation.

The visa sections of consulates and the offices of honorary
consuls—the country is not considered important enough, by
some countries, to have a more formal diplomatic mission—
are a scene and dialogue repeated in each. The script does not
change, she learnt now at first hand, after having known it
only recounted by him when she would ask for news; the
premises may be equipped to impress or intimidate with
chairs in a waiting area, informative brochures, framed texts
from national poets and politicians in some, at others only
queues proceeding under gruff orders, but all have large portraits of the head of state, President or Royal, gazing down at
the young men who replicate her own standing beside her,
and women hung about with babies and children who look at
her, and then away, as if it can't be that she is there among
them. At one of the consulates an official of some other Oriental origin, posted by a country of the West as perhaps likely
to deal best with fellow Orientals, questions her with the regard of distaste: the way this glance compares her with the
husband she has chosen shows that the choice, the world being the way it is, is inexplicable. Flanked by swags of the
Stars and Stripes flag and a bronze eagle on a standard, a

friendly black American official draws back from her papers
with a laugh—You really from Africa?—

It was right to have spared her the tedium of all this. She
had waited at the dentist's or the doctor's, but never before
had she shuffled along in a queue in hope to gain a right—
that had been the history of blacks in her country, but she's
white, Nigel Ackroyd Summers' daughter, yes. And even
when she took herself off to live in the doll's house, the only
queue she might stand in with the mates from The Table was
to gain entry to a cinema. *That's it*, for her; in the press of
supplicant-applicants, she slid her hand behind her to take
the hand of hers, among them. He whispered to her ear (his
smile in the tone), That fellow, he thinks you should be black.

She saw how impossible it was to tell, from the manner of
the petty official you didn't get past to anyone more influential, whether your application had a chance or not; whether
your credentials, your reasons for leaving your country, your
justification for expecting to be received by the one you were
applying to enter, were the ones likely to be received favourably—at least considered before the rubber stamp fell against
you.

The doors of consulates closed on the queues, before noon
prayers. When the morning was over there was the city she
had wanted to explore, getting off the plane as if it had been
one of those destinations of holiday anticipation. But what
they both were in need of now was something to quench
thirst and satisfy hunger. They walked and walked, the thick-
ets of vehicles and collision with bodies, the ricochet of
shouts, calls, vehemence of voices echoed from shop-fronts,
buildings, strung through by the cries from mosques, close by
and distant, like undersea calls of mythical creatures. In this
assault that is a city, the confrontation she had faced when
she got out of her car in another city, there are, of course,

what are called amenities to enjoy that don't exist in a village. If a McDonald's is to be included in the category, they passed one. Then there was a restaurant that also looked as it might have done in any city, closed off from the frenzies of the streets, potted plant either side of a handsome carved door. He was in a good mood, Ibrahim, perhaps it was a comfort to have a companion for once, on his routine quest.

How do I know this place? Uncle Yaqub one day brought me here.

They laughed: to prepare the favoured nephew for the kind of life he was to be offered. The laughter was as near as she and Ibrahim had ever got to referring to that offer again.

The restaurant was air-conditioned, the temperature of some other country; the food succulent and served gracefully by young men. She remarked on this service with appreciation; silently following the waiters' glide about tables, he saw in them likely rivals, brothers, yes, in the queue for visas. No wine, here, of course. Sorry for that.

I don't care. Everything's delicious—but even though it's so elaborate, it isn't any better than your mother makes at home.

They paid in dollars left over from the fee due at a consulate. The alley-way bazaars they passed, the street stalls— these were selling much the same sort of thing as in the village market, only more of it, and the shops displayed among tinselled robes, gold-framed mirrors and curlicued furniture familiar from the house of the Uncle and of Maryam's employer, the even more familiar international choice of Nike boots, cellphones, TV consoles, hi-fi and video equipment. The mosques—but did she really want to see government buildings and mosques? It's only the walls, anyway, you know they won't let you go inside. Then they came to a cinema complex that was a fair example of such a concept

anywhere. They had not seen a film since The Table had
trooped together from the EL-AY Café to a Brazilian film fes-
tival at an art house. Of the film posters' giant gaze outside
this complex, most faces were unknown to her and although
the names of actors were familiar to him, did not attract him.
They saw a James Bond film, subtitled, his choice. If they did
not hold hands as she had done with other lovers (he retained
some of the sexual decorum of the village) she kept her hand
on his thigh while they sat comfortably together in the dust-
mote dark. If the mosque and the church have been left
behind somewhere in life, the cinema can be a place of medi-
tation. As in a place of worship, the one prostrate, forehead to
the floor, the one on the knees, neither knows in what the
person beside him or her is lost.

Next time he went to the capital there was no need for her
to go along with him—he said. On his return in the early afternoon he did not come to his mother's house but to the vehicle workshop, took off the tie and jacket every applicant,
poor devils like himself, queueing at a consulate wore as
proof of respectability, and pulled himself into the stiff mould
of greasy jeans that hung on the wall; the Uncle must have
his money's worth from his ungrateful nephew, disgrace to
the family. When he came home to the lean-to she was lying
on the floor—he often found her reading there, studying her
Arabic, stretched on her belly for coolness; now she was
cleaning sand from between her toes. She looked up and saw:
no news. That night she began to caress him, down the silky
hair of his chest to his groin, but he did not rouse to her
hand, he was tense in some other state of concentration. She
had the odd vision of his mother when at prayer.

She lay angry, resentful at the officialdom, the require-
ments and provisos and quibbles of smug petty functionaries
who had the power to induce these states of tension in him.
And what for? What was it all for? The Uncle, the family,

had said of that world that shut him out, didn't even want him reduced to a grease-monkey—yes, they had said it, and at the time she had had to stifle a derisive splutter of laughter—Isn't it enough to have a cellphone and TV? Wasn't that more than enough of it? What else is really worth having out there in the world of false gods?

She was given the day. Maryam's idea.

What Maryam called her 'wish'; the father was to make one of his infrequent visits to the oasis where he had his connection with a relative who grew rice. Maryam asked that she and Julie might go with him.

Would there be no objection from the father? Perhaps he would prefer not to present the foreign daughter-in-law.

No, no, Maryam had told him Ibrahim's wife wished to see something of the country before Ibrahim left again, took her away.

Only . . . she, Maryam, would have to get permission from her employer to absent herself from her daily work. Her face pleated in embarrassment of presumption at the request: —You ask her, she'll give me the day.— So at the next conversational tea Julie told the lady of the house that she had the opportunity of a little outing (an English colloquialism for the gathering to remember) and wanted Maryam to keep her company. Permission was granted immediately.

The father borrowed his son Ibrahim's car. Rather, it was the son who insisted on this. Julie, you can't go driving around in his old wreck, it breaks down everywhere. Time my Uncle gave a new one my mother can be safe in, anyway. *Would* be, not *can*.

The teacher ran a hand over his hair, with the correction; he complained she helped everyone improve their English except him, to whom it was important.

You are crazy, in this heat, the desert.

I know. I know.

Maryam did not like to tell her to cover her head for this expedition, but brought along an enveloping scarf for her as a gentle instruction rather than an indication that she should have decided to wear something adequate of her own. A man accompanied the father in the front seat, and the two young women sat at the back. —It's all right for you?— Maryam whispered concern for comfort to be provided on her little expedition.

The two men talked all the way without pause, their language so voluble that a beginner, though making progress, caught nothing but the obeisance *in sha allah* and others she understood.

The road ventured out into the desert, the road parted the desert with the thin accompaniment, on either side, of lone outbreaks of small stores, repair yards of undefinable nature in their clutter of disparate wreckage, coffee stalls where men from nowhere sat and a few goats cropped among detritus of torn plastic and cigarette packs; but it was not the desert she came to herself; was received by. In passing stretches it was stony; the outcrop bones of dwellings, bones of animals and humans it had submerged, bared to the surface, like the stump of masonry where she sat on the house it had overcome. The desert withdrew from the interruption of the road; even when the road became hardly more than parallel grooves ground by the passage of vehicles in the sand that flowed over its surface. The experience of the desert she had anticipated from Maryam's expedition was refused her.

In the name of God   If God wills it

Perhaps it was the cocoon of noise which enclosed Maryam and her; the loud to-and-fro talk between the men, bound by winding plaints of car radio music that had the same cadence as their language, and the engine groan of the Uncle's hand-me-down car. Hot, yes, if there had once been airconditioning in the car, it didn't work. But Maryam had a local inhabitant's ability to rest back in the palpable heat, and she had learnt from her not to resist but to do the same.

They did not come upon the destination suddenly. At the sides of their track there glinted what might be a fragment of tin catching the glare, a shard of broken glass shining. But then there was continuity in the shine: water, shallow threads of water. And something like weeds, though not the tough flourishing wayfarer weeds in countries where there is rain. There were palms. At last. A group of camels rested on legs articulated beneath them, their heads rising like periscopes. They must have been hobbled; one struggled to stand with a lower front leg roped back at the knee to its upper half. She had forgotten how she had visualized postcard palm trees, back there. Now they came to a village only a little more formal and extensive, with its mosque, than sparse roadside occupation. The visitors were received in a palm courtyard where offices, like the image of another world (back there) entered through a television screen, had two young men seated at computers, a young woman, wearing the chador but with pursed thighs revealed by a gauzy skirt, used the intercom to announce an arrival in the seductive corporate voice.

The father's collateral connection came from an inner office slowly, as if the visit were something unavoidable rather than welcome. He was a foreshortened man, the compression

of whose aspect created the impression of concentrated ability. The father looked loose-limbed and flabby-bellied, before
him; a wordless vis-à-vis of their relative positions in a common fate. She saw that Maryam was sensitive to this graphic
statement, distressed, on behalf of her father, to be reminded
of what everyone knew but was not confronted with like this:
he was dependent on what was hardly more than the charity
of this man, for whatever his minor function in the man's affairs might be.

Maryam caught up and held breath while greetings were
exchanged. Mr Muhammad Aboulkanim showed no surprise
or curiosity when the European woman wearing a headscarf
was presented to him, a wife the son Ibrahim must have
picked up somewhere in emigration; the wife saw that this
was to make clear to the father that this patron had done for
him all he could be expected to, no question of his having any
interest in the affairs of his distant relative's family—if that
were some idea of bringing the woman along. But the father
was accustomed to dealing in a certain dignity with rebuffs
from this man as from his wife's brother, Uncle Yaqub. He
asked whether, once business was over, they could show
Ibrahim's wife how rice grows 'in our dry country'.

Aboulkanim had the women and the father's friend served
coffee and glasses of iced water while he ushered the father to
his inner office past lowered eyelids and clamped lips.

The three sat on steel-framed, jouncing chairs in the style
of office furnishings fifty years ago, and Maryam replied to
the secretary's bright questions with schoolgirl obedience.
The friend smoked and eyed the door of the inner office as if
he could monitor whether tactics discussed all the way in the
car were being pursued by the father, behind there.

Mr Aboulkanim drove them in his own car to the rice
field. The father sat beside him; there was in his voice a tone

that conveyed to those seated behind that his interview in the inner office had not gone badly; which was to say, nothing changed: he still had his connection.

For half-an-hour a road ignored by the desert led them as before; in vast spaces of the planet Earth like these the road is one road, not multiplied by alternatives. The father talked volubly as he had in the to-and-fro with the friend, although his patron merely grunted or cleared his throat of mucus in response, the radio was babbling news to which nobody listened, part of the smooth function of the handsome German car. In air-conditioned chill the pores on her arms contracted to goose-flesh; but Maryam pulled a little happy grimace and drew her nostrils to take in the coolness as if to store it prudently for the heat beyond the windows.

And then the road ended and there was a low cement-block building with a large efficient-looking pit before it where there were pumps and other heavy machinery whose purpose women would not know. The patron addressed Maryam with an explanation as if the other woman brought along were not there. Maryam translated softly. This is where the water is controlled and the rice is—the word she was looking for was understood: threshed. A barefoot worker, eagle-faced and blackened by the sun, stood by silently, breathing with open mouth like a patient attendant dog.

But she was gazing in concentrated distraction on what was suddenly there before her with its own-drawn close limit of horizon and dazzling density, man-high, what seemed to be meshed slender silky reeds, green, green, green. A kind of wooden walkway offered itself—dank water glancing between planks—and she turned away from the others and took it. The intoxication of green she entered was audible as well as visual, the twittering susurration of a great company of birds clinging, woven into the green as they fed; their trem-

ble, balance, sway, passing through it continuously like rip-
pling breeze, a pitch of song as activity, activity as song, filled
her head. The desert is mute; in the middle of the desert there
is this, the infinite articulacy: pure sound. Where else could
that be? That coexistence of wonder. A break in the rice-
canes, just at the side of the walkway; a low private glaze of
fallow water. A heron awaited her there, standing; she paused
and stood; the bird dipped its beak. Ringingly deafened with
the music of this sphere she did not hear human voices calling to her and took her own time to make her way back.

She had kept them waiting, the patron's eyes were hidden
by sunglasses, but the set of his mouth made that clear. They
were lined up as if for a photograph; indeed, it was for a photograph. The father's friend was trying out focus with an
instant-delivery camera. She was placed between her husband's father and Maryam; then Maryam posed her just before the building on the concrete surface where rice had
spilled. —Pick up, please, go on, in your hands—Maryam
laughed and mimed.

She scooped a handful of slippery husks and sifted them
through her fingers, smiling, the friend stepped back a pace,
forward again, and the picture was taken. The coloured print
came rolling out, he waved it a moment and gave it to her.

On the return journey the father and his friend included
Maryam in their exchange, expansive under the influence of
the lushness they had come close to, as if they had been
drinking. Maryam would not let her be left out, and translated. —They're saying it can be possible, they can buy some
part where there is growing now, or look for water—what is it
you say—

—Drill. Drill for water, you mean?—

—Yes, make a well. And grow.—

—Grow rice?—

—Rice, onions, potatoes, tomatoes, beans, many things. They're saying it can be, if they have the money.—

—You can get permission to drill a well?—

—If they had the money they can do it, even right now. They will if they had money. Just the money!— Maryam laughed, at them and herself—always it was just the money, for everything you wanted and couldn't have.

—And they'd know how to go about cultivation—growing the rice?—

—They know, Julie, yes, oh from years—learned from Mr Aboulkanim, of course they know . . . only the money . . .—

On this journey now she was in dialogue with herself.

What's the legal position with funds in a Trust—why hadn't she taken more interest in learning these things about money! All very well to scorn them, turn up your nose at the bad smell, when there's nothing you really want that you could buy with it; the second-hand car he found was fine. She had always known about that Trust—the family lawyer had told her father it was right and proper that she, the benefici-ary, be informed. So she'd once signed some papers thrust in front of her. The Trust had been set up, apparently, to avoid death duties when Nigel Ackroyd Summers died and his daughter would inherit a considerable fortune from him (even if he were to leave most of his wealth to his second wife). Tax reasons—to benefit the heir, of course, lucky girl. Always tax reasons for what Nigel Ackroyd Summers does. Perhaps—there must be—some way of drawing on that money? Nearly thirty years old, living in some god-forsaken country, isn't that a case of dire need, for a rich man's only daughter, without waiting for anyone's death? She remem-bered—summoned—a term, maybe one the lawyer had used?—pre-inheritance. If she had heard it from the lawyer, that must mean it came up theoretically, but as a possibility. So it could be done. Why not? You must write to someone—

the lawyer, of course. No, to Archie. Yes, always it's to Archie. Ask Archie to look into the principle, the possibility, with a lawyer—not my father's, that one would be alerted to objections on behalf of his client, knowing the daughter's reputation in the family . . .

She returned herself to awareness of the company in the car only once, asking Maryam to ask the men what sort of money a piece of an oasis where things were growing might cost? How much? There was some animated cross-talk of disagreement and agreement between the men, and then came a sum pronounced, impressively drawn-out as if the flourishes of written Arabic were being rolled forth on the air.

Maryam translated. But she had understood, and she had become used to rapid mental conversion from their currency into the hard currencies that mattered to the world: in those currencies, which the Trust certainly held, rely on Nigel Ackroyd Summers for that, the sum was extremely—unbelievably— modest, confirming the feasibility: the possibility. Probably a derisive sum in terms of what the Trust was worth (the lawyer had carefully concealed from her what that might be). About the dollar, sterling or deutschmark price of a new car on the luxury level Danielle would be provided with by her husband. —Stop sneering at the rich, you're thinking of making use of the fact of being one, yourself, aren't you! Abdu (still names him, to herself, by the one he had when she discovered him in the garage) was right, back there, when he reproached me for repudiating their value, the makers and shakers.

Dreamed green.

I dreamt it because it exists.

There is another way, not surrogate succession to the Uncle Yaqub's vehicle workshop, not the dirty work waiting in some other, the next country—here, a possibility. A possibility: his favourite dream-word: 'there are possibilities' in whatever country will let him pass through its barriers of immigration.

Here. You could have it both. The mute desert and the life-chorus of green.

When they arrived back at his parents' house he had already eaten with his mother. The mother enquired, through him, how his wife had enjoyed the trip.

I could never have imagined . . . Rice is so beautiful . . . wheat, maize—nothing to compare as a crop . . . growing . . .

Well we have left some for you to eat. He spoke, amusedly tolerant, in Arabic. His mother smiled royally at her, and lifted a permissive hand to the kitchen. Maryam had sped ahead to prepare a meal for her father, silvery husks falling from the soles of her worn sandals. Mother and son saw his wife pick up a few and examine them, lying in her palm.

In the privacy of the lean-to she was able to give him the kiss of her enthusiasm.

So you had a good time. Hot, ay. He tasted the salt of sweat on her lips.

Have you ever been there?

I've been there. I know Aboulkanim.

It seems a successful business . . . and producing food . . .

Maybe.

You know I understand now that you have to live with the desert to know what water is.

I told you before you came. Dry, nothing. In this place.

No, no . . . that's not what I'm trying to . . . Water's—water is change; and the desert doesn't. So when you see the two together, the water field of rice growing, and it's in the desert—there's a span of life right there—like ours—and there's an *existence* beyond any span. You know?

You are not believing. You always tell me. Not a Christian,

since you left your school, not a Muslim like my family, so what is this now?

He felt he was listening to one of those arguments about the meaning of life started by the rambling of the old man with white hair tied in a ribbon at that table in the Café he thought of as the home she had left behind to be with him in this annex to his family.

Not heaven, nirvana—this place where we are, what there is here. A kind of proof. Do you get me—I can't explain.

With the thumbnail of one hand he was taking the rind of garage dirt from under the nails of the other; his fastidiousness, more than anything he said, expressed to her, bringing an empathy of injury, the frustration and humiliation of his return to nothing more than the underbelly of the Uncle Yaqub's vehicles. She lay down beside him and stroked the hand, a moment.

I'm told you can buy part of the oasis already under cultivation. I suppose from a landowner. Or is it from the government? And you can get permission to drill for a well, in the desert. Did you know?

With money you can buy anything from the government. The landowners who call themselves a government. Same thing. That is what is *here*, in this place of my people. That is one of the first things for you to understand—what's true, about life in this place. There is no mystery about our life. Money—and the government will tell you the deal is done, *Al-Hamdu lillah.*

He was speaking in Arabic.

The price is so reasonable—I asked your father and that friend of his who came with us. I could hardly believe it. Something I could almost certainly raise—from back there, there's a Trust meant for, well, when my father dies, but there are ways . . .

You want to buy a rice concession! You! What for?

She did not look at him but at the unpainted board ceiling, aware of his attention on her profile.

For us.

He lifted his spine and let his body thud back to the bed with a grunt like a laugh. Julie, we do not live here.

Making our own living doing something—interesting? Useful, different, growing food. Something neither of us has ever done.

Once it was an agency for actors in Cape Town, now rice in an oasis, another adventure to hear from her, from her rich girl's ignorance, innocence.

For her part, she sensed it best to place before him something of hard-headed calculation.

That Mr Aboulkanim obviously makes money.

Not rice money.

He spoke now in fluent mix of English and Arabic, translating himself, leaping from phrase to phrase.

That is his—what do you say—his front, the beautiful rice fields. He makes money all right—plenty of it—and do you know how? Do you? He is a smuggler, he calls it import-export, he's a go-between in arms sales for a crowd of cronies over the border, and that's only what I can tell you about Mr Aboulkanim, there's much more of the same I don't know, that people who know admire him for because he's successful. That's *success*, here.

She sat up startled and confronted him. Your father works for him.

My father works for what makes *him* respectable. Your rice field. My father isn't let into the Big Business, my father is the poor devil, may I be forgiven to speak like that, who fills in the right papers to sell rice, only rice, and gets a cash handout every few months. So he uses my father's honest name.

And now she confronted herself. Why should I be so shocked at this story; how many lunch guests at Nigel Ack-

royd Summers' Sundays are involved in deals that are not revealed, and if known are not talked about along with the
price of Futures—not arms deals; but why not? Perhaps even
those, passing by remote control through the sale of dia-
monds in Angola.

If we had a concession it wouldn't have anything to do
with all that. Mr Aboulkanim. Just growing rice.

He rolled away from her, rose, and changed his shirt, took
from the canvas bag his folder of papers.

I've got a meeting tonight with someone. We'll see if he
turns up.

He came to where she sat flushed with the heat of the day,
dangling her legs from the iron bar of the bed, shook his head
over her, giving her the smile, that treasure so often withheld.

She had not shown him the photograph, the slippery
husks of rice sifting through her fingers. Until it faded it
would be proof that the place exists; could have been at-
tained.

From the canvas bag standing ready, that carried his life from country to country, he had taken the letters sent by the woman in California.

He said nothing to her; she had been completely dismissive of her mother's likelihood of knowing anyone whose signature could be of use, anywhere, in a situation remote as his. But more than that: his hopes had been raised so often—the thought of this brought that confusion of resentment and shame that was new to him, a result of coming back to this place. He could not face her philosophical encouragement, real or assumed, her patience, real, or a cover for the adventure soon to become another to entertain back round The Table; the beautiful suitcase she didn't value stood there, ready for her.

No more news. He would say nothing to her, nothing at all, of the progress he was making, this time, this one time, and she knew so little about the delicacy of such business, she was too ignorant to be able to read the signs. Taking her to a consulate or embassy for personal questioning indicated nothing to her. Better that way. When—if—no!—*when*, this time, he would have something to say to her, it would be: news.

And there was something else. There was an aspect to the triumph of his refusal to grasp at the opportunity offered by an Uncle Yaqub other young men stagnating in the village would give anything (of their nothing, poor devils like himself) to have, an aspect he had hardly known himself when the great decision—the best moment of his manhood so far—had been made by him: say no. Even if this girl had failed in the purpose he must not forget (in any tangle of emotion about her) he had counted on her as a source of Permanent Residence in her country, she had somehow in the meantime they happened to be living through brought about in him also an interim of meantime brooding contemplation, moving into thoughts of a kind he had never had before. When he had said, from the very depths of himself: no; it was also no to abandoning the man she had fallen in love with (as they say); no to what would have determined for sure that the adventure would be over, it could not become that of the wife of a future Uncle Yaqub. He would have been left in this place and married off and fathered more sons who could not get out.

He came from the capital that day and as he parked Uncle Yaqub's old car at the gate saw women coming along the street. She—Julie—with Amina and infant, Maryam and the little girl and—he had to look again—Khadija, they were coming from the market, female pack-horses loaded with plastic carriers from which green stalks and leaves overflowed. Onions or potatoes burst out of one, and gathering them was a game between Julie, the child and Khadija—apparently *madam* who kept to her own purdah of superiority now would venture out with the other women if Julie were one of them.

He waited in the car. What kind of life. For her. It presented itself in its shame, approaching him. The child pointed him out, broke away from the women and rushed up to demonstrate his presence as if his arrival were some special occasion.

It was.

He greeted and exchanged a few words with his mother where she sat on her sofa in the communal room while Julie and the other women chattered over unpacking the market shopping in the all-purpose kitchen. She waved as she passed through to the lean-to; she would not disturb him and his mother.

He came to her. She was dowsing face, hair and hands in the basin of cool water she kept supplied for them, placed on the chair she was kneeling before.

So hot! She turned and looked up, a streaming smile, as if with tears.

He opened his hand. Between finger and thumb were stamped papers round two passports.

What?

She stood up, wildly shaking wet hands. What?

Visas. Entry permits. The United States of America.

All in one movement he threw the documents onto the bed, overpowered her in a crushing embrace, a yell of triumph that brought their mouths together through water trickling from her hair.

I am going to America.

Told them, hadn't he.

So it should not have amazed them that he now had the authority stamped in his passport and his wife's. There were family embraces of congratulation implicitly apologizing for having doubted if not disbelieved him. Only Khadija referred to that—You were just boasting then, weren't you.— He did not take the jibe kindly; Julie saw this in his face but did not understand what had been said.

Others in the family could not rejoice. Maryam cried: Julie would miss her wedding. He embraced his father; his mother. For forgiveness, for their blessing, once again. When he came home with his foreign wife his mother had allowed tears to mark the cast of face she had bequeathed to him, now she allowed no emotion to change the sculpture of years and the discipline of prayer. Or perhaps features and flesh could not express what she experienced in this departure; yet again. Only she, and her son, could know what that was. He said to her under the voices of others, I will send for you. To come; to visit us. It was as well, he knew, that she seemed not to hear.

The visas in his hand.

Still a number of practical details to attend to. He must go back to the capital, present his passport to his own government's authorities, fill in forms pertaining to his emigration. He must return to collect the passport when behind the files and the computer screens whatever the process was has been completed. The airline would not accept a booking until both passports and visas were brought for scrutiny; and of course once this had been done, tickets could not be issued without money to pay for them.

They sat on the iron bed in the lean-to reviewing their resources. She had a few dollar traveller's cheques left but these would have to be kept aside to provide for immediate needs on arrival. His final hand-out pay from his Uncle, if they managed to leave, as he was determined to, within not more than two weeks, must go to Maryam as a wedding gift; her brother could not do less.

Your father.

She stared in alarm.

Just say the word.

No. No, no.

Your father. He can pay for the tickets there and have them sent to you. That is the way. We will pay back.

I can't.

Again.

He had to fix her with his mother's eyes while he kept control of himself, kept his voice soft and reasoning, held down, as he had had to do countless times in immigration offices, his frustration, and swallow the reflux of evidence that privilege can never be brought to understanding of reality, of what matters, the dignity of survival against principles.

How to make him understand: her voice sharpened.

You wouldn't ask your Uncle Yaqub, would you!

I asked. He said he would not help me to run away again. He enjoyed himself.

She put her head on his shoulder and buried her face in his neck. And he had not told her of this, the latest refusal. He had spared her.

Back where she came from she had been the one in charge, the one with status; here, in what was his home, his place, ineradicable birthmark that defined in him that place's ways of going about things, he had done—and only he could do—what was necessary. Alone with her in the lean-to now, he talked more than he had ever talked, taking her step by step out of her ignorance. The brother-in-law of a cousin had been in the United States successfully (that means legally) for six years. The family had lost touch with the man but through the months of asking everyone who might have heard where he was, in the days of sitting it out in coffee stalls, nights in the backroom bars in the streets where she had seen the bloated body of a dead sheep, he had been slowly gathering the information he was after. He had been able to get in touch with this cousin's brother-in-law. And this

one, somehow, *Al-Hamdu lillah* (the usage of home came unnoticed to his tongue as The Table would exclaim 'Thank
Christ' when some secular dispensation could be acknowl-
edged only through a deity), had done everything he could,
and more, to offer a start for them at the other end—America. America. He was janitor in a large apartment block—
she'd been to the States, she'd know how they are twenty,
forty storeys, plenty of people living there—as janitor or care-
taker or whatever he was called, he had a place to live, an
apartment down at the bottom—

Yes, she had been there, to America, she had seen how
some people lived in the apartment buildings of the affluent.

—In the basement.

The cousin's brother-in-law knew a lot of people who had
found work to get started with, and knew how from that base
you could move up towards the kind of position you wanted,
so long as you had education where you came from and
could learn to speak the language well, learn the skills. Night
college courses, schools of technology, advanced computer
training, computer science—that's it! This man had all the
information, addresses of institutions, foundations, openings,
opportunities. Chances.

America. To him, beside her, it was a single concept: but
America, its vastnesses, so many Americas, from the casinos
in California to Idaho (where she had skied) to New York
(where she frequented museums and theatres), Char-
lottesville (where one of her lovers came from, she remembered), to Seattle, to Florida . . .

Where is he, in America? What city would we go to?

Chicago. He's in Chicago. And his brother and a friend
like a brother are in Detroit, there's work there. For a start,
that's all right. They say they could find something for me.
We might go to Detroit. You been there, you know it?

Her upper and lower lips are drawn, mum, into her closed mouth; her head moves as if she is searching.

He watches: ah yes, thinking back to another adventure.

She never was in Detroit but she knows, remembers, the other kind of distances in the vastness of America. From the houses of Sutton Place with their doormen attired as royal flunkeys (Daddy Summers had sent her to be received by his friends at an address) to the slums of Chicago and New York where a worn old man or blowzy woman sits on the broken doorstep of a decaying building where emigrants 'of colour' find lodging, a bed-space, along with the black American poor, born down-on-their-luck.

For the first couple of weeks Ismail says we can stay with them, they'll make room for us in their place, Chicago. They have this janitor's apartment—I told you. They must be very nice, wonderful people—don't know us but of course we are family.

And then.

He rose, away from her, and began to walk about the room; so confined that only a few paces took him back and forth. Her eyes followed him to read what the movement might mean. His unaccustomed expansiveness had dried up; she was back to reading him in other ways, as she had learnt to. Was he pacing the cage of refusals for the last time, ritually, just before it was about to swing open wide, on America; never easy to read him.

Depends what happens. I'll go to Detroit. That's it. I think it will be.

Have they found a place for us? To live, in Detroit.

Well, I'll sleep somewhere, wherever they do. They are without wives, not been able to send for them yet. They've only been there a year . . . a bit more . . .

He had come back, to stand before her, his legs touching her knees where she sat. I'll look for something for us right away. An apartment. Even some rooms.

You. 'You'. Was she understanding him. What d'you mean?

It will be good if you go to California. To your mother, just for some days.

She bent forward with the flesh over her cheek-bones lifted in anguished pressure against her eyes, her head tipped to him, trying to scrutinize what might be written for her on his smooth tarnished-gold forehead under the fall of black silk hair.

How did you think that.

He had come to know the power of his particular smile, she had made him conscious of it, so that what he had been unaware of, when the impulse to smile came, was now a tactic to be employed; this is one of the possibilities of power that come with what he had though he couldn't afford; what the privileged call love. The smile offered himself to her.

Julie. You are not always right about your parents. Of course they are not like you. Not in many ways. But in some ways they are there— He put the flat of his hand on her breast-bone, just above her breasts. It was touch, a gesture, very different from his seeking out her breasts in a caress; it brought him closer to her than any sexual advance.

It is like with my parents.

It's nothing like with yours. Your mother. What can I say. Then there came to her as a slap in the face, something that had been intended to be a pleasant surprise: How do you know my mother would want me there? Around-thirty-year-old daughter to prove to everyone that my mother is much older than her latest husband.

And then what there was to be read in him was deciphered: Have you been in touch with her? Have you?

On the phone, yes. The letters she sent, from her husband. They were a great thing—help—to get my visa. We won't ever know how much. Until I took those letters, nothing happened. You know that.

California. Take on the casino style, for my mother and
her husband. Her voice was backing, away, away. California.
The smile had opened a flow in him again. It is good
sense. You don't understand what it is like. Come in a country like I do. I have done—how many times? Even legal. It's
hard, nothing is nice, at the beginning, Julie. Without proper
money to live. You are a stray dog, a rat finding its hole as the
way to get in. I know you don't mind, you even seem to like
to live . . . rough . . . it's like a camping trip to you. But this
is different, it can be bad, bad. I can't take you into it. I don't
want you to experience . . . I don't mind for me—because this
time I have the chance to move out of all that, finished, for
ever, for ever, do what I want to do, live like I want to live.
That is the country for it. There's plenty of chances again
now, there; you don't read the papers, but the unemployment
is nothing. Lowest for many years. Work for everybody.

And the meantime. —She seems to force herself to speak.
What is that?

Before the chances to live the way you want to. What
work will you do.

Same as immigrants, always. Anything. If you have some
brains and education, it doesn't matter. I tell you, you don't
know what happens there. It isn't your country, never get out
of the garage! You don't know—one of the biggest, the most
important financiers in the whole world today was an immigrant from Hungary, he started there in New York as a waiter
in a club. He was white, a Jew, yes. But people where I come
from make it, there, even if not so high as that, they're in
computers, in communications, that's where the world is!

Women here—his home—do what their men tell them to. Is
that what is happening in the makeshift walls of the lean-to,
are there listeners with ears to the clapboard door hearing

what is being said, is he who 'runs away from home' (Uncle
Yaqub) yet taking an assumption from all he abandons? He
and she won't go on talking about it: California. That may
mean anything. That he has accepted her rejection; that she
has accepted her assent.

*J*ust say the word

There was no strain between them and that cannot be explained. Better not. For either to try to. Not everything between two people can be laid before The Table for resolution. *That's it.* He was sorting out the contents of the canvas bag, there were things, time-fingered documents, to unburden himself of forever, now; legality is light to carry. He looked up to give her the smile as she opened the door . . . going out to his sister or somewhere about the house.

She walked as a somnambulist slowly down the street to its end, the desert. The bean rissole vendor must have seen her, the man with a donkey cart hawking melons must have passed her, the nasal harmonies of house radios and the electronic call of the mosque trailed round her familiarly unfamiliar figure. The dog was waiting. If there is not The Table, there is always someone. She sat on the clump of masonry that had once been a house and the dog stood on its splayed thin legs a little way off. The desert. *Always.* The true meaning of the common word tripping off every tongue to suit every meaning, comes from the desert. It is there before her and the dog. The desert is always; it doesn't die it doesn't change, it exists.

But a human being, she, she, cannot simply exist; she is a hurricane, every thought bending and crossing its coherence inside her, nothing will let her be, not for a moment. Every emotion, every thought, is invaded by another. Shame, guilt, fear, dismay, anger, blame, resentment at the whole world and what it is—and names come up, names—for the sight of him as he is going to be. Again. Living in a dirty hovel, a high-rise one or a shed behind a garage, what's the difference, with Christ knows what others of the wrong colours, poor devils like himself (as he used to say), cleaning American shit—she has seen the slums of those cities, the empty lots of that ravaged new world, detritus of degradation—doing the jobs that *real people*, white Americans, won't do themselves. At least in her home, that city of the backward continent, lying under a car's guts was a better human grade. And then the assault comes at her: in *your* city? Your country? All *real people* by law now, but who still does the shit work, neither Nigel Ackroyd Summers nor his daughter Julie. And even the 'better human grade' was denied the grease-monkey there, he was kicked out of that better grade, wasn't he, right out; of your country.

And again: America, America. The great and terrible USA. Australia, New Zealand—that would have been something better? Anywhere would be. America. The harshest country in the world. The highest buildings to reach up to in corporate positions (there he is, one of the poor devils, the beloved one, climbing a home-made rope ladder up forty storeys); and to jump off from head-first. *That's where the world is.* He thinks *I* don't know; *he* doesn't know. He is standing before her, conjured up by her rage against all that threatens him, waits for him: so young, his slender hands hanging ready for anything, at his sides, his defiant elegance—that silk scarf round his neck with its strong tendons, the black hair down his breast and again round his testicles

and proud penis she sees beneath his clothes whenever she
looks at him, the black eyes that never reveal what's going on
behind that face she discovered comes from his mother, as the
traits of an ancient Greek, Egyptian or Nubian image may be
rediscovered in far-removed living descendants.

But there is no-one. Nothing imprinted on the desert. It is
always; and what is thudding inside her like a road-worker's
stamp in a street is *now*.

She is at one with the woman, his mother, to whom she
should have been able to run, at one with the woman with
whom she could not exchange, did not have, the right words
for what she now shared with her. Only she herself, who had
discovered him disguised as a grease-monkey—not the father,
not Maryam, not anyone at all in the family where people
were so close to one another—only she and the mother could
experience the apprehension of, the rejection of what every
emigration, this emigration, was ready to subject the son to.
But the mother was at prayer; his mother had prayer. She
should not be interrupted. Even if one were to have had the
words in the right language.

The dog went silently away. She sat on until the tumult
slowly cleared within her, disentangled. The sands of the
desert dissolve conflict; there is space, space for at least one
clear thought to come: arrived at.

When she came back to the house the prayer rug had been
folded away. Mother and son were together in their privacy
on her sofa. He looked up and signalled—come. Where he
sat, he put an arm round her waist; Where have you been? A
walk. Fresh air is good if it is not too hot, the mother said to
her, speaking slowly so that she would understand. They
looked at one another for a moment; she thought his mother
knew—if not where she had been—where experiences were
taking her.

They retired to their lean-to together—that was the formal feeling of it before the following eyes of the mother. He had her by the hand, it was a gesture more for his mother than for her: as if to say, my foreign wife is with me, I am not alone.

She dumped herself on the bed that had complained so much under the weight of love-making.

I'll write to Archie. My Uncle.

Dear Archie,

You won't be too surprised to hear from me, and you'll know that it probably means I'm coming to you—for something. Because you've always been the one I could ask. This time it's money. Ibrahim has been granted a visa for America. It was never a problem to get one for me, but it has taken months and endless hassle to arrange for him. He's been turned down by every other country he's tried. I still don't know how he's done it—better not ask! You'll understand that, after his experience in S.A.

So we have the green light for the USA. But my dollars have run out. We couldn't have and wouldn't have expected his family to keep us. His earnings here (work he's had as a favour from a relative) and the small sums I've been able to add by having the nerve to teach English, are not enough to pay our airfares and give us a breather when we get there. Could I ask, I *am* asking, could you possibly, somehow, let me have the equivalent of about 5,000 dollars? I know exchange control regulations may make this difficult, but any currency you could arrange to come to me from your contacts anywhere, would be fine. Ibrahim has a friend at a bank in the

capital who will take care of the draft and get us the proper
rate of exchange at this end. I am enclosing a sheet with all
details of the bank for the transfer, however you can do it.

Dear Archie, I would hope to pay back some time. I
wanted to write to you, anyway, not long ago, about the possibility of a pre-inheritance from the Trust you know was set
up—but that's no doubt something complex that would take
time, and we really have to have cash right now. So to be
honest, I won't be able to meet the debt too soon because we
don't know what our situation will be in the USA. But eventually, I'll write again for your advice on how I could perhaps
draw on that Trust. I suppose in America I could most likely
get the same kind of work I used to do. I could contact the
principals there, of the people I worked for in Johannesburg,
it's an international spider, legs down all over the place. If
they make some sort of in-house request to employ me apparently a work permit won't be a problem. For the moment,
Ibrahim's been granted one, I'm just the wife he's supposed to
provide for while she sits and watches TV.

Archie, I don't know how to say how grateful we'll both be
to you.

You know I can't ask my father.

With much love, as it's always been,

Julie

It came to her from herself with reproach, only now: she had assumed, in her outrage at the preposterous charge against Archie, that it had not been, could not be pursued; must have been dropped before evidence of his life-long professional reputation. Only now; so in the emotional conflation of what had happened, all at once, to him and (in her hand) the two airline tickets to take her and her lover out of the country, she had not written to him as she meant to do! Hadn't written although in all her adventures round the world she was free to roam she carried in her address book, on Archie's insistence—just in case—his fax and telephone numbers at his consulting rooms and at home.

Ibrahim had talked to her about calling, but she was reluctant, and no point in pressing her now that she had come forth with the solution for them; he sensed it was better to let her achieve it in her own way; she seemed to shrink from some emotional complication in speaking to this uncle of hers. They went together to the capital to a friend-of-a-friend who was in the import business and sent the letter by fax.

The draft came with incredible promptitude—in their experience, anyway, so accustomed to protracted patience, sit-

ting it out isolated in the village in the desert that knows no
time while officialdom teased with promises from week to
week.

Archie had sent six thousand dollars, not five. Following a
day later there was a letter faxed through Ibrahim's friend-of-
a-friend. My dear Julie, What a relief to hear from you and
know that your life is working out. We were told you came to
the house before you left, whether it was to say goodbye or if
you had heard about that crazy unpleasant business with a
patient—sorry to have missed you. It was difficult to prove
that the woman was a so-called borderline personality (psy-
chiatrist's diagnosis) but there'd been leaked information to
my defence team that there was a history of such incidents in
her past and they were able to obtain corroboration of this. I
privately think, poor thing was concocting deliberate revenge
on *any* man—happened conveniently to be me—in the resentment and anger she felt against some other man she
couldn't get at to damage. You cannot believe how incredibly
supportive my patients were, there were more wanting to give
evidence on my professional conduct and ethics than the
lawyers could use. There I was advising you to engage good
lawyers for your problem, when I was about to need them for
myself! Never thought I'd be the male victim of sexual harassment—but there you are, there has to be a first time for
some man. Tables turned. She was the one making unwelcome sexual demands on her doctor, not t'other way about.
Test case. It went against her and I could have claimed damages but decided on the facts of the way medical colleagues
as well as my patients indignantly rallied round and publicly
vouched for me, not only in court but perhaps even more im-
portantly in the press, I hadn't been damaged . . . Sharon dis-
agrees, she says the forgiveness and reconciliation we're busy
with in our country doesn't extend (I think she means descend, eh) to the level of someone who could have destroyed

me. You know redhead Sharon, she wanted to go up to the woman in court and slap her face this side and that—those were the damages she thought of, just to start off with. What's come out of the whole thing is that many of my fellow doctors have become afraid of their patients . . . I continue to trust mine, how else be their doctor?

It's over, we're intact, we're well. Please keep me posted wherever you are/go. Let me have an address. After I was told you'd come to the house that time, I asked Nigel for yours, he said he was not in touch with you, did not have it. I'm sorry it's like that. Time will mend. Good luck in the U.S. to you both. You're a brave girl. Love, Archie.

Along with his generosity there was this, to her, another kind she would always need to know existed; Archie was as he had always been, unharmed, not making judgments others did, his own man; a surety to be found in no-one else, nowhere else.

She had that uncle, this was the response from the family she cut herself off from! Under his dark gold skin there was an elation of red that added to the deep brilliance of those eyes.

Now there is something good will be left over from the air tickets, I will have what you need to put down in deposit when I find a place for us, I can buy things to make it ready—for when you come.

But with this money we'll be able to get somewhere to live right away. Even some cheap hotel, Chicago, Detroit, whatever.

They were thrust back to what they had not talked about since the first time he had spoken of it.

Hotel? What hotel. How long can the money last if we start off like that. I can live very cheap with the other men in Detroit and look around and when I know if it's going to be

there, Detroit, Chicago—how can I say—I'll have the money
to find a decent place for us while you are all right in California.

But you must have understood. Abdu! I never said I could
do that.

What is it you're saying now. Julie—I told you, I can't
take you to live the way immigrants start, they must, unless
money is going to fall on them from the sky. Now we have
something, and I know how we must use this . . . luck . . . this
from your uncle . . . like from the sky, but it is not millions, is
it! Is it? It is from heaven, yes, but we can't spend like a holiday, I must find work, I must find somewhere where you can
live . . . can't you understand that? We have to thank your
mother, her husband for the letters that got us in, we have to
thank your uncle for the money that buys even the air tickets
that let us go. Your family is good to us. What is the matter
with seeing your own mother, she wants it, she likes to have
you with her for a while, that's sure, and how do we know—

What don't we know?

He breathed out exaggeratedly at her obtuseness, her lack
of reality.

He was smiling; he drew new breath. They, he—her husband got the letters from important people so easy. Yes? He
knows people. We see that. It can be he will find something
good for me, he'll put me in with the right connections. Connections are everything, believe me, I know. We could be able
even to go and live there, there are big centres in communications technology, it's a nice climate, warm, like you have at
your home, not hell hot as this place—never cold—Chicago is
cold, isn't it. California—wonderful. Everyone wishes to live
there.

His arms open wide, he doesn't have the words, he is em-
bracing California; or her. His gaze will not release her although they are standing apart.

A creature caught by a light in the dark of private being. Just say the word.

He recognized the moment, came over and put an arm round her, a hand against her cheek, mumbled soft sounds through the screen of her hair at her ear.

There is something beguiling about submission, for one who has believed she has never submitted. Something temptingly dangerous, too: The Suburbs; The Table; a third alternative.

Maryam was planning an elaborate farewell party for them.

She meant it to be a surprise but Khadija made an oblique reference in her usual sharp way. —You never had a wedding. Everyone wants to wish you well on this other occasion—they say.— Ibrahim chaffingly asked his sister what she was up to and she began to cry. —You will also miss my wedding.— She could not say to this brother whom she knew so little, he had come and gone, so long, that her tears were because he was taking his wife away from her. His understanding was indeed different: so this party was to be a substitute for all that had been missed by the family—his marriage to a girl of their choice, the grandchildren, nieces and nephews, cousins, the common celebrations and mournings, the communion with brothers in the ritual of Holy Law that made right and righteous decisions, uncomplicated, for them, armed them against the other world into which, unwanted, unprotected, he wildly cast himself. But blessings are never to be dismissed, they are even secretly longed for, in the core of self, the seed from the genetic granary that remains embedded beneath all that is assumed elsewhere, among other places and people. There were gifts for his wife from the conversational tea ladies and the parents of school children whom she had taught, brass trays and phials of perfumes, a length of

sequin-embroidered cloth; for him a souvenir someone had
brought from Mecca (kindly encouragement to make a pil-
grimage from whatever ends of the earth he might find himself). His father presented the couple, son and wife, with a
beautiful old Koran. The mother there; no need to utter, the
words came to him from her. He spoke at length and the
weight of solemnity in their graceful language was translated
to her to supplement her understanding: The Book is for the
education of your children and your children's children. Then
there was even a gift from the wife of his Uncle Yaqub to
prove to his sister, the no-good nephew's mother, that if the
Uncle refused money for the abandonment of familial, religious, community and national heritage, he was not mean. It
was a table lamp very like the ones in the Uncle's house,
made in the flashing golden form of some overblown flower,
unlikely to be a tulip, perhaps a water-lily, from whose metal
petals small electric globes rose on gilded stamens. Leila had
climbed on Julie's lap to show the present she had made: they
sat together looking at her drawing, the child watching the
woman's face to see her reactions to the offering. The picture
showed a ship, which was something the child could never
have seen, except on television, a tower or building, something between the tallest structure in the village, the minaret
of the mosque, and an apartment block, which she must also
have seen on television, a broken wall where two stick-figures
sat, seen from the back, one big and one small, but both with
large heads. Their one-line arms were looped round each
other, the loops scored deeply. Two bodiless heads, front face,
split by huge smiles hung, suns in the space above that was
neither land nor sky. A painstakingly-striped watermelon
(they both loved the messy orgy of eating together the fruit of
the market) lay at the edge of one corner. A stick-dog with a
drooping tail stood at the other. The child stayed proudly on
Julie's lap, holding her gift while Julie's attention was drawn

this way and that in talk with other people anxious to wish
her well. Some composed what they had to say in the English
they had learnt from her. There was interruption between
them, laughter at mistakes.

Maryam, in her sadness at all these symbols of parting,
was happy for the couple: Wedding presents, she said. Everything in the life of this brother and the woman he mysteriously had had the good fortune to find for himself was
differently timed, different from what she knew or could expect within the family.

The whole street that, vision awake and asleep, Julie had
in her mind, having taken the way past the same parked mo-
torbike against the same fence, the same music coming from
the same windows, the same veiled grandmother talking to
herself on the same peeling leather-covered chair, to the path's
end in the desert, must have been roused by the high volume
of chatter in the to-and-fro from the kitchen as the women of
the house, of whom she was one, and the guest wives wove
past one another with a balance of laden dishes, and every
voice rose with the stimulation of feasting. The human cries in
expression of their occasion must have sounded out beyond
the stump of last dwelling-place abandoned to the sand, wa-
vered to be lost in the desert as the calls of the muezzin were
and the cries that she had been told were of a pack of jackals
in expression of their occasions where they roved, far off, at
night. Then the bowls and plates stood around emptied of all
except some leavings of an ingredient not to someone's taste,
here, and the juice swimming from some succulent dish de-
voured, there; and Maryam—it was she who had asked her
employer's wife for the loan of some discs—set dance music on
Khadija's CD player carried in, invading with decibels of its
own. There was new laughter: what was this? It was music
from the country where Ibrahim and his wife were going, its
confident pulse, its dominant rapping voice shouting down all

others. The old people sat calmly undistracted; the shoulders
of the young moved irresistibly to the beat. She whispered
something he couldn't catch. I said, it's great that people can
get lit up without drink or something to sniff or shoot up.
Come on—let's dance.

No—not here, men and women don't dance together—not
in front of parents, no.

The lively shoulders of the brothers were revealing a fa-
miliarity of body with a mode of pleasures they must have
learnt in forbidden places. It was a fine night. Later they sat
talking under the awning at the back of the house while the
women washed dishes and re-created the events of the party
with the supplement of gossip and anecdotes about the departed guests. On a final look-around for dirty plates, she
was alone in the family room: the empty sofa where the
mother had her place. She happened to glance out of a window; there, at the gate, a summons, sat the dog. She went to
the kitchen and, unnoticed, retrieved a handful of scraps. It
was late; the street was deserted. She held out her hand, but
the dog wouldn't approach, she should have known by now, it
would never come to her. That was all it had, in its hunger:
its dignity that can't be understood. She went through the
gateway and put the food down in the dirt; it had its eyes familiarly on her, unmoving. She turned her back and went
into the house. From the window she now saw the dog come
to the food and eat.

There were final, retreating sounds and voices of everyone
going to bed in this house that was not large enough yet ac-
commodated each in his and her place, home. Even a lean-to.

The wedding presents were on the bed and the floor, lying
or propped anywhere.

They laughed to one another.

Looks like a pawn-shop, remember, near the Café.

It was a nice old Jew who kept it. One time I had to take

my watch there, until the end of the week when the garage paid.

What on earth to do with this? —She lifted the lamp by its bright metal petals, exaggerating its weight in the effort.

Khadija. Give it to her. She is collecting things like that for the fine house she's going to make my brother buy for her. But some we will take of course.

Of course; was he thinking of the Koran, beautiful edition, a kind of family bible; the one she had sent for, the translation she read, was humbly mass-produced. But not the brass trays. He could not get the brass trays into the canvas bag. And what place would there be for such things that belonged here.

In America.

The kind gift of these strong flower-perfumes; to permeate everything you take away. Her attention wandered to the suitcase; elegant suitcase Nigel Ackroyd Summers' Danielle had chosen: waiting there. Tiredness rose to her head, the lean-to held the heat of the day. She pushed the window wide as it would go and there (like the dog) was the splendid night, waiting. She gave way to an impulse to let him in, into something she had not before, the kind of impulse—indiscretion? but he is her lover, her discovery—she used to give way to after too many drinks or too many joints in her old life. Let's walk a while in the desert, it'll be cool. The stars fantastic.

The desert. —His answer was to begin undressing.

Only down the street. Not far to go. As if he doesn't know, he was born here, this is his place, not mine.

Let's sleep. It's late, who wants to go out there. Anywhere. Let's sleep.

He stood before her as he had done every night in the doll's house shed of his grease-monkey overalls like a prince freed of the spell cast upon him.

Whether she dreams or whether a streaming profusion of thought was what she decides she must have dreamt, does not much matter. On the eve of moving out of some tentative anchorage it is either way the natural return of comparison, attempting the matching, somehow fitting together images, years, days, moments. The relative duration of these may be reversed in their significance. The moment is longer than the year. Whether this is a raided store of the subconscious or a wakeful night—when so-called dreams are recounted to yourself in the morning, how much is being invented in the urge to find the coherence between the conscious and subconscious; *that must exist*; is unattainable? Must be found. And if it could be found—there would be certainty. Of what? What does that mean? Of why you live as you do. And how that ought to be. No rules, not those of The Suburbs or even (not any more!) those no-rules of The Table—the elusive coherence is what there would be to go by—something of what is known grandly as the truth. But avoid big words, for Chris' sake, for the Prophet's sake. Well, the individual truth. Nobody else's.

The stream of vision, thoughts, re-creation has a kind of narrative of its own; the desert is a good place for it to relate itself. On the terrace in California (which, like the child's ship, she had never seen except in prototype in the media) there are assembled the guests of Nigel Ackroyd Summers' Sundays, Danielle and her mother; or Danielle-and-her-mother one and the same. Men beside a sauna (sauna! where does that detail come from!) are talking about winnings and losses at Black Jack and buying into the Future on the stock exchange. The latest husband introduces Ibrahim to the right people, there's the international website man who emigrated to Australia and the black lawyer turned business entrepreneur. Her mother/Danielle introduces Ibrahim/Abdu to women, bringing him forward by the hand: my son-in-law, an oriental prince (as The Table, she knew, used to laugh about her pickup behind her back) in Gucci shoes, Armani pants and Ralph Lauren shirt Danielle's bought him, his beauty is an exotic dish to sample along with the pool-side lunch. He's still wearing his old elegant scarf round his neck. All that is left of him. Whatever he was, had been, is? Sliding himself out from under the vehicle, sitting in silent judgment upon us at The Table, flung upon his back on the bed in the cottage, now carefully repacking the canvas bag in the lean-to. What was it she'd read. There was a poet's novel, she didn't remember the title or the writer, The Table poet had given her, insisted she must read—something in it was dredged up now its time came to be understood: for her to understand what she had done. 'I was occupied in picturing him to myself; I had undertaken the task of imagining him.' But he is himself. Nobody's task. Tell it to the desert; that is safe. Each time she faced the desert from the stump of a wall and then rose and walked out a way, never too far, could be the last time; meanwhile she was continuing to do what she had discovered she could do, occupied

her final days as she had since she bought the two air tickets
and came with him here, to his place. Right up to the date
they boarded the plane, she would continue; it was her small
farewell gift to the school children, leaving them with another
few words of the language he had to apply himself to acquire
more fluently if he were to get what he wanted where he and
she were going. It was her small way of thanking the conversational tea circle and others who had come to her, for—
well—their need of her.

There is no last time, for the desert. The desert is always. It does not matter that she has turned and gone back
up the street, buying three circles of warm fritters from the
vendor as she returns to the family home, the lean-to for
transients.

Out to buy fritters.

They decided together, often disagreeing and then giving
in, each indulgent to the other, on what to take and what to
leave behind. Some abandonments were reversed.

One of the brass trays? Just that little one. If you can
squash it in at the bottom.

They regarded each other mock-questioningly a moment,
laughed. With Maryam she had bought a supplementary suitcase at the market, a cardboard affair with tin locks instead of
the digital combination one on the elegant suitcase. His
mother, through Maryam as emissary, had provided two sets of
flower-patterned bed sheets as a start, wherever they might
find the next bed, and it was not possible to distribute these
discreetly, like the other 'wedding presents' they couldn't carry.

All right. Between my mother's sheets, if you want.

They wrapped the family Koran like a mummy, to protect
it in his canvas bag, and then discussed whether it wouldn't

be safer to have it in the cabin. She taped it once again in plastic film so that toothpaste or deodorant, which might leak under pressure changes in an aircraft, could not harm it in her overnight pouch.

What about that perfume stuff the women gave you. You like that.

No . . . no, Maryam and Khadija have it, I know from experience what can happen with perfume . . . and those phials don't have proper stoppers. I wouldn't think of putting them in there with the Book. And the sheets—you'd never get the scent out.

Her books, her humble Koran, were all that was left to be packed; they went into the cardboard case; Ahmad, handyman of the family, home from the butcher's yard, supplied a length of rope and strapped the case to take the strain off cheap locks. He remarked something to his brother and he and Ibrahim both exclaimed and laughed.

What does he say?

Ibrahim's face crumpled wryly. Emigrant's case. It must break . . . if it even gets to the other side. Piece of rubbish.

And now there was nothing left, of them, him and her, in the lean-to, except the bed they still slept in, made love in, for a few more days. He had insisted that they should be ready, no object, nothing to look back for, roll out the elegant case (it has wheels, of course), pick up the canvas bag and the cardboard acquisition and walk out to the taxi already ordered in advance for when the day and hour came; so he had them on the point of departure three days ahead of the day.

That night, after he had slipped from her body and rills left of her pleasure had ended, she spoke; but then sensed from the rhythm of his breathing that his silence did not mean he had heard what she feared and shamed herself with so that she could hardly goad herself to say what she had to say. He was asleep.

Just say the word

It was better perhaps to be less cowardly and not choose the dark, where you would not have to see the other's face. More honest in the morning. They were dressing two days before their departure for America when she chose the moment, the close space of the lean-to round them when his brother had long left for the butchery, his other brother had gone to his post at the café, the women in the kitchen, except Khadija probably still in bed, the children, little Leila, off to school, and the mother—the mother perhaps at her prayer rug asking divine help to protect her son on his endless journey— that was the moment to say to him, not with *I have something to tell you* as a useless preparation, but directly, right out for what was between them; I am not going.

Where's it you're supposed to go?

For him, they've already left this place; but she might have one of the women she'd known here who expected still to see her.

I am not going—coming to America.

What is it you're saying?

His voice was normal, as if sometimes when he needed a simplified phrase for something she had said in English.

I'm not going to America.

Of course you are going to America. On Thursday.

No. I'm not going.

Julie, what are you afraid of? What are these nerves. You are never like this.

He is ready to come to her, embrace her, soothe her, they must get away from here, this place has taken the spirit out of her.

Her hands are up, palms open, fingers splayed, holding him off. No. It's not that. I'm not going.

What is she, who is she now, this woman who beckoned him to her, if ever a woman did, who followed him to this place—bewilderment, rage, what is it you feel that you never knew before, never would get yourself into this kind of provocation. Are you mad? His whisper is louder than a yell. You have gone out of your head. We are going on Thursday, Thursday, Thursday. That's it.

Are you mad? Are you mad? Saliva filled his mouth, spit flew from his lips. Her silence was a wall of obduracy he could not pummel his fists against. He flung himself from the space that held them, stumbling against the iron bedstead, the chair, the obstacle of the charged canvas bag as he made for the door: it was too flimsy to bang behind him, he stood faced with the communal room of his mother's house, aware at his back that she—the girl who picked him up, the lover, the faithful follower, the wife—could see him there through the gap of the sagging board. The family room was deserted; the sofa from which his mother surveyed all was unoccupied by her form. He did not know what he was looking for, for whom; if he had come out to look for—what? The one certainty in a life—it is not known until it suddenly is not there. And what does that mean? That his mother was not there for him on her throne; not now, this moment, not when he is in Africa, England, Germany, in Chicago, Detroit, not ever. That *she*, everything she has been, lover, follower at his heels, something called wife; she is not there. Not in the cottage, the café where she lured him for coffee, not on the iron bedstead in the lean-to, not in America. Not ever.

He did not want to see them, any of the family, no-one; and he needed at once someone. Anyone upon whom to lay 'I'm not going'. To see from outside the self the effect of this statement. But it is never 'anyone' who is being sought; unacknowledged, in the deviousness, the reluctance to admit what is lodged deep, it is *someone*. He passed the warm voices coming from the kitchen; no, no, not the women; he found himself approaching the angle of privacy in the passage: but she was at prayer, his mother, her head bowed to her mat. He was the small boy who had burst upon her with the tale of a lost ball when she was in the middle of her devotions and had been shamed by reprimand; he slowed and turned away without her being aware of him.

And it happened to be Maryam he came upon. As he stood, back in the room the whole family lived in, every chair and cushion moulded to their weight, worn places on the carpet designed by the concourse of their feet, Maryam came smiling greeting to him on her way to the front door, leaving to clean her employer's house. What she saw in his face and stance made her halt where she was; immediately she thought of some accident or illness in the family that somehow had been kept from her. So many dear ones, Ahmad working with knives at the butcher's yard—she lived by tender concern for all. —What is wrong? What happened. Julie?—

—Nothing.—

—But you are— She feels her intrusion.

—Just woke up, that's all.—

But he had now been assaulted from within by something he had not said, unable to think beyond *Are you mad* in response to a single meaning of *I'm not going*. Not going to Chicago, to Detroit, to California.

He left Maryam looking aside from him in her tact, and burst back to the lean-to, dragging the door shut behind him.

She was standing at the window. She turned with the

agony of composure drawn in tight lines between her brows and around her mouth.

So you're going back. There. Where you come from. I thought it all the time. One day. The day will be that you go home where you always say is not your home. But you see I was right. You do not know what you say. That is how it is with you. So you don't know what you do. To people. Good luck. Goodbye. Tell them all at the Café, this shack you live in, this dirty place, and tell them you're too good, you're very fine, you won't what is it—sell out, they say— you don't live with the capitalists in California, tell them, you'll think of everything to tell. Goodbye. Go and tell. Goodbye.

He began transformed by anger, his face dyed with rising blood, his eyes narrowed to chips of black glitter, his body strangely gathered as if to spring, and ended—as if by a knife thrust within himself—in dejection.

She was afraid of the dejection, not the anger which she had, his violent breath—taken in with open mouth. She came to him, stumbling as he had done over their baggage and he tried to fend off her hands and arms as she clung to him. Don't say. Don't say.

No right, hers, to say now what was eloquently unsaid ever since—certainly the first nights in the doll's house—*I love you.*

Listen to me. Where did you get the idea. I'm not going back there. I don't belong there.

She has taken his head between her hard palms and forced his face before her, she feels his texture, the nap of a day's growth of beard against her skin. She has the image of him, one of those habitual and dear, pressing his tongue against the inner side of his cheek to tauten the flesh as he delicately shaves round his moustache; the image stored.

You know that. Saying both at once: the unsaid (that
stored image is love) and what has been said, I'm not going
back.

What are you talking? What is it. You are not going to
America. That's what you say. You are not going to your
home. That is what you say.

And now she has to tell him what she thought he must
have understood. I'm staying here.

The passion of dispute that erupts like this abandons intimacy that has been respected; through the makeshift door of the lean-to it flowed to the family living-room, through the whole house, invading, overtaking the pre-occupations and concerns of all who lived so closely there; as if each, even the children, looked up from these, through the day, as at a sudden sound or sight. What happens between man and wife, that's their business, it is customary to main-tain the principle of privacy even to the extent of appearing to be unaware that anything is happening. In a house crowded with relatives this is particularly stringent; not only the door of the lean-to is too thin. The surface conventions of blood ties and religious observance are able to contain sub-sumed almost without a ripple, for example, the presence of Khadija and its implications. But whatever is happening in the lean-to is different, it thrusts itself in demand upon the house. As son, brother, cousin he has no option, no other re-source but to come out and repeat to each relative the same account of what has happened in that lean-to—from where she, the foreign wife he brought to them, does not appear, either because she accepts that he speak for her, or because he does not allow her to speak for herself. Who can say. But even when her favourite, the small Leila, is seen by him making for the lean-to door, he sends the child away.

Everyone is confronted with this account, even those who are only embarrassed and bewildered by a situation they cannot understand, they shouldn't be admitted to. Something that belongs to the life of this family member so different from theirs, lived unimaginably in worlds they do not know. As if he could expect some explanation, support, from them in their innocence, the ignorance he has always made them aware they live in. His brothers Ahmad and Daood listen to him in disbelief, a woman does what her husband says. They are too loyal to him, too respectful, to reveal what this makes him immediately alert to again: the stigma on his manhood. The women—she'd now joined them, the kitchen was the neutral ground from which to take the right of entry by way of household tasks, playing with their children, exchanging pidgin-language—when he approached the women their embarrassment emanated from them like sweat. It was from their gathering under the awning they spoke at all. She is a very good person. It will be all right. She will do what is right, she is a wife. Sometimes we just get upset, you know, for a while, then it passes, *ma sha allah.*

His insistence drove them into silence. —There is no time for a mood to pass. Two days. That's it. I want to know, has she talked to you. This business. Staying here. In this place. Have you said anything like that to her? Have you? I need an answer. Has she been talking like this?—

Amina looked round over the bundle of her baby at the others and shook her head conclusively, earrings swinging, in mandate of denial.

He had the thought of getting one of the women to speak

to her; but he now felt no one of them really was to be trusted. Never mind teaching a few words of English, she had influenced them with her rich girl's Café ideas of female independence.

In his father's face, the slow lowering and raising of thick eyelids and the twitching parentheses at either corner of the mouth, he saw that the response was silent reproach, brought up, deserved, for being too proud and foolish to have taken the chance offered him, *Al-Hamdu lillah*, by his Uncle Yaqub to stay where *he*, a son, belongs.

Again the laconic response: a wife follows what her husband wishes.

This from a father who the son knew did what his wife in her wisdom and character, yes, *Al-Hamdu lillah*, knew was right.

Facing himself this way and that, where to turn— Maryam. Maryam, alone. With the other women, she had said nothing. Maryam: of course, who was the first to see blazoned on his face as she left the house for her work as a servant, *I'm not going.* Maryam made herself the friend, acolyte, it is his little sister Maryam who had the idea of the occupations, the English teaching, Maryam who made his wife at home in this place, well, all right, gave her something to do in the meantime, waiting with a poor devil all those months applying for visas. Whom else to turn to. Like a blood-letting, confront her.

Summoned on her return from work for charges against her, and she knows it at once, it slows her feet as she comes into the house from the place beneath the awning where the child Leila has been sent to fetch her. Alone; he'll see her alone, without the twittering support of the women.

—What does she say to you. I want to know. What do you tell her, you are the one, you tell her what to do here, you

make her your sister here, afraid to be without you, the ladies
that offer tea and learn English, the schoolteachers who flatter her. I want to know. What have you done. Who told you to
do this. Did you ask me, your brother? Come, I want to hear
from you what you have been saying to her.—

He has a power over this girl he will never have over his
wife Julie, and that he would never want to have, it is part of
what he emigrates from, every time he gets away. While he
exerts it, it sickens him, the anger his sister fearfully sees rising in him. —Come. Speak, speak. What have you done.—
She has been weeping through his tirade.

He cannot make out what she's saying now. —What?
Speak!—

The girl is an idiot. What else can you expect. Never getting out of this place, accustomed to being spoken to as I am
speaking to her, by brothers like me.

Where else to turn to.

He cannot evade any longer. Her presence has been following him about the house from confrontation to confrontation, hearing him, aware of his frustration, his failure to
extract from anybody any answers real to him; her authoritative version of his face is before him all the time. If she is at
prayer—she is the only one from whom he will hold back, the
others have been burst upon. He will wait. Everyone keeps
out of the family living-room. Away from him. Even the children are hastily snatched when they linger at the leading
doors. He sits in one of the upright chairs second-hand from
Uncle Yaqub when his house was redecorated. Facing her
empty throne. Biding his time. There is no cyclone of emotion
of which she does not occupy the still eye of his respect.
Nothing, ever, can take precedence over that.

He does not have to wait long. She comes into the room as
if it is at her summoning that he is there, and occupies her

sofa. He gets up to greet her and takes a chair nearer her she indicates with a half-tilt of a hand from her lap.

She knows what has happened. Or rather what threatens to happen—it's seeped through the house in whispers and in the supersonic of thoughts. She must have had related to her many versions. But he tells her all, over again all comes from his own mouth as only he can know it. She asks questions, gives no opinions.

This girl did not have a family at home in her country.

Well, of course she has, but she does not get on well with them—her father.

Her mother is dead, *inna lillah*, may the Lord have mercy on her daughter.

Her mother remarried and she's well-off—she lives in America and will welcome her.

She found our life here strange to her.

Well, yes, of course she must have but you know she has made the effort—to fit in—just for while we had to be here.

This time, is there suitable work for your ambitions already arranged for you in that country.

Not yet—wonderful opportunities there that have not been where I've been away before!—other times, those other countries.

She wished to have a child.

Yes and I would wish it, but not until I know we are settled, my work, and a home where we are going to spend our lives.

She gets up, weighty in her robe. Her left foot falters for balance.

She's getting old; this is what you return to, abandon, each time.

Mother—

But she, who always has advice and a solution, for everyone, whether this is welcome or not, has none for him. My son—she gives him her blessing—*Allah yahfazak*, and she leaves the room, he knows, for her place of prayer.

Mother?

Ah, an ally, that's it; but not his. An ally of the foreigner—*she* will be the one to restore the son to the mother, lure him, bring him home at last.

There is a terrible strength that comes to a dread decision aghastly opposed by other people: their words, supplication, silent condemnation, are hammer blows driving that decision deeper and deeper into its certainty.

Maryam's clinging affection and unexpressed joy at the idea that her unique friend, from another world and closer in understanding than any sister, would stay in her husband's home, like other women, was the only support; his mother—no indication, no word or sign transmitted from her, her usual stately presence supervised calmly in the kitchen where the girl, Ibrahim's wife, continued to do what was assigned to her, just as if the mother were not aware that she was supposed to be emigrating with the son in twenty-four hours. And the girl slices onions as if she cannot be aware of this either.

Twenty-four hours. The decision that has been growing in her, changing her as the cells in the body renew themselves spontaneously, becomes a clench of panic: it's happening too quickly, too soon, the time has come before she's really ready—

Funk.

Way back, The Table has the word.

But it's all been thought out, felt through, dismissed, re-jected as crazy (yes, he's not alone in making that accusation; become self-accusation), renewed, taking over—final—many times in the months: the meantime, as he called it.

He would not allow himself or her to lie down on their bed, to submit even to exhaustion that night. If he could plead, reason, argue, bargain, reproach, rage long enough the time that was left would sweep her in this flash flood to the airport, onto the plane that would carry her away with him just as she had carried herself with him, deported to this place.

Listen . . . we'll make a good life there. You want me to do something I want, the kind of position . . . use my brain, study—you always tell me that. You are the one who knows I can do it. You'll be happy. You're happy with me—I make you happy—yes, and you, how can I be without you. A couple of weeks, while you're in California, I don't have to worry if you've got everything you need—all right, but we have some money, I can even come there to see you. I will. You've followed all this way with me, I'm so lucky, I know, so how can it be—

So why? Why? Why did you come? Why—you bought that ticket for yourself? You hung on to me? What for? Don't say it! Just don't say it. *Not now.*

His conviction that 'love' is a luxury not for him has found its proof. Yes.

Won't have her say it; she sees. Say something else that has the same meaning.

Ibrahim, you'd think I was leaving you, the way you take it. I'm not going anywhere. I'm not going back there, I've told you, told you. I'm in your home.

You are a liar. Why did you never say one word to me? You were lying to me all the time. Here in this bed with me kissing and lying. Fucking and lying.

I never lie to you.

Ah no? You only lie with the mouth? Keep quiet when there is what you must say, that's not lying?

I thought, I really thought you saw how I was beginning— you make it so hard to explain—to live here. Oh my god. How I was different—not the same as I was back there when you met me. I thought we were close enough for you to understand, even if it was something you—didn't expect . . .

Not lying when you got the money from your uncle for the tickets? Not lying when you signed the papers for the visa, not lying when you went smiling to the embassy to show them your face, my wife 'accompanying me', you saw it written on my visa? No? That was not lying? Or was that true then, and now—I don't know, out of the sky something somebody has changed your mind, driven you crazy? Where did you get the idea from, how, where?

And while his anguish batters them both she now knows where. The desert.

But she cannot tell him that. The stump of wall in the sands where the street ends. The dog waits and a child places a hand.

She cannot tell him that.

He shuns the desert. It is the denial of everything he yearns for, for him. And if he should remember—the enthusiasms of some members of The Table—his next derision could be that her decision was a typical piece of sheltered middle-class Western romanticism. Like picking up a grease-monkey.

Confusion is singing in his ears. But what is the confusion? No confusion; I should know that. Like me, like me, she won't go back where she belongs. Other people tell her she belongs. She looks for somewhere else. *I'm staying here.* Here!

The elegant suitcase is standing packed. Finally he can't stop staring at it. He lunges to it and struggles with the digital lock, the combination comes to him and he gets it open and begins to throw out all her things; on the bed, on the floor. Now she will do it. Put them back, give in.

She comes to him through the mess. She tries to draw him against her tightly, breasts to chest, belly to belly, but he resists wildly and the embrace becomes a parody of the violence that has never existed between them. Some short time before dawn of the day on which they are to emigrate, like corpses laid out side by side on what was their bed: sleep drugs with its ancient promise from childhood, it will be all right in the morning.

He got up dazed and dulled with the hang-
over of emotion and went to his brothers. She woke to their
low voices behind the lean-to door. She left the bed, dizzied
for a moment, and then collected the contents of her suitcase
scattered everywhere. She folded some garments on the wire
he had rigged up for her and the bright plastic hangers she
had found in the market, hung the pants, dresses and shirts.
The shoes went to their place in a row under the window.

He came back into the room with a bucket of hot water.
He saw her things, the clothes hung up, folded, the shoes
where she kept them. He looked only for a moment; and not
at her; he poured water into the bowl on the table and began
to shave. Although his back was turned, she could see his
face in the little mirror strung to the wall in which he met
himself as he was on this morning. She saw, once more, his
cheek thrust taut by his tongue as he delicately shaved close
to his glossy moustache.

From the neat pile of underwear on the bed she took a bra
and panties and began to dress.

He was aware of her movements somewhere around him,
somehow slowed, as his own were. When he had shaved and

washed he poured his water into the empty jar kept beside
the table and refilled the bowl from the bucket he had
brought. He heard her washing as he dressed himself for the
journey in jeans she had learned to iron just as well as the
black woman she paid to do it, back at the cottage, a shirt
she liked best, and the silk scarf that was his plume. While
her back was to him he happened to glance and saw in the
little mirror the gestures of her hands, the upward tilt of her
neck as she looped her earrings into her ears; once more.

He spoke. Are you coming to eat?

She looked round as at a call. Yes, in a moment.

Everyone was at home; apparently Maryam, the brothers,
had been given leave to arrive late at work, be present for this
latest farewell. The brother-in-law was unemployed at present, anyway. Over food there was subdued chatter, suitable to
an imminent departure, on the route to be taken, the country
where a connecting aircraft would be, the time-change in
space, a further separation of the voyagers from kin. She appeared, dressed in what became her best, a combination of
pants made of handsome hand-woven local textile and a
jacket bought long ago on some jaunt in Italy. A necklace
given her by Maryam brought the exchange of a slight smile
between them. When Ahmad asked her how long was the
wait between connecting planes, she answered round about
three hours. Ibrahim corrected, more like four or five, there
are always delays on airports this side of the world—drawing
laughter in which she joined. Daood the coffee-maker turned
fondly to his brother. —Maybe you'll be lucky and everything
will go all right, for you, on time.—

Muhammad, excused from school, was quick. —And
when Julie goes next month, it must be lucky for her too!—

So she understood what the low voices behind the door
had been about: it was arranged among the adult brothers
that the official family version of what had happened would

be that their brother's foreign wife would be following him as
soon as he knew in what city of this immigration he would
find himself established.

He kept away from her, in the company of the family,
making sure there was no chance for them to be alone until
the hour of the taxi arrived for him. Let her have an idea of
what she doesn't realize, all his pleading, arguing, of no effect, that she will be in this house, this family, this village,
this place in the desert, without him, without the love-
making she needs so much, without anyone to talk to who, as
he does, knows her world, without—yes, he can admit it to
himself only, without his love for her. That weakness that is
not for him.

She could not approach him. He held her off by his right,
as she had asserted hers. She was not going; in all the pain of
seeing him return to the same new-old humiliations that
await him, doing the dirty work they don't want to do for
themselves, taking the hand-out patronage of the casino king
(stepfather, is he) as the chance of being the Oriental Prince,
quaint way-out choice of the mother's daughter. *That's it.
That's reality.*

Neighbours came to see off the lucky one bound for America. The taxi ordered so well in advance drew up in the home
street before the family house exactly when expected. In the
gathering she stood with him now, their clothes touching in
contact, they would keep up together the version he had
arranged with the brothers; it was all she could do for him for
the present, her lover, her wonderful discovery back there in
a garage. Everyone embraced him, children ran to him to
touch the great adventure, the achievement that is emigration, not understood but sensed.

Muhammad rushed up with the canvas bag and neighbours added plastic carriers with gifts of food for the journey.
The son embraced the family in the order of protocol they

knew, embraced his father and then, last, his mother. She
blessed him. And made a slight movement as if directing: her
son embraced his wife. Before them all, the women who
watched from behind curtains across their street, the men
who looked away from her where they mended their cars and
motorbikes, the close neighbours who flitted in like swallows
to visit, the children Leila brought along for games—he and
she held one another, and there was a kind of gasp of silence.
Some old man with the loud voice of the deaf broke it.

—She's not going?—

—Couple of weeks.—

—*Bismillah.* That's much better.—

—When he has a place.—

He was walking to the taxi. The owner-driver everyone
knew stood grinning, door held wide, a kindly man with a
fierce face resurrecting genes of some ancient desert warrior.

He bent his head to enter and held himself straight in the
sagging, tattered passenger seat, looking ahead as if he had
already left. The driver banged the door several times to get it
to hold shut, laughed to the gathering and capered round to
take his place at the wheel.

Ibrahim had abandoned this place again, his eyes were on
the road, the arrival at the same airport, the initiation
through security body-check, handing over of ticket and
passport where the visa is plainly stamped, cannot be
doubted this time, sight of the same canvas bag borne away
on a moving belt, the pressure of other bodies, leaving, push-
ing close at the boarding call. The plastic bags of gift foods
like those he's been given shoved into overhead lockers, the
blocked gangway where he will thrust and jostle to find his
seat. Close on either side their breath, their heat, you can't
get away from them, poor devils like himself. The rites of
passage.

He does not look back at the raised hands and faces, some

smiling at his happy chance, one or two crumpled in tears not for his departure but in reminder of another, closer parting, endured.

Everyone continues to stand about until the taxi has turned from up the street, out of sight and hearing. The children jump and scuffle in excitement as they do on any sort of occasion, whatever brings adults together. Maryam nervously goes to whisper something to the mother and apparently is given consent; all are invited to come into the house for refreshment.

Ibrahim's wife is asked kindly questions, when will she expect to follow, what city will they make their home, is she preparing warm clothes for the climate, it's said the cold is something you have to get used to. She has the appropriate kindly answers for them.

Unnoticed in the house's customary bustle of hospitality and the rising voices of the company, she took her tea and went to the lean-to. She drank it slowly, placed the cup and saucer on the window-sill and was standing at the window when there was a tap at the door. Before she could answer it was opened; Khadija there. Khadija has never come to the lean-to. Khadija dragged the ill-fitting door closed behind her with her often-heard scornful sigh, dangling a bunch of dates, her strong red-painted lips twisted as she savoured what was in her mouth.

Khadija put an arm round her conspiratorially, smiled intimately and held out the bunch of sweetness, smooth dark shiny dates. She spoke Arabic, the foreigner understands enough, now.

—He'll come back.—

But perhaps a reassurance offered for herself, Khadija thinking of her man at the oil fields.

Notes

21 *Too long a sacrifice*   W. B. Yeats, 'Easter 1916', *Michael Robartes and the Dancer* (Churchtown: The Cuala Press, 1920).

28 *Whoever embraces a woman*   Jorge Luis Borges, 'Happiness', *Jorge Luis Borges: Selected Poems* (New York: Viking).

35 *I decided to postpone our future*   Feodor Dostoievsky, 'The Meek One', *The Diary of a Writer—Feodor Dostoievsky*, trans. Boris Brasol (New York: George Braziller, 1954).

66 *Rose thou art sick*   William Blake, 'The Sick Rose':

> O Rose thou art sick.
> The invisible worm
> That flies in the night
> In the howling storm:
>
> Has found out thy bed
> Of crimson joy:
> And his dark secret love
> Does thy life destroy.

'Songs of Experience', *Songs of Innocence and Experience with Other Poems* (London: Basil Montagu Pickering, 1866).

88 *Let us go to another country*   William Plomer, 'Another Country', *Visiting the Caves* (London: Jonathan Cape, 1936). In his *Collected Poems* (London: Jonathan Cape, 1960), Plomer published a slightly different version of this poem.

144 *And remember Job*   'The Prophets', Sura XXI, *The Koran*, trans. Rev. J. M. Rodwell, with an introduction by Rev. G. Margoliouth (New York: Everyman's Library, 1948), p. 156.

145   *And make mention in the Book of Mary*   'Mary', Sura XIX, *The
      Koran*, p. 118.
146   *The God of Mercy hath taught*   'The Merciful', Sura LV, *The
      Koran*, p. 74.
173   *And she conceived*   'Mary', Sura XIX, *The Koran*, p. 118.
178   *al Kitab wa-l-Qur'an: Qira'a mu'asira*   The views expressed by
      the young men are based on quotations from this book by
      Shahrur Muhammad Shahrur, as cited by Nilüfer Göle in her ar-
      ticle 'Snapshots of Islamic Modernities', *Daedalus (Journal of
      the American Academy of Arts and Sciences)* (Winter 2000).
245   *I was occupied in picturing him*   Rainer Maria Rilke, *The
      Notebooks of Malte Laurids Brigge*, trans. John Linton (Lon-
      don: The Hogarth Press).

Grateful thanks to my generous mentor, Philip J. Stewart of the University of Oxford.